MARTHA GELLHORN

was born in St Louis, Missouri. Leaving Bryn Mawr College, in a hurry to get started, she arrived in Paris less than a year later, after two jobs, on the *New Republic* and the *Hearst Times Union*. She had decided to pay her way around the world as a reporter and write about it in fiction. Returning to the U.S. in 1934, she was hired by Harry Hopkins to report on the way the Federal Emergency Relief program really worked. The result, in 1936, was a widely acclaimed book of four linked novellas about Americans in the Depression, called *The Trouble I've Seen*. In Spain, in 1937, she sent to *Collier's* in New York an unsolicited article on daily life in besieged Madrid, and so began her career as a war correspondent which lasted for nine years and covered five wars: Spain, Finland, China, the Second World War and Java. In intervals between assignments, she wrote two novels and a book of short stories. After 1946, journalism became occasional and free-lance, a means to see for herself whatever absorbed her interest and concern, ranging from the Eichmann Trial to Nicaragua. She wrote short stories for American magazines and nine more books. She observes that you also use a lot of interesting time just living.

Martha Gellhorn has written five novels: *A Stricken Field* (1940), *Liana* (1944), *The Wine of Astonishment* (1948), *His Own Man* (1961) and *The Lowest Trees Have Tops* (1969); two collections of short stories: *The Heart of Another* (1941), *Honeyed Peace* (1953); four books of novellas, *The Trouble I've Seen* (1936), *Two By Two* (1958), *Pretty Tales for Tired People* (1965), and *The Weather in Africa*(1978)Her non-fiction is *Travels With Myself and Another* (1978) and *The Face of War*, originally published in 1959, reprinted to include Vietnam as a paperback in 1967, and republished with additional wars by Virago in 1986. Virago will publish *Liana* in 1987.

Martha Gellhorn now lives in Wales.

VIRAGO
MODERN
CLASSIC
NUMBER
206

A
STRICKEN FIELD

MARTHA GELLHORN

With a New Afterword
by the Author

Published by VIRAGO PRESS Limited 1986
41 William IV Street, London WC2N 4DB

First published by Duell, Sloan & Pearce, 1940
First published in Great Britain by Jonathan Cape 1942

British Cataloguing in Publication Data

Gellhorn, Martha
    A stricken field.—(Virago modern classics)
    I. Title
    813'.52[F]   PS3513.E46

    ISBN 0-86068-735-X

Printed in Finland by Werner Söderström Oy

There were young knights among them who had never been present at a stricken field. Some could not look upon it and some could not speak and they held themselves apart from the others who were cutting down the prisoners at my Lord's orders, for the prisoners were a body too numerous to be guarded by those of us who were left. Then Jean de Rye, an aged knight of Burgundy who had been sore wounded in the battle, rode up to the group of young knights and said, "Are ye maidens with your downcast eyes? Look well upon it. See all of it. Close your eyes to nothing. For a battle is fought to be won. And it is this that happens if you lose."

from a Medieval Chronicle

1

FROM this height the Rhine looked narrow, sluggish, and unimportant. When they were over Germany everyone leaned close to the windows, staring out as if they hoped to see something special. But the land looked the same as when they flew across France, summer green and rich, with the pompons of the trees, and the white roads, and the farm houses. Perhaps the roofs are steeper, she thought, but the land doesn't look any different. In the plane, everybody waited, tightened and ready.

Later someone said, "This is occupied territory," and again they pressed at the windows, expecting some change in the land to equal the change on the map. There was nothing to see. What are we looking for, she wondered, maybe a swastika painted on a roof? In the distance the wand-like church steeples of Prague rose into the sun.

She thought she was the last to leave the plane, but sitting deep in his chair, with his face turned away, was a man who apparently did not know they had arrived. The stewardess came into the plane and touched his shoulder and spoke. He shook himself, and smiled, not really seeing her. He was a young Jew, about thirty years old, with good but mussed clothes, who looked as if he had been traveling for days with no time to sleep or shave.

She felt the motion of the plane still; the ground rolled and swayed beneath her. The weather had changed from the blowing brilliance of Bourget. Later, over the Vosges, there was a misted autumn sun but the air was thick now and smoky. Two silver monoplanes, with large swastikas painted on their tails, were parked close to the entrance of the airport building.

"Heil Hitler," one of the passengers said, talking to himself in a soft, furious voice.

The regular transport plane from Berlin had landed a few moments before their plane from Paris and the customs was crowded with German tourists, wearing belted suits and swastika lapel buttons. They carried cameras, by straps slung over their shoulders, and seemed very much at home. The people from the Paris plane stood apart and watched the Germans without friendliness. The Czech customs officials appeared to be embarrassed by the Germans who talked loudly with each other and argued about having to open their suitcases. Then the Germans drove from the airport in a special bus and the place became quieter.

When their luggage had been stamped, the passengers from the Paris plane went to their bus. The stewardess came with them, carrying a small patent leather hatbox, and took a seat in front of two of the younger Czech passengers. The bus drove down wide suburban streets, heading for the center of Prague. The streets were lined with square cement-gray houses and heavy apartment buildings. There were few trees, and the streets, houses, and buildings looked merely well-built and clean. All

4

the windows had been criss-crossed with pasted strips of brown paper to keep them from shattering during the air-raids that never came.

The stewardess turned to the men behind her and said something and they laughed and the one with the tweed cap answered her.

The young Jew, sitting next to the American, stirred and noticed where he was when he heard them laugh.

"You are English?" he said.

"No, American. A journalist," she said, as if you would have to explain why you were coming to Prague this October.

"Do you understand what they are talking?" He nodded toward the stewardess.

"No. I cannot speak Czech."

"The girl says, 'What, no pictures of Adolf in the windows yet?' and the man says, 'Be quiet. Do not talk Czech. It is forbidden.'"

"Oh," the journalist said. "Well, it's nice that they can make jokes."

"They are not real laughing," the Jew said. Then, as if he were paying her a personal compliment, "It is fine to be American."

"Yes. I suppose so."

"I wish I go to America. Perhaps later I get a visa."

"Yes," she said. Everywhere, now, people spoke to her of America and visas. It was not a topic of conversation you could develop very interestingly.

"I left from Germany in 1933," the Jew said. "And now I am Czech citizen. They are wonderful people— very liberal and intelligent and good working. And they had a wonderful country."

5

"I like them too."

"You were here once?"

"I was here in May, for the mobilization."

"Not to permit to fight!" the Jew said, his face changing from the polite conversational look into one of darkness and anger. "You do not know how we could fought. With what readiness. What joy."

The journalist turned to watch the Czechs and the stewardess. They were not talking now. Seen from the side, their faces looked hard and lonely.

"If there is anything I will do for you in Prague?" the Jew said.

He took a card from his wallet. She had a great many cards. She would very likely never see again the people who gave her these printed or engraved reminders of themselves. But if you accepted the cards, they felt they had some claim on you. It was not that they wanted anything ordinary, she thought, they did not want to borrow money or take you out to dinner. They wanted to know an American, in case they would have to leave the country suddenly.

"Thank you," she said, and shook hands with him. "My name is Mary Douglas."

His wife was meeting him at the airline office. Mary Douglas smiled and bowed, and moved away from them, beckoning a taxi.

"Good afternoon," the desk clerk said. "We received your wire. Mr. Lambert has been asking for you. He is staying here. So is Mr. Thane. Mr. Tompkins is at the Metropole and wishes you to telephone. Mr. Berthold is here too."

6

"All right," she said. There were small stone-topped tables in the hotel hall and straight chairs with greenish tapestry seat covers. Waiters carried trays of towering pastries and coffee cups and cocktail glasses. The people eating and drinking and talking (but never in clear voices, so that each table kept its own secrets) seemed all to be making money on something or arranging to make money.

"Have you given me a nice room?"

"The best, Mademoiselle. On the front. Times have changed since May, have they not?"

The older clerk frowned. He did not want his assistant to have political discussions with the clients. You could no longer be sure of the opinions of the clients and there might be trouble later.

"The times are now," she said, with the frankness her American passport allowed her, "disgusting."

Someone called to her as she went to the elevators and she saw them all, some she knew and strange faces which were already familiar. They were here as they would have to be, and when we were younger, she thought, we covered three bell alarms and the morgue, but now we are successful and cover large international disasters. Their table was disorderly with many glasses and they sat around it, each in the pose that would some day become famous in a photograph on the cover of his own book of reminiscences (if not already famous), and if you did not know their legend or appreciate their special genius, they seemed to be only a collection of pale, rumpled men who never got enough sleep. Those who always drank looked a little drunk, at six in the afternoon, and those who did not drink more than taste or

7

politeness demanded, looked as they always did, like foreign correspondents.

She liked them very much, and she did not know them at all. They had met for years now, in various capitals, in trains and boats and on odd roads. They were warmly intimate and affectionate with each other, though sometimes pompous too (when you showed off that you knew the language better or were more informed about local politics or had just lunched with a big native statesman), sometimes flirtatious in order to rest the mind and change the conversation, sometimes honest because after all they were people working on the same job, needing help or advice.

This is going to save me a lot of time, she thought. She had no particular respect for what they wrote (let the subscribers approve that), but they knew more than they could ever sign their names to, and she admired the way they worked. Besides, she thought, I'll have someone to eat with. The worst of this business was the solitary meal in the strange restaurant, with a paper-bound book propped up against the water glass.

Tom Lambert, very good-looking in a way that you never remembered and holding his cane which he had learned to carry twelve years ago as a brand-new American in Paris with no job, stood up, took her by the shoulders, kissed her a little drunkenly on the forehead, and said, "When'd you get here, beauty?"

"This minute." She hugged him back, hampered by his cane. She was very fond of him. "How are you, son? I telephoned you the last two times in Paris but you didn't seem to be around."

"Hi," Thane said. "You work for the goddamdest outfit. The story's already dead."

"Me," she said to him pleasantly, "I do not write news like you gents. I write history."

"Yah."

"Seen old John lately?" Tom asked very casually.

She answered him the same way. "We were in Spain together. John's still there." She needn't have said his name, but it gave her such pleasure.

"Pretty quiet now, isn't it?"

"There may be something doing soon at the Ebro. Hello, Louis."

Louis Berthold, an airy and talented Frenchman, who could not keep the same political viewpoint for more than three months at a time, said, "I did not think you were going to speak to me. I thought you would ignore me because I am a Fascist. You look lovely. Spain agrees with you."

"She likes Spain, don't you, Mary?" Thane said.

"Sure I like Spain."

They smiled at each other. I must keep it off my face, she thought crossly, why don't I wear a sign. It's indecent to beam this way.

"I am sorry to hear that you and John have gone over to the Reds," Berthold said.

"Oh, really, Louis, what rot."

"You mustn't mind," Tom Lambert said. "He's been a Fascist for a month now. It won't last much longer. We let him stay around while we're waiting for the change."

"What's going on in Paris?" a new one said. He was

9

blond and about twenty-six and probably a Harvard man.

"Mr. Luther, Miss Douglas," Tom Lambert said. "Mr. Luther of the *Dispatch*. The Mr. Luther of the *Dispatch*."

"How do you do?" she said. She had heard his name in the last few months. The standard of beauty for correspondents was definitely rising. "Paris? Nothing much. Some people say: well, we couldn't have gotten there to help the Czechs anyhow. And some people say: what is Czecho, not really a country, just something Wilson invented. They're doing their best to find excuses."

"Always loyal to the losing team," Thane said.

It was the beginning of an old argument between them. She smiled and said good-by, bowing to them all, and to three others who had not been introduced. "I've got to clean up. Where will you be later?"

"We're eating at the fish place at eight-thirty," Tom Lambert said. "It's the one up this street on the same side, with a neon fish hanging over it. Remember?"

"I'll see you there."

Looking back over the hall, from the elevator, she thought how like a cheap international-spy story it was: the too fat, too tailored men at the tables with gaudy blondes, the women alone wearing veils, the men in couples whispering to each other and eating pastry with their faces bent close to the small plates. These people, who had no apparent existence outside the lobbies of large European hotels, seemed to be the usual camp followers of catastrophe. They thrive on it, too, she thought, noticing their well-fed, satisfied faces.

Mary Douglas remembered the room from the last time. It had the same bright blue satin wall-paneling and grimy cream furniture, and also the cardboard notice stuck under the glass on the desk top, which told you exactly what to do in case of air-raids. They can begin throwing those away, she thought.

She opened the windows to take away the hotel smell, and went out on the balcony. The Wenceslaus Square was poorly lighted, as if all the street lamps were slowly burning down. The row of shops across the way, with their names painted in the strange, untidy Czech lettering, did not shine as they used to, and only Bata's neon sign flowed at this end of the street. The other neon signs gleamed, pale glass threads, reflected from the street lamps but not running color as she remembered them. The Bata shoe store was as bright as ever, the windows clogged with homely inexpensive shoes, but the linen shops and glove stores were in shadow. The windows of the apartments opposite were shuttered too. In the next block, the wide open door of an Automat let light onto the pavement.

From this corner, all the way up to the Narodni Museum, the street was laid out in parallel strips of trolley tracks and asphalt roadway for automobiles, so that there were four moving lines of traffic, suddenly cut by a pedestrian crossing from one side of the long square to the other. She listened to the trolley bells and to the taxi horns, but of the people she heard only the slur and scrape of their feet on the pavement.

It was a very stony street, with the flat granite faces of the buildings rising six stories above the shop fronts, and tonight it looked cold and shabby. From here, she

11

could not see the spreading walled fortress that is the Hradcany Castle, nor the bulbs and spires of the churches in the old town, and she thought, this was never a good street, I'm making it all up, it was always just a prosperous business street, like one in Chicago or any place else, it hasn't changed. But she remembered the flower vendors on the corners, and the book stores and the jewelers' and the place where you got fine Czech stockings cheap, and the wonderful mayonnaised hors d'œuvres on trays in the Automat windows, and the newspaper stalls with the papers from everywhere, full of effort and excitement and fury, all of them loud in such various prints and languages. She remembered the people hurrying, and those who dawdled eating large whipped-cream puffs, and those who sat in pairs on benches under the short city trees, admiring the traffic or enjoying the noise, and she remembered the beggars who had looked so neat and worthy, and the extra-sized, pink-faced policeman. She remembered it as a pleasant, bustling street, and the people on it had always seemed contented, attending respectably to their business. It's because it's night, and there's something wrong with the electricity, she decided, that's all.

But when she had gone down into the street, and was walking along the curb against the stream of people, she knew it was another city, and unlike any place she had ever seen before. The crowds moved slowly, as if they too were strangers, uncertain of directions and having nowhere to go. She could not find one face to remember. They all looked alike and no one seemed to have slept, or eaten, or gone shopping, or made love, or transacted business successfully or unsuccessfully, or done any of the things that leave a mark on the eyes or mouths of passers-by. They're all waiting, she thought. She began to watch them closely, looking for anger somewhere, hoping to see perhaps two men talking together in sharp voices, with a little crowd collecting, and the anger spreading. But the people held apart from each other. She imagined that on the faces of the women there would be some sign of what had happened, even despair would be better than this, despair would have shape, and bring the faces to life. But these people looked gray and empty and she thought, so that's the way it goes; they learn to keep quiet fast.

She was walking quickly now, as if to leave behind whatever had silenced these others. She swerved to avoid a woman with a black felt hat, pulled down like a pot, and cracking shoes and a loose black coat, who carried a bundle wrapped in newspaper. A cleaning woman, Mary decided, going home from some office building to get supper, and tired anyhow as she is every day, but now more than tired. Two young girls, with their hair chopped into stiff short bobs, very blonde, unpainted, walked along not noticing the men or the shop windows. They must be salesgirls, Mary said to herself. A man passed her, with a dog on a leash, and she could not place him, because he was too well dressed, and showed no marks of work. There was an errand boy in a white coat with his shop's name embroidered on the breast pocket, two painters in spotted overalls, then a stream of dark-clothed city people mostly wearing glasses, their shoulders curved by desk work. She thought, but you can't be a private citizen any more, it doesn't matter what they are, or where they

13

work, or if they just get money from a bank every month. They're all caught, and now the city has shut down on them like a prison and they must obey the rules, and they have to like the prison and cheer the rules. Or escape. Or escape. Get out somehow. Run from it.

She went into a newspaper stall, thinking that she needed the foreign papers, she would like to remind herself that there were other places in the world and they weren't cut off forever in this heavy quietness. A small woman was pulling German papers from their wire racks, counting them to see she had them all, then rapping on the counter with a coin she paid quickly, and as she turned to leave the shop they faced each other and Mary put her hand on the woman's shoulder to stop her and said, "Rita, wait a minute."

"I thought you would be here soon," Rita said. "Come outside."

"How are you?"

Rita did not answer. How could you suddenly put it into words, standing on the street, scraped by hurrying strangers, and having to lean tight together or talk in raised voices to be heard? Mary saw what could be seen at once: the inexpensive dark blue tailored coat, the dark blue dress, and the beginning of a round white school-girl's collar that showed under the coat, the neat childish feet in oxfords, a small flat bag (with nothing in it surely except a handkerchief and a comb and a few coins for carfare), the beret Rita carried, the well-brushed black hair that was cut straight around below the ears, with a single lock that fell down across her forehead and her right eye. Indian hair, Mary thought, but how young she looks in her new clothes, and rested and sort of pert. She's all made over.

"I am well," Rita said finally, and smiled.

"You look wonderful."

The clothes were two months old, but every day they were as new and miraculous as when she bought them, and every day she was astounded to be walking wherever she wanted to go, she, Rita, dressed as well as anyone (oh, better, she saw no other coat she envied, no other dress with a white piqué collar that was nicer). A week ago she had bought a lipstick no larger than a capsule for five pennies, and at last she had dared smear some of it on her mouth. It was the wrong color but she did not know, and only saw herself as brilliant and gay, with a face she need not hide. She saved the lipstick now, not wanting to squander it, or use it for every day. She wished that she had worn some this evening, for Mary to see.

"Rita, how is it going to be for you now?"

"Ah," she made a gesture, turning her right palm up, and Mary thought, but what has changed her, she looks so well. This is not the time or place for people to be looking calm and healthy and all right.

"I do not know," Rita said. "The police have not come to us yet. The police come to the new refugees, the ones from the Sudetenland. You should see the station: the refugees come in and there they are sent back where they escaped from. You should see it as a writer," and Mary remembered the passing, bitter smile.

"What are you doing?"

"I work now in the Solidarität. It is a party organization. We help the new refugees, the best we are able.

15

There is not much we can do, you understand. All the people ask," Rita said, speaking with a new angry voice, "is some ground to sleep on in a country that is safe. And they are not allowed."

Her anger was as surprising as what had been before, the smoothness and serenity. Mary remembered the first time she had seen Rita, the evening Thane brought her in after dinner for coffee, saying, by way of introduction, that Rita had come from Germany ten days ago. That was last May. She remembered the way Rita looked at them all, as if they were crazy and a little dangerous, with their talk and their laughter and their easy eyes. Rita mumbled *"Es freut mich sehr,"* and found a chair in a corner where she could be by herself. After an hour, her silence embarrassed them and they made remarks to her, which she ignored, and then, asking her direct questions, they got short furtive answers in a voice that was just above a whisper. She's terrified of her voice, Mary thought, not knowing that Rita had simply forgotten how to use it.

Mary could not remember Rita's clothes, except that they had seemed much too big for her, and she remembered only Rita's face, a small face with round black eyes, and an expression of exhausted but unrelenting obstinacy about the mouth. She looked as if she had fought everyone with silence, which was all she had to fight with. After that, Mary met Rita in the street several times, and once Rita had come to her room to ask help for a friend (she had nothing herself, but she would not take money or the concealed gift of money that the journalists regularly made, offering to translate and place magazine articles). And she remembered how

16

Rita walked then, as if she were marching in line with people she could not see, slowly, to the orders of someone standing invisible alongside, shouting and threatening.

Rita seemed to fear that sooner or later they would use what they knew of her, and identify her, and from the three years which they would never understand or share, she kept distrust of everyone. All she wanted then, Mary had guessed, was to disappear, to be alone, not to be noticed ever again, not to be caught.

Now Rita turned to look at a clock that stood before a jeweler's window, a few doors down the street. *"Wie spaet ist es!* I am late. Now I go home." She said "home" shyly but with confidence, bringing it out as if it were a rare word, and one that she wanted Mary to hear. If it weren't so idiotic, Mary told herself, I'd begin to imagine that she has a fine house, a fine husband, four fine children and at least a British passport.

"But when will I see you, Rita?"

"At the office of the Solidarität, or perhaps at the noon hour. I am usually with the comrades to eat in an apartment on the Truhlarska Street, twenty-seven. I wish to tell you many things of what has been happening here. But now I am late. You excuse me?"

"Certainly," Mary said. "By all means, old girl. See you tomorrow. I'll come and find you."

They shook hands and Mary waited a moment, watching Rita weave through the crowds, half running in her hurry to get home. Home, Mary repeated to herself, hearing Rita's voice again. Then she walked up the street towards the fish restaurant, to dinner, to meet again her own odd portable world, but she no longer

17

noticed the muted people around her. She thought: Rita's not a refugee anymore. It's finished. She's lost that floating, empty-hearted look they have. She's happy. That's the same thing as having a country, anyhow.

2

THEY were all, with the addition of a famous Polish-American novelist, sitting at a round table in the corner of the restaurant. From the look of the table they had had many drinks with their hors d'œuvres and were now bowed together, arguing hotly. Mary saw Tompkins rising forward in his chair, so that his wide flannel-covered rear shook as he hit the table to make a point. Thane was leaning back, drinking vodka in a tiny glass, taking no part in the talk and watching the fierceness of the others with a certain professional contempt. He had long ago learned that to be quiet, and doubt both sides, gave you a position of superiority.

They rose when she joined them, and Berthold said, always personal (though wearily and without much conviction), "Your Spanish sunburn is very becoming, Mary."

Exactly as he might say, "Have you ever had measles?" she thought, and wondered if they acted in character naturally, or if they were always just a little tired, a little bored, so that it was less effort to stick to one pattern of behavior. But she had known them so long that, on the whole, making or acknowledging compliments was a waste of time (unless by chance you found one of them melancholy and distressed and then you

19

said all the pleasant things you could invent, to tide him over the bad place; and he, loyally, would do the same for you some day).

She smiled at Berthold and asked Tompkins, "Why isn't Mike Ames here?"

"He left two days ago for Palestine," Tompkins said. "That's a story. People shooting at each other. Not just disappearing or shooting themselves the way they do around here."

"Do you know Mr. Novak?" Tom Lambert said, turning towards the novelist. She cast about rapidly, trying to pair up well-known names and places, feeling she had surely met him, and it was probably Geneva, but maybe it was Rome. Take a chance on Geneva.

"I think we met in Geneva," she said, "years ago."

Mr. Novak agreed to this and went on with the talk where she had come in.

"This is the greatest crime of our epoch," he said, and Mary could tell from the faces of the others that it was a remark he had made before. "Today I have been to Pilsen. The Germans have carved the frontier so as to ruin Czechoslovakia economically. The frontiers they supposedly decided on at Munich simply do not exist. The Germans take what they see, and from one day to the next, no one knows what more they will grab. Now at Pilsen they have taken the most important electric power stations, the way they have here." (Ah, Mary thought, so that's why everything's dim.) "They have seized the land in such a way that Skoda workers who live in the suburbs must cross Germany to get back to Pilsen for work in the factory. They have taken the coal mines. Now Skoda has to haul its coal in trucks, because also the railroad is cut. Everything is like that. The economy of the country is ruined."

She would have liked to ask him many things, since he was a thorough man (from his work), and knew this part of Europe well. There were the flat basic facts that you had to assemble: how many coal mines had the Nazis taken; how much of the textile industry, the glass, the porcelain, the sugar was lost; how many hectares of timber, hops, flax, tobacco, had been seized; what had happened to the railroads; was it true that the Tatra car plant had been confiscated, though it was well inside the Munich-agreed frontiers? How many Czechs were now living in the new Germany? It would take much running and asking to bring this information together and check it and spread it out smoothly so that it made a complete picture. Statistics were only black marks on paper to her, and if she learned that an unpronounceable Czech manufacturing town had become German it meant nothing, until she thought of the people who worked in the factories, and where would they go now: you would see them on the roads, with bulging sacks over their shoulders, walking from place to place, looking for jobs that had disappeared forever behind an unreasonable line of barbed wire: the expanding Nazi frontier.

She would have liked to ask questions, forgetting dinner, and she began to feel in her bag for a stub of pencil and an envelope to write on, but she saw that her colleagues were bored with this, and counting on her wordlessly to change the conversation, she being a woman, and therefore by right inconsequent or frankly ignorant. They probably know it all, Mary thought, or else they don't need such information for their stories; and by simply turning her head and smiling, she gave Tom Lambert a chance to talk. The others relaxed. The novelist was too earnest for them.

"I got my chauffeur out of jail in Carlsbad," Tom Lambert said, grasping his cue, "but they beat him up some first."

"What do you mean?"

"Oh, you missed it, Mary; you missed the fun. That was last week, when the Heinies were taking over. We kept driving up to the Sudetenland, watching them come in. You know how they did it: they'd enter and occupy the country by zones. The first few days we got shot at by the Freicorps, they're the local Nazis, the Germans who live in the Sudetenland, and a finer bunch of thugs you could scarcely hope to meet. So that was interesting. But then the Heinies came, regular army and the Gestapo running alongside. They were more serious. Then one day we went to Carlsbad."

"Yes," Thane said. "Dopes."

"We went to Carlsbad," Tom Lambert explained, "to try to get a look at one of the new concentration camps. Very thorough, these Nazis. In the first five days they were in Czecho they had five concentration camps running, and packed full, and one of the best ones was at Carlsbad. So we went snooping around and they caught up with us. They couldn't do much to us on account of our passports and foreign press and all, but they got the chauffeur."

"I've seen people scared," Luther said. "In China, when they bomb for instance. But this boy was scared of something you couldn't see."

"So we argued," Tom Lambert went on. "We drove around to the police station and demanded to know his crime, but that's old-fashioned stuff and doesn't count, and after a while we saw that the next thing would be that they'd shut us up too, passports or not. So we left him, but we felt pretty lousy."

"Gave me the horrors," Luther said. "He was a social democrat, and there were plenty of people who knew him around there and could denounce him. He came from some village close by, Ostrov or something like that. Nice-looking young fellow too."

"What did you do?" Mary asked.

"Our consul here," Tom Lambert said, "and the Czech foreign office, and then we went to the Henleinists' propaganda bureau and told them we were going to write such stories about them, and their Nazi friends, and their idea of law and order, that they'd never get the smell of it off them. That was what worked it, a little blackmail. Would have written it too. So they let him out, and he came back to town today."

"How does he look?" Thane asked.

"So-so," Tom Lambert said briefly; but you could see that he wasn't forgetting it, and that he hadn't cared about it. "Messy. A little messy on the back above the buttocks."

"Ai," Mary said.

"Listen, sugar," Thane said to her, "if you hang around the frontier, up beyond Kladnow and in that general direction, and go to the places the refugees are staying, the schools or the hospitals or wherever they've got them parked, you will see things that will alarm and surprise you. In the way of messiness, I mean. You

23

will also hear things that are worse, but you can't check them, so you have to throw them out."

"The only one who has seen a first-class atrocity," Tompkins said, "is Markton."

"Don't know him," Mary said.

"No, he's from London, from the *Daily Clarion*. My paper wouldn't use it, but his gives him a bonus. And he's an honest lad; he wouldn't make it up the way most of their men would. He really did see it."

None of them asked to hear the story. Thane had nodded his head, so she guessed he knew it already, but the others were shying away from it, as if they had heard too much, and seen too much, and as there was nothing they could do, they would rather go on with dinner, and forget about it.

"Let's talk about something cheerful," Luther said. "Don't you want to eat or drink?"

"Yessir," she said. "Both. Drink first. Double dry martini, please, and for food, whatever's quickest and easiest."

Berthold said, "I wrote a beautiful story about the refugees. Very poetic and emotional but my paper wouldn't use it. My paper approves of Munich. I called my story 'Mr. Chamberlain's Orphans,' though I would rather have called it, 'What that Cow Monsieur le Ministre des Affaires Etrangères Georges Bonnet Did.' But even putting the blame on the English they wouldn't print it. I had made a special trip to the frontier too, to get the material, though I could have written it from here with much less trouble. I do not know what they pay me for, as they have almost stopped using my articles."

24

"He's on a Fascist paper now," Thane explained, "but you can see his politics are changing. In about three months he'll be working for the Socialists. Then as soon as he's with them, he'll become a Royalist. It's a wonder to me that Louis eats at all."

"I am the most talented journalist in France," Berthold said affably. "Everybody knows that."

"He is too," Luther said. "That's what's so funny."

"How's the Czech censorship?" Mary asked.

"You can't understand it," Tompkins said, "unless you realize that the Nazis already own Prague. Every time we try to get something out that shows what a raw deal they're getting, the censors tone it down or cross it out. They're so scared they're going to rile Adolf, they act as if they were working up for jobs with Mr. Goebbels."

"I don't know," Tom Lambert said. "What difference does it make to them now? After all, the Czechs got a pretty good idea of how world opinion stood nobly by and defended the weak and virtuous. I think they're right to please Adolf and let the rest go. Adolf's who counts in Europe."

"Anyhow," Tompkins said, "unless you can sneak stuff out, you better plan to write in Paris. You can't give the facts from here. Especially about the refugees. Adolf wants it to look like everyone was welcoming him with flowers and heils and the English and French would rather not know what a stink it all is."

"The story's dead," said Thane. "The Nazis have won again, and that's all there is to it. The only place that's interesting now is South America."

"My food," Mary said. "Have none of you men a heart?"

The waiter was called and instructed, in German by Thane and in Czech by the novelist, and left, startled by this flow of language.

"I saw Rita on the street," Mary said to Thane.

"Poor old Rita," Thane said.

"No, she's fine."

"Well, if you mean she hasn't got cancer, or tuberculosis of both lungs, I guess she's fine," Thane said. "But not otherwise."

"Who's Rita?" the novelist asked, interested again in the conversation, hearing a name that meant a face, a story, something you could store up and later alter in your imagination until it had a shape. You could almost see him reaching for a minor character, with that nervousness and groping need of someone who would have to pull out of his brain, year after year, people and situations, whether he was able to or not.

Mary let Thane talk. She was not going to hand Rita around as dinner table conversation. Thane would not understand Rita, or care, and he could talk of her, and she would stay a stranger to them all; but Mary would protect Rita's privacy, because Rita deserved that.

"She's a little woman," Thane began, "who is probably thirty-three and looks twenty-five. I met her in Berlin in 1930. She had a brother then who was short and skinny and ugly and ran an unreadable weekly magazine of the extreme left. It seems Rita had always taken care of him since they were kids because her mother died just after he was born, though why she was so devoted to the miserable little guy I never understood. Anyhow, they lived together in one room and were always kind of hungry, so I gave him something every month for keeping me up on Communist politics. He would bring me in an article as long as a book, full of fine phrases about the party and what wonderful things it was doing. Rita helped him. They were mousy people but nice, and I took them out to dinner once in a while. Of course they were crazy, the way honest Communists are, you know, believing in it like the second coming of Christ, and making nothing for themselves, and having a tough life, all sweat and no pay, but they weren't important in the party or dangerous. They were just little intellectuals who worked for a better world. There used to be thousands of them in Germany."

"And then?" the novelist prompted: he could invent this part himself. Mary tried to fit Thane's story with her own; she knew he would have the facts straight, but beyond them, beyond the dates and the places and the acts, he would not go. He could not accept the idea that people would risk and perhaps ruin their lives for something that never profited them.

"So then came Adolf," Thane said. "Came Adolf and the Gestapo. Whereupon Herr and Fräulein Salus caught it. They didn't catch it as fast as the important left-wingers, because they had to be dug out like moles, but the Gestapo got around to them in due course. In about 1934 or 1935, long after I'd been kicked from the country. I saw Rita in May here, and she told me just what had happened and the rest I could figure out from what I knew of other people like them in Germany."

"Hurry," Tom Lambert said. "My God, man, come to the point."

"Okay," Thane said. "I am telling a wonderful story in about one thousand words and I get hurried. I'd like to see you do it any quicker."

"I can tell five in the same time," Tom Lambert said.

The novelist made a little sound of impatience and Thane went on.

"They arrested her brother because he ran a treasonous Bolshevik paper. The paper of course had stopped in 1933, and Rita and he went underground together with all the Communists, but the Gestapo found them. They got Herr Salus in one of their jails and decided to beat him to make him talk. He was supposed to give them names of other party members, because he hadn't been doing anything much since Adolf arrived, but he knew Communists naturally. So they began and beat him with a belt buckle. And the skinny little guy wouldn't say a word. Then when they'd just about killed him, which wasn't very hard as there were eight big Nazis working on him and he was a runt of a man, they brought in Rita. The idea was that they would show her her brother, and she would talk to stop them from beating him. He just managed to tell her not to talk, and they held her there and went on beating him. They slapped her face so she'd keep her eyes open and watch it, and they kept it up with the belt buckle until they'd laid his kidneys bare and after a while he died."

"Right there?" the novelist said, in a quiet voice. "Right there in front of her?"

"Right there in front of her."

Mary did not know this, and hearing it now in a well-lighted restaurant, where they were all safe, not believing a thing like this could ever happen to them or to who they loved, she felt it anyhow, creeping along her skin and making her throat tight.

"What then?" the novelist asked, and the others waited.

"Well, she wouldn't talk either so they got tired of using the belt buckle on her and they put her in prison. It's a woman's prison that is famous in the Third Reich. They didn't bring a charge against her or have a trial or any time-wasting procedure like that. After all, she was either a Communist or the sister of a Communist, or the sister of somebody who thought Marx was pretty good, and her mother was a Jew, though she'd died about twenty-five years before, and that's all you'd need for a crime. So Rita stayed in that prison three years, and then they threw her out and gave her two days to leave Germany and she came here. That's when you met her," he said, turning to Mary. "Some of the other German refugees I'd known in Berlin told her I was in town, last May, and she looked me up. I think just to see someone pre-Hitler, but aside from telling me what I've just told you, in about four sentences, she didn't say much. So I don't know what went on in the prison, or how she got out, or how she lives here, or any extra details. But that's who Rita is."

"Some story," Tompkins said. "I wonder if I could use it anyway?"

"There must be about five thousand others, as a minimum, just like it in Prague alone," Thane said.

"What does she look like?" Tom Lambert said.

"Like nothing," Thane said. "Like a she-communist."

In May, Mary thought, Rita didn't really have a face: just eyes, a mouth, a nose, set coldly and without color on the taut skin. But she was wonderful to look at anyhow, or why did we all keep turning towards her corner, when she never said a word. She had something none of us had, certainly. This evening, on the dark street, when she said, "Now I go home," she wasn't pretty. Only you wished you could look like that yourself; you knew with envy how the way she looked would enter into the man waiting for her; you wanted to reach out and touch her and take for yourself what she had behind her skin, behind her eyes, and her smooth throat. Mary thought, with scorn, a man who knew anything about women would know what she looks like.

"Here's your food," Tom Lambert said. "What are you doing tomorrow?"

"Nothing."

"It's Sunday and there's no news around here. I've got a car. Want to drive out to Cesimova Usti and try to get an interview from Benes?"

"Christ," Tompkins sighed. "And I bet you get one too, with Mary to vamp the gatekeeper. I've been hanging around that country estate all week, and never even got up to the fence."

"He isn't talking," Tom Lambert said. "But I used to know him when he was a big shot in Geneva, and maybe, just maybe, we could get in. Anyhow it's a nice drive and you'll get a look at the country. And if we get a story, it would be something."

"Fine, Tom," she said, thinking: but that isn't the story. It doesn't matter any more about Benes. He's got an aeroplane. The story is those who have no aeroplane.

3

THEY were parked at the entrance to the garage, having explained in sign language that they wished to fill the tank with gasoline. Mary held a map on her knees, and together they attempted to trace a route through Prague out to Benes' country place.

"Did you ever see such names?" Tom Lambert said. "We couldn't possibly ask the way."

"I think I've got it," she said. "We go down the Wenceslaus Square and turn to the left at the bottom and go straight down Narodni to the bridge, and then turn left again on something I can't pronounce. That ought to bring us out to the Cesimova Usti road."

Tom paid for the gasoline and they started off at twenty miles an hour, Tom saying that until they left town she was not to speak to him, so that he could concentrate without emotion on the Prague traffic.

"The Wenceslaus Square beats all," he said. "How's a man to know which side to drive on? Besides those street cars racing to and fro in the middle and people ambling about like damned chickens and me with no driver's license."

"Take it easy," she said. "You go down town on the left."

The Square was scantly alive on Sunday morning

31

with window-shoppers and bicyclists who changed their minds in mid-traffic, and near the center on narrow cement pavements, groups of people, the women in Church black, the men Sunday-starched and aimless, waited for street cars. They drove with jerking stops (Tom Lambert being more careful than accomplished) for three blocks, and then a man, with his back to them, stepped suddenly from the pavement by the street cars, swung into the street ahead of them, and walked under their car. He was hit by the right fender and thrown back and he folded up softly, in a gray bundle against the pavement he had just left.

They ran behind the car to where he lay. Four men were helping him up, awkwardly. He stumbled, trying to rise, and his arms sawed the air, stiff and wooden. His hat had rolled off, and his hair grew like dry coarse moss and his eyes were empty with shock. He did not speak. Mary dusted his hat and gave it to him, as he stood with one of the strangers holding him on his feet. There was a short scratch slanting across his forehead and no other mark; nothing seemed to be broken. He looked as if he would faint.

"Get him into the car," Tom said. "And for God's sake, let's get out of here before the police come. Tell him we'll take him to a hospital."

Without explaining in words, but only guiding and shoving the little man, and the four who had picked him up, Tom managed to get the man into the back seat of the car.

"Hurry, Mary," Tom said. "We've got to get out of here."

She closed the door behind her and turning to the

little man, she said, "Hospital, clinic," trying to make it sound German, in her alarm forgetting the word *Krankenhaus.*

The little man nodded, not hearing or understanding. He was looking at his hat as if it were precious, and he was about to lose it forever, and she repeated "Hospital." Then surprisingly his eyes were brilliant with fear and he said no, no, and fumbled with the door of the car.

"It is nothing," he said in German. "Nothing, nothing. I will go now. Excuse me please."

They all heard the police whistle, and Tom said, "That tears it. I hope you will send me nice canned foods to the jail, and reading matter."

Mary had been watching the little man. He closed his eyes swiftly, as if the long pointed notes of the whistle hurt him. Then he slumped into the corner of the car, and his mouth sagged and trembled, and he could no longer keep back the despair that was blurring his face and bringing sharp tired tears to his eyes.

"He's much more scared of the cops than we are," Mary said to Tom. "He's really scared."

"I'd like to know why. He didn't run over anybody without a driver's license."

The policeman came alongside the car and Tom rolled down the glass window. The policeman said something in Czech and they smiled, politely and stupidly. Mary asked the little man in the back seat whether he spoke Czech and he said, *"Nein,"* shaking his head.

"Now what?" Tom said. "This is going to be dandy. Jailed in a language you don't even understand."

33

The policeman climbed into the back seat and prodded Tom's shoulder and pointed where he wanted to go. With prodding and pointing, they drove through Prague until they came to a quiet street, with high round trees along it, and stopped opposite a yellow stucco building. The policeman indicated that they were all to follow him.

The policeman walked ahead, with Tom beside him, Tom unable to speak but hoping that if he smiled and looked respectable, reliable and charming, some useful impression would be created in the policeman's mind. He wondered whether he should produce ten kronin, and get it to the policeman, but the Czechs were notoriously honest and filled with a passion for citizenship, and it might prove fatal to try money. If only this were France, Tom thought, oh, God, or Italy, or any nice crooked country.

The little man came last. At first Mary thought he would let them get ahead and make a break for it, running until he got back into the crowded part of town. He could lose himself wherever there were people, you would never see him again, he would fade into the pavement, being the same color, he would look like every other old man who was a little down on his luck, humble and frayed and trying hard to keep clean. But he knew, and so did she, that he couldn't run far enough or fast enough: they would catch him: and after he had stared once down the street, his whole body pulling towards that safety, he followed her. Mary waited for him, and coming closer, he smiled, timidly, and said in German, "It was nothing, Fräulein, now all this trouble for nothing."

"Yes," she said, thinking: what is he afraid of?

The policeman was talking with a stout, helpful, overdressed young woman, just inside the door. As soon as they came in, they smelled that it was a clinic. The young woman nodded several times and began to translate for the policeman in stiff English.

"The wounded must follow the police. He will become treated. Then all must go again with the police to the police house, where must be given names and a statement."

"Thank you," Mary said. "Will you tell this gentleman in German?"

She told the little man who shook his head anxiously and his eyes begged the woman, since she spoke his language, to stop all this, to tell them it did not matter, he was not harmed and he had no grievance against the two young people, and he would like to go.

"It is nothing," he said to the woman. "I am satisfied. I wish no trouble for anyone. Can they not go, and I too?"

"It is the law," the woman said to him. He knew about the law, and how strangely and fiercely laws appeared, and how relentless they were so that one man could change nothing, but would have to obey. He followed the policeman through a door into the dispensary, and Tom and Mary leaned against the wall and lit cigarettes, and from time to time made half-hearted answers to the young woman who was happily practicing her English on them, while she waited for a sick friend.

The little man returned, barred with iodine, and the woman told them they must now go to the police house.

They had grown very quiet. In the car, Tom said, "Mary, you haven't by any chance your French driver's license, have you?"

"Yes."

"Give it to me, I may be able to get away with it."

"It's got my picture on it, so say I was driving the car."

"Don't be silly."

"Don't be heroic. You know they'll make less trouble for me, and anyhow, Tom, I'm sure nothing will happen to us. It's our poor old pal who's going to catch it."

"Why the hell should he get in trouble? He was just a half-wit who walked backwards into a car. It's always the driver who's guilty."

"It hasn't got anything to do with automobile accidents," she said impatiently. "It's something else."

"Ah," he sighed, "you would have to get intuitive at this point."

The little man said nothing that you could understand, but sitting in the corner, as far from the policeman as possible, turning his hat in his hands, then slowly examining his frayed left cuff, noting with wonder that he had somewhere and somehow lost the third button of his overcoat, smoothing and brushing himself, patting down his hair and passing his hands over his face, and the new iodined scratch, he mumbled softly, so that the sound came to her as a sigh.

"I think he's saying *'Lieber Gott, Lieber Gott,'*" Mary told Tom.

"If he had any sense, he'd be saying, 'Ten thousand kronin, ten thousand kronin,' and slapping himself on the back."

"He won't ask for money."

"Mary," Tom said, "you are beginning to madden me."

"All right, darling. All right, sweetie. All right, angel."

When they had stopped before the high dark stone door of the police station, none of them moved. The policeman was already in the street, holding the car doors open, and beckoning to them, with many smiles and gestures, as if they could not be expected to understand that when a car stopped you got out of it.

Tom said, "Come on. We're up to our necks in this. We may as well get it over with."

They filed up shallow steps to a glass door, down a brown-walled corridor, smelling of wet cleaning rags and tobacco, knocked at a door that was lettered in Czech, were shouted at from inside the door, and entered. Tom revived at once, being able from a certain international experience with police to place an atmosphere quickly. This was all right. A tall iron stove in one corner warmed the square room. The walls were plastered with notices, posters and maps, all faded and scratched. Behind a wooden railing at the far end of the room stood a big roller-top desk and three tables, at which were seated five Czech policemen with their tight military collars unbuttoned, smoking. They looked sleepy and after all it was Sunday morning, almost lunch time, not an hour for being too aroused by duty. Tom walked to the wooden railing with confidence and a friendly smile. Mary stood beside him, but the little man, as quiet as fog, had drifted to the other end of the room, turning, with his back to them,

37

to face the stove. Then, hoping that if they did not see him they would forget him, he stepped behind the stove and pretended to read the Czech police notices and traffic posters on the wall.

One of the policemen spoke German and Mary, with an expression of sweet helplessness, blundered in that language more than she had to, explaining the details of the accident. As the officer who had arrested them had seen the accident too, from the corner by the traffic light, this part passed easily, was noted in a ledger and dismissed.

"Reisepass?" the German-speaking policeman asked.

Tom and Mary produced their passports, and the policeman handled them with respect: good red-covered American passports, always valuable, proving that the owner was a serious, law-abiding, probably wealthy citizen.

"Zeitungsberichterstatter," Mary said, hopefully.

"What's that?" Tom asked.

"Telling him we're journalists. Useful in France, England, Spain, and probably here. Bad in Italy and Germany. I never know, but it's worth trying."

It seemed to be a good idea because the policeman said, *"Ach, so?"* and smiled wisely.

"He can see anyhow," Mary said, "that we're not the sort of people who go out on Sundays to run pedestrians down for the fun of it."

"Wait," Tom said, "we haven't come to the driver's license angle yet."

The policeman then asked for the driver's license. Mary frowned as if she did not recognize these words. Tom made shrugging motions and began turning out his coat pockets in a false gesture of helpfulness. The policeman placed his hands on an imaginary wheel, steered it for a moment, and then tapped the documents.

"Ah," Mary said, with sudden understanding, and gave him her French driver's license. "International," she said firmly.

The policeman looked at it, puzzled but not unwilling to be convinced, decided that it would do, did not ask who had been driving the car, and nodding his head, showed them that their business was now terminated.

Then they called for the little man. The policemen could not see him behind the stove and for a moment they became irritated and alarmed, since to have the plaintiff disappear was a marked irregularity.

"I hope he got away," Mary said and Tom looked at her as if she was purposely trying to annoy him.

The officer who had arrested them went behind the stove and led the little man back to the wooden railing, and the questions. The little man came quietly, as if he always intended to do exactly what was wanted of him, but on the other hand, how was he to guess their desires. He assumed an expression of calm innocence but his eyes flickered about the room and he could do nothing with his worn, shaking hands.

It was very hard to get a description of the accident from him. He said, "I have no complaint to make, it was nothing at all. These ladies and gentlemen have already wasted much time," with wistfulness, sadly, as if he were deeply ashamed of having been hit by their car. "I wish no inconvenience to anyone. As you can see, *Herr Wachtmeister*, I am not hurt, not at all." The policeman would call him back from this, and ask for details, and at last three identical versions of the accident, from three sources, were properly written down in the ledger.

"Papers?" the policeman asked.

"Right here," the little man said, and began feeling through his inside pockets. "Right here, I had them a moment ago." His hands were loose on his wrists and unbearably clumsy, and he would look at no one. They waited in silence, the policeman knowing already how this would end.

"I am from Romberg," the little man whispered breathlessly, still searching his pockets, tearing at them, his back twisting and bending to find something that did not exist, "I am a democrat."

"Yes," the policeman said in a flat, not unkind voice.

"In the Sudetenland," Tom said to Mary. "The second zone, I think. The Heinies got there last week."

"You are a refugee?" the policeman asked.

The old man let his hands fall to his sides as if he would need to stand as straight and strong as he could to answer them now.

"I do not know," he said, and Mary turned, unable to look at this any more. "I went away when they came, in the night, with nothing. My mother is still there, a very old woman who cannot move quickly. I am from Romberg," he repeated, giving out the name as his reference, his last link with an ordered, reasonable world. "Many good citizens know me there, many Social Democrats."

"There is a law for refugees," the policeman said,

40

still in the same voice, as if he had used the voice, and even the words often before and had memorized how to do it because it wasn't easy. "The present rule is that you may remain in Prague a pair of days; after which all refugees, having registered with the Prague police on arrival, must return to their own communities."

"I cannot," the old man said, not begging, not hoping for help or that the relentless law which spared no one would spare him, but only stating in a thin weary voice what was a final fact. "They do not allow Democrats."

"Your address," the policeman said, and Mary thought, he's too honest and he'll tell, then they'll have a record and they'll find him. If he lied he could hide for a week anyhow, and get out into the country, and cross the frontier somewhere at night, but what frontier, she stopped herself, what is there to cross into?

"I do not have an address," the old man answered, speaking far from them, and without fear for them or their rules anymore. He had a home in Romberg where he had always lived, and his mother had kept it clean, and he painted the white walls and the porch and the flower boxes every two years, and tended the dahlias in the garden. He was sixty-two years old and he had always had a home, and people had said to him on the street, *"Guten Morgen, Herr Brecht,"* as should be said to a man who owned property and paid taxes and was always decently dressed and sober. Now he slept in the street, and he knew he was dirty.

He could not return to Romberg, where the people had gone mad, and hunted each other like animals. He remembered how it had been before he left the town,

41

not caring where he walked, talking to himself, sobbing like a sick man. There was the butcher from the Hermannstrasse whom he had known all his life, and Plauen who ran a restaurant and Gutberg, the gymnastics professor at the high school, and he had seen them with crazy faces going through the streets, armed, walking as men could not walk but only as terrible hungry animals moved, going through their own streets in their own town after other people, his friends (but their friends too surely), to beat and torture and kill. They had been Henleinists for years, but nothing would excuse what they had become, only last week. He remembered the German soldiers entering his town with heavy shoes and square steel hats, and their faces mocking, cold, distant, watching these cruelties as if it did not concern them. Then there had been dreadful people, swift and sharp like rats, wearing ordinary clothes and going smoothly to the houses, at night, and his mother told him how Frau Klaus wept and was like one insane because her man had been taken away. But why, but why?

He would sleep in the street and be without a home or anyone he knew, unclean, walking all day, yesterday and tomorrow, hoping only that he would not fall from weariness or hunger (he who had always eaten hot meals in the kitchen with his mother at noon and six-thirty, not talking, listening to the steady tick of the clock), hoping only that he could go on walking and pass unnoticed, trying even to breathe quietly and keep back the horror and the fear that were screaming inside him. He would not be hunted down simply because, all his life, over a pipe and a glass of beer, he had mused placidly on politics, without wishing to change anyone else, but enjoying his own thoughts and guarding them. He would not be caught by the mad ones and hurt so that he was forced to cry out whether he wanted to or not. But if he could, a little later, by himself and in his own way, arrange to die, that would be sensible and respectable and he would not be ashamed of it.

"I sleep in the street," he said, and the policeman flicked papers on the table rather than face the old man's eyes, because there was no denying the overcoat, the soiled shirt, the shredded satin tie, the shoes that had been wiped, and you knew this man never slept in the street, carelessly, like a tramp or a drunk. "Like others from my land, like thousands of others," he said, in a fine mourning voice that asked no pity from strangers.

"I must give you a paper," the policeman said, "an order to leave Prague in two days. If you do not, and are found, it will be bad for you."

The little man seemed to come back from wherever he had gone, and again the police were standing before him, with power, and Prague was real and he alone in it. He said eagerly, "That is good. I am going to Zurich, you understand. I have already my ticket for Zurich. There will be no trouble. Naturally. I am planning to leave tomorrow."

He began again to search his pockets for the Zurich ticket. The policeman did not bother to wait through this small hopeless deceit. He filled out a printed form, a flimsy slip of paper that was the expulsion order.

"Do you wish damages from the lady and gentleman?" the policeman asked, reverting to the accident.

"Oh, no," the old man said, shocked. "It has delayed them so much already. It was nothing, and not their fault. I am so sorry," he said, turning to Mary. "You excuse me, please."

He held the expulsion order as though it were breakable. Tom shook hands with the German-speaking policeman and they left the building. The old man still plucked and tapped at his pockets, walking behind them, as if—so late, far too late—he might fish out some odd scrap that would at least cover up his lies, his lie about having identification papers, and his other lie about Zurich.

"See," he said to Mary, smiling, "I have a ticket for Brunn," and he brought an empty hand out of his pocket and looked at it with disappointment and shame and Mary said, "Of course, of course," hoping he would think she believed him.

"Have you any money?" she asked Tom.

"About four hundred kronin."

"I seem to have three and a little over. You give it to him. I'll walk ahead. It will come better from you."

She heard them behind her, the little man protesting, saying No, in a gentle but hurt voice, he wanted nothing, he was only sorry that they had wasted the whole morning when they were going for a vacation surely, on Sunday, to eat lunch in the country pehaps. Tom, not speaking German, kept saying, "Please take it, really, it's all our fault," in an embarrassed unhappy voice, and at last there was a brief silence, as if the little man, probably wrinkling up his face, sick ashamed of having to do this, accepted the money. Mary did not turn.

44

Then the little man came to her and took off his hat and thanked her for her kindness to him and set off down the street.

"We've sure got horseshoes," Tom said, but as if he no longer cared. "It might have been a hell of a mess. Shall we call off the trip and get rid of the car and go to the movies or something?"

"All right," she said. "Do you know any good movies?"

4

YOU came in through the gray stone arch of the door and had a choice of stairways, narrow, very clean and marble, which wound up into different corners of the building. She thought it would be this one on the right, and climbed three floors, past the white plaster walls, the high doors with shining nameplates, and stood before a door that said *Schultze* in black paint on a brass plate. She rang and heard them stop talking inside the room. There was a wait and then a thin girl with a long neck, wearing a beret and a trench coat, opened the door and asked what she wished, politely, but not letting her pass.

"Rita," Mary Douglas said. "Is Rita here? She said she might be here at lunch time."

"A friend of Rita?"

"Yes."

"Come in," the girl said, and Mary stepped carefully into a room, avoiding the mattresses spread on the floor. In a corner of the room, sitting on the mattresses, were three young men and a girl playing cards. All around the room, on nails (but so tidy, correct and German) their clothes hung, very few clothes, per nail, and per mattress. She saw through an open door another room like this one, mattresses and clothes against the wall and

46

alongside some of the mattresses small packing boxes which were bed tables, bookcases and bureaus, all in one.

The girl led her to the left into the dining-room. It had a round table, eight chairs placed against the walls, maps and a large calendar tacked up; and from the kitchen, beside this room, lunch was now being handed out by a middle-aged man who wore a cap, bedroom slippers and the motherly expression of someone who likes to care for the young. There were six or seven young men, not much more than boys, in this room, and a few girls, and they were eating lunch, watery soup in a tin cup and a hunk of dry bread. They were eating it willingly and had been talking until she came. Now they watched her and no one spoke.

"A friend of Rita," the thin girl said, but this was not enough. Let her prove she was a friend of Rita's. Did she have some note, some word, some sign? They were used to people, friends of friends, who turned out to be something else. Mary tried not to fidget. All the eyes, dark and light, cool, not unfriendly, but simply careful, watched her.

"I'm an American journalist," she said. "Rita told me I could find her here at the noon hour. If you would rather that I waited outside, I will go."

"No," the thin girl said. "Take a place. She will soon come."

Mary Douglas sat down and looked them over, wondering which one of them would talk to her, about the weather for instance or some subject equally unlikely to get anybody in trouble. On the other hand, being here at all was what was dangerous from their point of view, if she could remember faces. She might be anything as far as they knew.

A young man with slanting green eyes and thick hair and a mouth that had probably been beautiful, turned to her and said, "What do they think of Hitler in America?"

"I have not been home for a long time. I have been in Spain mostly these last years. But I don't believe they like him."

"Spain?" the young man said.

"Which side?" another asked, a sandy-haired one with a pale face.

"Madrid," she said, and then the question angered her and she said, "I have asked you no questions and do not wish to ask you questions. I do not care who you are nor why you are here. I am a journalist and not a police spy, and if you would like to see my passport I will be happy to show it, in case you wish to see passports. Meantime, I am waiting for Rita."

Then like children who have been scolded for bad table manners, or she thought, what is worse, like Germans who always respond, even the good ones, to the firm voice of authority (even the good ones, she thought, they are almost a hopeless people), they moved around the room uneasily, consulting each other without words, while she stared at a map and wished Rita would come to end this foolishness.

The green-eyed boy, who seemed the most confident one, decided to take a chance on her.

"You know Rita a long time?" he said in English.

"I didn't know you spoke English. No, not very long."

"I learn English in prison," he said, laughing, and they all laughed with him, as if this were a fine old joke which they shared. "The university of the people," he added, the beautiful mouth curving into a very young, delighted smile.

"Me too," said the sandy-haired one, "not so good like him. I also learn Morse Code and French."

"Very fine prison," the green-eyed one said, and now they were all enjoying themselves. "That comrade and me, we get in only the best prisons. That one," he pointed to a boy who was sitting in the corner, a dark frail boy with glasses and bony shoulders, "he get in concentration camp and learn nothing. Just how to sing."

"I beg your pardon?" Mary said.

"How to sing, don't you, Jacob?"

Jacob nodded, smiling from a great distance. One of the girls stood beside him and put her hand on his shoulder, most gently, as if she knew he would not mind the joke but he could not help them with it, and she did not want him to feel left out or lonely, now that they were all laughing.

"He just get out since two weeks," the sandy-haired one said, and pointed swiftly to his head, explaining the boy's strangeness and silence. "So anyhow, Jacob he was in the finest concentration camp since two years. In this camp is many kinds of criminals but mostly Jews. They do outside work, like with hammer on stones and roads and such, from early nach six to when is dark. But in this camp is the fun of the guards to make the criminals sing. From when they get up all day

49

long, walking, working, eating, everything they do, up to bed again, they must sing."

One of the girls, a little one with a square chin and a soft child's throat, said now, in German, "It is horrible. You understand it?"

"Yes," Mary said. "I understand it all right."

The boy with green eyes said, "Jacob is now a little ferucht with this, from the nerves. It is also very hard, work and sing, work and sing. The old ones fall down, too tired from doing this and the guards beat them to stand up, and say, "Sing, go ahead, sing."

"What did they sing?" Mary asked, trying to talk as they did, about plain facts.

"Anything," the sandy-haired one said, and shrugged. "That is the comic. Anything, so they keep singing. Sometimes the 'Internationale,' don't you, Jacob?"

Jacob nodded, his eyes puzzled, his face helpful but sad, he not yet used to thinking of all this as the past, something you could talk about out loud, and carelessly.

"And the girls?" Mary said, hoping they would not mind questions.

The middle-aged man who took care of them spoke now, "They come also from fine places."

The girl who had opened the door said in German, "Rita and I met in prison; that is how we are friends. Three years in the same one."

"The best prison of all," the green-eyed boy said. "Better as mine."

"We did not learn anything," the girl said, "because we were not allowed to talk."

"What do you mean?" Mary asked.

50

"No. That was the rule there. There were five hundred women in that prison but we were never allowed to talk."

"At night they could knock on the walls," the sandy-haired one said, "from one cell to the other, you know how to make the alphabet, the simple way, not Morse, one knock for A, two knocks for B, and so? They can do that at night but it is not the same as talk."

"We made a revolution in the prison, the second year," the girl said. "We made a revolution, arranging in the night by knocking on the walls. This revolution was to get permission to say to each other, 'Guten Nacht' when we marched back to the cells after supper. Just 'Guten Nacht,' not a big revolution. It was a failure."

"What happened?" Mary asked. She tried to picture it: five hundred women planning and scheming through the stone walls, waiting in terror for the appointed day; then what, a delegation of pale, half-crazy women making their demands to a warden whose face you couldn't even imagine, or was there instead a mass refusal to leave their cells; all for the right to tell each other good night.

"The ones who were leaders got beaten. For all there was less food for a time. The leaders after beating were put in the cellar."

"Ah," said the green-eyed boy, remembering the cellars where he had been.

"It is cold and dark in the cellar and wet on the floor and not big," the girl went on. "You must stay there alone without light for sometimes two weeks, with

51

bread and water and more food if you become very sick."

"She and Rita," the little girl said, as if she forced herself to think about it, "were more in the cellar than any other women in that prison."

"How did you get out?" Mary asked.

"They let me out. They let Rita out too. We did not have trials, either one. I do not know why they let Rita go, but I have now the tuberculosis so it is not necessary to keep me."

"She is a big criminal," the green-eyed boy said bitterly. "They talk in her *büro* at lunch time about Nazi and Hitler and politics. She is not political, you understand, just a typing girl from a poor family. So she says, well, she do not know about politics but she is believing in freedom. So one denounces her, she is a communist he says. She is not a communist then. She is a communist now."

What a way to be young, Mary Douglas thought, hiding and waiting. If they lived for hate, or for revenge, it would show in their faces and the way they talk. But they seemed to her only pitifully, nakedly young, and strange because they were hunted, and untamed like all very brave people. Oh, my, she said to herself suddenly, why aren't they older, why can't people have more fun, why does it have to be so hell cruel and desperate and without end?

Rita came in on their silence. She did not see Mary but asked them all in a sharp unquiet voice, "Has Peter been here?"

"No," the green-eyed boy said.

"He has sent no word?"

"Nothing."

Looking up she saw Mary and said, "Hello, no, don't go. We will talk later."

"Children," Rita said to the others, to all of them, those from the sleeping rooms crowding into the doorway to hear her, "it is bad. Now they are sending back the refugees from the Sudetenland with only twenty-four hours' wait here in Prague. The police have been to the Jaures Heim and to the Deutsches Haus."

She explained to Mary, "Those are new refugee homes. Very big. The Socialists manage them. It is all new people, all refugees since a week. Perhaps nine hundred people in both."

Mary nodded.

"So," Rita went on, "for us it is the same as before. But it is bad that they drive back the new ones, faster and faster. Many among them are in great danger. Many of the Socialists, the Jews, and some of our comrades from Eger and Carlsbad."

"Where are they to go?" the little girl asked. "Where are we to go?"

The men looked at her with affection and pity. As if those in authority bothered to ask that question or answer it. One could see she was new to the profession of exile.

"This time," Jacob said in a queer, deep, and halting voice which surprised Mary, who had not heard him speak before, "there is no place to go."

"Nonsense," Rita said. "We will find a way."

Mary thought: is she lying for them, or does she believe it? But she could see that neither Rita nor the others thought now of themselves, or what might hap-

53

pen to them. Their anxiety was for those who were measured out a small twenty-four hours' worth of safety. (Count it as it goes: it is eleven o'clock now, and now it is one. It is three already: look, the street lamps are going on, it must be nearly five . . .)

"But where is Peter?" Rita said. "He was to go this morning with a committee of Czech and refugee writers to see the authorities. He told me to meet him here."

A man who wore oil-stained blue denims said thoughtfully, "From now on, perhaps it will be better to keep away from the authorities."

Rita looked at him swiftly. "Not yet," she said. "We still have time."

"The town is full of Gestapo," the green-eyed boy said.

"Be quiet, you fool." This was the girl who had been in prison, Rita's friend.

"Naturally, Katy," the green-eyed boy said. "I did not mean anything. Peter will be here soon."

"I want to talk to Mary," Rita told them, and they left, closing the door behind them.

Mary asked, "Who is Peter, Rita?"

Rita waited before answering. She did not want to lie to Mary, but she could not tell her everything about Peter.

"Now he runs our newspaper," she said. "It is printed here every week for the German and Austrian refugees. It is a party paper. There are others who have the same danger, most of them would be killed too if they were caught, but he is very valuable. He is a fine man, Peter."

She had said that night, I must go home. Home

54

would be Peter. Peter would explain the new clothes, and the new serene face, Peter would explain all Rita's hope. Mary suddenly thought: nothing more must happen to her. Peter has to come back.

"I'm sure he'll come back all right," Mary said.

Rita knocked her forehead as if to beat away her thoughts and said, "Naturally. I am only upset from what I have seen this morning. It is silly. He will come back."

"Is it final about the expulsion orders?" Mary asked.

"We can always work to stop it. Otherwise it is final."

Mary took cigarettes from her bag and offered them to Rita, who refused. She did not know what to say, she feeling soft and alien, protected, possessed of every safety and every guarantee, and doing nothing to save these others, and unable to do anything. I suppose our turn will come some day, she thought, but she would have liked to go away from this room. She was ashamed to stay.

"Will you help, Mary?"

"Of course, if you tell me what to do." I can always give them money, she thought, making rapid calculations on her salary, but what good does it do to have money and not be able to buy a train ticket?

"I do not think this is the fault of the Czech government: I think they do this because they are ordered from Berlin, and because also they have no money to take care of thousands of homeless people. There is feeling against all Germans in Czechoslovakia now, naturally, even against us because German is our language. But I do not think the government is moved by this reaction alone. The only chance is pressure from England and France and America. You must write about this, you and your colleagues, quickly, to make an opinion in your countries."

"All right," Mary said, but without enthusiasm. After they had public opinion all properly shaped, what good did it do? It was immensely easy to make people hate but it was almost impossible to make them help.

"All right, Rita, I'll speak to the others. They write what they can all along, you know. But you better not count too much on the moral indignation of the world. It has not been something you can count on. And if you have it, there's not much you can exchange it for." She knew what she was talking about.

"Will you come with me to the places the refugees live, so that you can see yourself? You will be better able to write then."

"That's what I wanted to see you about today. I knew about the expulsion order. There was a little man yesterday . . ." She stopped.

Rita was thinking about something else. Mary Douglas did not really want to talk of the little gray man anyhow. It had been bad enough to have thought of him in the night, bad enough to wake feeling it was all your fault, that tomorrow they would put him on the train and it was your fault.

Rita would think it only natural anyhow that she should help. It's like war, Mary thought, people ask you to do something, there is very little time, they have to trust you because there is no one else handy, or perhaps it is that they hope more than they trust because they have to hope. You say what you will do, fast, and then you try to do it. You don't stop to think out all the explanations or reasons; by the time you got through doing that, the wounded would be dead. I ought to believe in something, some party program, some definite pattern for a future society; then the reasons are ready-made and you don't have to think up an explanation. She knew she would always say yes, when she was asked for help, because she did not feel she had a right to her privileges: passport, job, love. She only felt she was lucky and lucky and luckier than anybody could be, and you had to pay back for that.

The little gray man in the police station was not one, he was anyone. No, he was one; and one alone matters and she would never believe in any system where one is not important. She knew she would have searched through her pockets for the ticket to Zurich; she knew she would have lied uselessly, with shame and with fear. The little man was one and she was one too. But she was a lucky one.

"How about tomorrow morning," Mary said. "Will you come by the hotel at eight-thirty, and we'll go together?"

"Good."

"I know Peter will come soon," Mary said, as if in repeating it, she would make it true.

She opened the door to the other room and saw them all gathered in a corner, kneeling and squatting on the mattresses, bowed together over something the green-eyed boy held on his lap. She wanted to say good-by, but did not like to interrupt. They were talking quickly to each other, pointing and asking questions. They seemed excited and eager, as people look who are studying travel folders, and steamship schedules and the glossy hotel advertisements of summer resorts.

"No, no," the sandy-haired man said suddenly, "it is a Fascist country. What are you thinking?"

"You know the Swiss will not let us in, Sofie," Katy said to the little girl. "You remember the letter from Louisa in Berne last week. It was never easy in Switzerland."

"But, no, that is an English colony," the green-eyed boy said.

"Well, where?" Sofie asked, close to tears, like a tired, disappointed child.

"Be patient," Jacob said. "We have all the countries here. We will find one."

Mary looked over the shoulder of the man in blue denim. The green-eyed boy held on his lap a geography book, a school text, dog-eared, and with soiled pages, open at a map of the world. It was a simple bright-colored map, with only frontiers and capital cities marked. Suddenly Katy leaned forward and put her finger on a tiny yellow dot on the left near the bottom of the page.

"That one," she said. "What is its name?"

"Nicaragua," the green-eyed boy said, holding the book up a moment to read the small print.

"Has anyone ever heard of Nicaragua?" Katy asked triumphantly.

"No," they said. "No."

"Well, Katy said, offering them hope and a future, "maybe we can live there. Maybe it is a democracy."

5

THERE was a slow determined rain, falling from a gray-white sky. Taxis moved with a slushing, clanking sound, rubber on wet asphalt, chains on wet cobblestones. People walked past the hotel, buttoned closely into raincoats or bending under umbrellas. A narrow cold wind picked at doorways and street corners and blew the rain flat against the houses. The leaves would all be washed from the trees in a week, to rot in brown drifts along the roads. September that year had been beautiful enough for the end of the world; the winter began drearily, an ugly winter, Mary thought, as is only fitting.

"Go ahead, get in," Mary said. "Don't get wet. It will be a long day."

Rita ducked into the taxi and gave the address, a Czech name that Mary did not understand.

"Did Peter get back all right?" she asked.

"Oh, yes," Rita said, smiling away her secrets. "He came home."

Home, Mary Douglas thought, with wonder again. "Are we going far?" she asked.

"Yes," Rita said. "It is in the suburbs, but we go even farther in that direction later. I take you to two houses; there is no reason for them any more than others, but I know comrades in both and wish to talk to them, and these places are typical also."

"All right."

"I have a letter this morning from my father," Rita said. "Will you excuse me? I have no time to read it before I come."

"Naturally." Mary settled back in her corner and watched the up-and-down, gray, sweating faces of the houses. She would have liked to sleep but the taxi bumped in car tracks and skidded gently turning corners. She was not tired from need of sleep, she was tired from being awake, from remembering yesterday and guessing at today, and she shut her eyes against this steady chilling rain on a dead city. She's got a father, Mary thought vaguely. I wonder what he does and what he looks like. Rita was so truly alone that she could not imagine her ever having been a child, living in a family, dependent and protected and taught and scolded and put to bed and taken to the museum on Sunday afternoons or to open-air concerts in summer. Having a father changed Rita; if you have a father you have someone to count on.

"Ach," Rita said, shaking her head.

"What is it?" Mary asked.

Rita shook her head again. After a moment, when she was sure of her voice, she said, "He is sixty-five, my father, and he lives now in Greece. Without a passport. He does not know how long . . ."

"In Greece?"

"Yes," Rita said. "That is where he found himself. He does not write to worry me, it is just to give me the news."

60

"Here," she said, and handed the letter to Mary.

The letter was written on cheap ruled paper, in the watery black ink that you find in European post offices, an old angular German script, very fine from a pointed pen, with careful punctuation and all the sentences neatly spaced down the page.

It began: "My beloved daughter."

Mary Douglas remembered with homesickness, suddenly, letters she had received (better ink, better paper), beginning the same way. The handwriting was not easy to read.

"The weather is very soft, like the month of August at Wannsee. . . . I have moved to another room which I am able to share with two gentlemen I met here, one of them comes from Hamburg and one is from Breslau. They are very nice intelligent men and sharing the room is a convenience to us all. . . . There may be some difficulty because I have no papers and therefore I am not going out much in the daytime. . . . I received a sad letter from old Mrs. Herzog, whom you must remember, she lived on our block. They took her husband away one night, though I do not know what he can possibly have done to offend them, as he was very old. She waited for two weeks to hear of him and was too frightened to ask, and as she is quite old herself and alone in the world, she probably did not know what to do. Then they notified her to come and call for his ashes as he had died in protective arrest. She is now in Switzerland but I do no know how long she will be allowed to stay. She seems to have a little money. . . . You remember poor Willi Boden, who used to play with you at school? I do not think you have seen him

much these last years but his father was always a great
friend of mine, as we had our coffee at the same coffee
house for ten years. I saw him quite by accident three
days ago. He ended up here as I did. Do you know how
we call it? The Refugee's Strength-Through-Joy Tours,
extremely cheap, see Europe, personally conducted by
the police. . . . He looks very badly and very aged. I
did not ask him about it because I did not want to dis-
turb him. All the teeth of the top row have been
knocked out. I do not know how he escaped. He has
no money but I have been able to help him a little as
I have been giving some extra German lessons to two
children of a postman. . . . I trust your health is good
and that the winter is not too cold in Czechoslovakia
and that you have a suitable coat. It grieves me not to
be able to help you, my dearest child, but as you said
in your last letter that you had a room and enough to
eat, I believed you would rather that I gave some aid
to Willi. I hope that next month I will have a little
money saved and will send it to you as I wish to be sure
that with winter coming on, you have a good pair of
shoes. Your mother was always very susceptible to colds,
and as I remember, it is damp there in the winter. Perhaps we will see each other at Christmas time. . . ."
Ah, Mary thought, with the money you make from giving German lessons to a postman's children, with no
passport either of you, but if you can write it like that,
as if Christmas were still a festival for a family together,
maybe you can both believe it.

"He was a music teacher," Rita said. "But of course
he could not afford a piano these last years."

"My dear," Mary said helplessly. She thought: to be

62

in Greece, just because they are lax at their frontier, or don't have a careful police check on aliens; to be sixty-five and sharing a room with two other old men, nice intelligent men, being matter-of-fact and cheerful about the poverty and the lack of privacy. He could still worry for those whose dangers or sorrows were greater. (Mrs. Herzog lived on the block and had no one but her husband; I drank coffee with Willi's father every afternoon for ten years in the same *café-haus*, quietly, happily, reading the newspapers and later perhaps having a game of skat. I knew the boy when he was little, how could I have guessed, and I would never have believed, that one sunny day in October in Athens I would meet a man already old, too old, with a deformed face and deformed eyes. His father anyhow is dead, fortunately, fortunately.) She thought: to fear for your daughter and to be helpless, without money or means of making money, without papers, not sure yourself where you will be next, not daring to tell her your anxiety or doubt, knowing what weight she already carries. And how lonely he must be, she thought, gone farther than he ever wanted to go, to Greece, with no time left for anything except to die wherever he could find a country to die in.

Rita said, "I have not seen him for four years. He could not live in Germany anyhow, it would break his heart. But if he was not forced to leave perhaps he could take his piano with him."

"Why did they make him go?"

"He helped anyone who was in trouble," Rita said, and her voice was gentle and proud, remembering the old man, with his white hair and his flowing black satin

63

bow tie, who always hoped he looked more like a musician than a music teacher. "He helped anyone and soon he was in trouble himself."

"What are his politics?"

"Politics?" Rita said with wonder. "He had no politics. He plays the piano. Poor Willi Boden. He was a good swimmer, when he was a boy, and he had a bow and arrow."

"Do you think you could get to Greece?"

"No," Rita said. "My father does not believe it either. But I will write and say we will surely meet at Easter and later I will write and say we will meet in the summer. It makes him happy to hope for it."

"Maybe you will too," Mary said, suddenly thinking, Why shouldn't they? Why shouldn't they have some luck too?

Rita laughed and put her hand on Mary's arm. "Of course," she said, "I will sometime." If it made it easier for anyone, she was ready to tell comforting lies. She did not lie to herself because it was too dangerous to play with hope. If you loosened for a moment into dreams, you became careless, and if you were careless, they would catch you sooner or later.

"We are almost there," Rita said.

They had crossed a narrow unmoving river. (What river, Mary thought? She knew the Mississippi, the Loire, and the Seine: but how many rivers you crossed and did not notice and never knew the names and did not remember in what country there had been willows along a deep brown stream, and washing hung out to dry on the lower branches, and boys diving like frogs; or where it was that the bridge curved up slender and

64

high and down below were three rowboats, pink and blue and yellow, like water lilies. Where had it been that they ran the car through fast shallow water, prob-ably Wyoming, Colorado, Arizona, somewhere. But she would always remember the Ebro and the day the bridges were bombed, the river in flood far below, the sky as flat as ice and ice blue and the little silver planes droning so sweetly over the hanging bridges and the broken burning town. What river is this, she won-dered.) Now they drove slowly up an unpaved road, rutted with mud like paste. Limp trees bordered the river on the right, to the left were wet, untrimmed hedges, behind them houses. She would never recognize the place again. It was neither country nor city, you could not see the shape of the houses, they were with-out color, and the trees were not elms or oak or maple, just thin pale trunks and branches, soggy leaves, against the gray sky.

"Lovely neighborhood," she said.

"We will leave the car here and walk," Rita said, leaning forward to stop the chauffeur. "The road is very bad with the rain."

She led Mary up the road to a gate. There was a gravel path under the trees and beyond a low house that looked abandoned. They knocked at the door and stood under the shingle porch, shoulders hunched against the rain. It was cold now.

A man opened the door and they went into a room that had once been the taproom of an inn. The inn must have failed long ago and been left to stand empty with the rain coming through the broken window panes, the rough board floor unswept, dust settling on the wooden bar and on the scratched tables and chairs. The bar slanted across one end of the room, the bottles on the shelves behind it were empty, the labels were all faded and half worn off and an uneven row of glasses lined the bottom shelf. The tables and chairs had been pushed against the windows. The people in the room did not seem to have been doing anything, neither sitting at the tables talking, nor reading, nor working. Mary Douglas felt that they had been standing, stony and unthinking, wherever they found themselves. She had never seen people with such faces.

They did not speak and Rita went to the tallest man in the room and told him in German who she was and who Mary was, and he did not answer. They don't hear, Mary said to herself. The man turned away from Rita as very sick people turn away from noise, turning on a bed, face to the wall.

For a moment Rita too was helpless before their isolation.

"Where is Friedrich?" she said, in a stern voice, to order them alive.

"Gone," the tall man said, and the room remained as it was, the people stiff in their places, with the blank unanswering eyes.

"Gone where?"

Mary thought he was going to strike Rita. He had turned, his body at once taller and bent over, his fist closed in a quick unreasoning movement of fury. His eyes were shiny, aching, and a little crazy.

"Where do you think? What have you come for, you and the foreigner? Leave us alone. We do not ask you to come and stare at us as if we were animals."

66

"Where has he gone?" Rita asked again.

He looked at her in silence. He seemed suddenly to have forgotten this room, or why they were all here, and he looked at Rita with indifferent flat eyes. Mary thought, it's much better for them to keep quiet, even if it's like this, as if they had gone blind. But she felt that, without warning, the silence would burst and they would rush and swirl around the room screaming.

No one moved. They seemed to be growing where they stood. Mary felt that if they moved some disaster would happen, the floor would cave in, the walls would collapse. She found she was holding her breath, staring at them. They stood in rows, without any particular order or plan, and she saw them from wall to wall, the denim work clothes, the corduroys, heavy boots, muddy or dusty, caps, white shirts and blue shirts, a green jacket, a black city coat, gingham dresses, aprons, a straw hat with a flower on it, a handkerchief bound around a woman's hair; but all the faces were the same, narrow with weariness, with trouble marked painfully on the foreheads between the eyes, the bitter mouths close and curving down.

A woman stepped out from the line, and the line shook and lost its form, shoulders and hands moved, someone coughed, someone wiped his face, and then as she stopped in front of Rita, the room settled behind her, immovable again, with all the faces silent, fixed and similar.

In the life that ended only last week, this woman must have been a scrubbed, spare, practical and hardworking housewife, caring for her children and her husband, seeing that the glass in her front windows

67

shone clean and the kitchen floor was as white as a table. Now she had no one to serve and no home to care for, and her body had worn away until she seemed made of wire, the hair scraped into a knot on her head, the skin of the face pulled violently over her cheeks and forehead, the eyes hollowed out and dark, bony hands on flat bony wrists, her cotton dress and apron somehow bound around her, as if she had lashed herself into her clothes. She was perhaps forty-five and looked older; she had not so much walked as flown towards them, like a furious, ugly, wounded heron.

"I'll tell you where he's gone," she said to Rita, the voice like a heron too, high and harsh, all on one note. "There were one hundred and twenty of us here; now there are seventy-two. Little by little. That's where he's gone. With the others. My husband is gone too. So many must go each day; they draw lots. You know what it means to go back. But if they resist, then we must all go. So they draw lots, leaving some time for the rest of us. Now do you understand? Are you satisfied?"

"What does she mean?" Mary asked, not taking her eyes from the woman. The room had fallen back into the waiting, watching silence.

She looked for an answer and saw Rita, pale and remote like the others. It is a sickness that spreads among them, Mary thought; they listen for something that makes no noise.

"What is it?" she asked again.

They turned towards the man in the corner by the window; it was a new voice in the room. The man

68

talked simply and easily and all the time his voice was low and warm like the sound of weeping.

"They took the children to one refugee home, we do not know where and we will never see them again. They took our wives to another and they are gone too. We can find no one, we do not even know where to look. We do not have the right to be families any more." His voice no longer mourned, it came at them, strong with accusation.

"We are not people, we are exiles. So the women go. Then they come and say: your wife is back home, in Eger, in Carlsbad, in Reichenberg, in Teplitz, wherever we came from. Your wife is home alone, they say, what are you going to do? We know that the wife is there in our place, to pay for us, they will hold her until they can get us. Some of the men return at once, knowing what they do, but hoping first to save their wives. Friedrich went that way. We heard from Johannus, who returned to Teplitz and again escaped, that Friedrich was dead."

Now that their fear had been spoken out with dignity and made plain and reasonable, the people seemed to take back their separate faces, and they watched Rita, all the eyes awake and questioning and sane. Since she understood what had happened to them, she would explain it and tell them why and tell them what to do. Rita knew what they expected of her, but what good news could she bring and what advice could she give? She would be ashamed to trick them with hope.

"I will translate for this comrade," Rita said, "if you will permit."

Rita turned away, afraid to see their eyes, as she

69

abandoned them who had been abandoned by everyone.

"Who are they?" Mary said, following Rita to a corner of the room. "Where do they come from?"

"They are Germans," Rita said. "Several millions of them who lived in the Sudetenland were Democrats or Liberals or Socialists or Communists or Jews."

"But aren't they Czech citizens?"

"Certainly," Rita said, "but they are Germans, by race, and the Czechs have had enough trouble with Germans already, so even these who were always loyal to the Czech republic are sent back to Hitler."

"But they can't go."

"Child," Rita said, "no one can go. No one dares go. But they are forced. And you see, before the German army entered the Sudetenland, there was a little quick war between the Czech police who were very few and the Sudeten Nazis who were very many. These Germans, who are faithful to the republic, fought along with the Czech police. Here they are not wanted and are driven back to the towns they escaped from, and there they are killed for treason to the Third Reich."

"But, Rita, it can't be. It can't be allowed. Somebody must be able to stop this."

"I told you. England and France and America."

"Oh," Mary said, thinking: they'll all be buried long before then, if that's the help they're going to get, they're dead now.

"It's too slow," Mary said. "Didn't they tell us that they were being shipped back every day?"

"These are only seventy-two people."

"But," Mary said, lost in it, thinking we can't go off

70

and leave them, we can't just say good-by and good luck, and go away and leave them, there isn't anybody to help them except us, there isn't anybody in the world who even knows they exist, no one will know they are dead. "But seventy-two people is enough."

"Not in this world," Rita said. "Not seven hundred or seven thousand or seven million. It does not matter in this world."

It is like being buried alive, Mary Douglas thought, people deserted everywhere, scattered about in empty houses going crazy, and alone, and no one knowing who they are and no one hearing them, and no one helping. And no way to help, she thought. But it cannot be. It cannot be.

"What is worst is not to know what will happen," Rita said, who remembered too well. "Not to know whether it is concentration camp, or death, or torture. And then not to know where are their families, or what happens to the women, or if the men are still alive."

"We could at least get them food," Mary said desperately.

"In case they have time to eat it," Rita said. "It goes very fast now. It goes so fast as drowning."

"Comrades," Rita said to them, "how do you live here?"

"As we can," the tall man answered gravely. "This is not important. You understand that a little hunger is nothing, a little cold, or to sleep on straw. The neighbors here help us when they are able with food, and some Czech comrades have made a collection in their factories for Sudeten German workers."

A young woman with a white face and weaving hands opened a door. "Here is how we live." They saw the next room, a long bare hall, paved in stone, with two rows of straw down either side.

"Like cattle, worse than cattle, and always waiting for the police. And next time," she whispered, "it will be Hugo's turn." She put the thin frantic hands over her face, her head far down. A young man went to her, and with his arm around her shoulders, held her tight against his side.

"You will excuse her," he said to the others, not to Mary and Rita, but to the others who must still fight the contagion of terror or despair. "She is young."

The room had again settled, the people painted against the walls, growing from the floor, the woman with one hand on her hip as if she had always been standing in just that position, the man at the table with his head leaning on his hand, the man at the window holding a cold pipe, the one with his arms crossed on his chest, hugging himself for warmth. Mary Douglas felt the hard, controlled silence coming back over them.

"They will not get me," the tall man said, talking in a dream, slowly, and to himself. "They will never get me."

Mary shivered in her coat; no one moved, no one listened, the man talked into the emptiness, before the unchanging, unseeing eyes.

He took a knife from his pocket, the kind of knife that a man carries who mends things. He opened the blade and looked at it a moment and then laid the steel against his wrist.

72

"Shall we go?" Mary whispered. "The rain's stopped. Shall we go now?"

Rita told them good-by, but no one answered; they had lost interest in the two strangers coming from a world where people were safe tomorrow as today, an unreal world. They left the room as they found it, furnished with still bodies, waiting in their places for whatever would happen next.

The car stopped. They sat listening to the wheeze and click of the windshield wipers. Smeary gray sky rimmed the flat land. There were no trees and the untended fields spread mud-brown, rough and wet around a huge building that might have been a factory or a prison, gray like the sky, with small black windows and rain-streaked walls. Mary could see nothing green or growing, no one moving, and the great square building rose high and empty from the silent empty land.

"People live here?" Mary asked.

"Many people."

"All right, let's go in."

The path was cut by streams of muddy water; the mud stuck to their shoes and splashed on their stockings. Rita pulled at the gate bell and Mary thought: if only they don't answer and we can go away, oh Lord, she said to herself, the places people actually live in.

A blond child with a cropped head opened the gate, and ran from them, laughing to himself, shy before the unknown women. They went into the first door they saw. There was a wicket window on the left (so it was a factory, Mary thought) and a narrow office behind this. They knocked at the office door and were greeted cheerfully by a man with a bookkeeper's green visor on his forehead, who seemed to be in charge.

"*Salud,*" he said.

The other men rose and shook hands and there were many introductions: Genosse Müller, Genosse Wilhelm, Genosse Schwarz, Genosse Gottfried, and Mary Douglas and Rita smiled and repeated their own names, in the neat continental fashion, after each introduction.

"So," the green-visored one said. "I am glad you have come. What would this journalist comrade like to see?"

"Show her everything," Rita said.

The man led them down a gray cement corridor, sunless but clean, and up narrow iron stairs.

"We have all ages in our hotel," he said amiably. "Now we are very crowded, this is the touring season for refugees. People come in every day from the Sudetenland, and we were already crowded with travelers from Austria."

He explained that in all these rooms lived couples, some young, some middle-aged, some old, that single men slept in the tool sheds, that on the fourth floor were old people, and a few large families. There was even one family of three generations who had somehow managed to stick together during years of exile in four countries. They lived like gypsies in their own room, cooking over an iron pot, not unfriendly, but bound so close by the effort of surviving together that they had no need for other people.

"The children live here," he said. "We have put them all together. It is best for them. We may see them two hours a day. Those who have lost their own now can watch these children grow. We do not let anyone talk sadly or with fear in front of them. The children are happy and every day we have that to see."

He opened the door and his face changed before them as if he had come home to a safe country.

Children played together in corners, rolling woolly balls, stumbling and falling and shouting with laughter. Three little girls stood demurely at a table with stiff beribboned pigtails on their shoulders, and had a tea party for three broken dolls with a few chipped coffee cups. Four small boys, like wonderful mannikins of bright wood, with round red cheeks, round black heads, round blue eyes, bent together in the center of the floor over a toy train made of a cigar box, a very clean sardine can, and a spool hitched together with string. You knew it was a train because one of them said Ding-a-ling, one of them said Chuff-chuff, and one of them said formally: Halt. They drove their train in a circle, and occasionally stopped to discuss where the stations were. A boy and a girl, eight years old possibly, deeply in love as anyone could see, sat together at the long center table and drew pictures with two crayons.

"They are making pictures for their newspaper," the guide said. "I think they are the editors this week."

A tiny figure, wrapped up in a muffler and a pink sweater, wobbled in from the next room holding a toothbrush firmly in his hand. With him was a girl of about seven who seemed to be his temporary mother. "Be careful," she said to him. "Do not drop the toothbrush. It is dirty to drop a toothbrush."

Mary stepped out of the way to allow a procession to enter the room behind her. The children walked two by two, holding hands, tightly, because that way they could keep their balance better. They were bundled in small coats, sewed together of any bright scraps that the women could find or beg, topheavy and with that comic careful uncertainty of the very young. They had been out for their afternoon airing and returned now, with wind-shined cheeks, to be greeted by screams of delight from the other children. They were dignified and important, having been on a trip and wearing their overcoats, and paid no attention to the other children but marched fatly and contentedly through the room to another door at the far end, into their own home.

"They will have supper now," the guide said. "The youngest eat first."

Around the walls were pictures the children had drawn, strange bright yellow chickens, green dogs, very red flowers bigger than the trees in the same picture, a few self-portraits labeled "This is Me, Trudie Neumann six years," or "I look like this, Fritz Kraus, I am seven now." There was a small low bookcase in one corner, with shabby books neatly arranged on the shelves. Mary opened one and saw it was a volume of fairy stories and the green-visored man explained that the older children had stories read to them before they went to bed. Their beds were pushed out of the way, lined against the walls to give more room for playing. Some of the beds were regular iron cots and cribs, but some were made of packing boxes, and one was ingeniously constructed by nailing two chairs together.

They come to these rooms, Mary Douglas thought, for two hours a day, to remember and to hope.

"Will you watch the dinner of the little ones?" the man asked.

In the next room, the little ones, unruly as rabbits, and like pink teddy bears in their flannel pyjamas, were being scrubbed and having their teeth brushed. There was a great deal of laughter, the mouths bubbly with suds, the faces dripping, much squealing and wriggling and at last they burst away from their nurses, and rushed to the table, clambered into the small chairs, worried themselves into their bibs and waited. From a bowl in the center of the table a young woman picked up bunches of dark red grapes, one bunch to each plate. From a platter, she handed to each child a big piece of black bread. There was water in the glasses.

"Is that all they have?" Mary asked Rita in English, shocked.

"There is almost no money left," Rita answered. "No one will contribute any more to help refugees. Even if they want to still, they are afraid what will happen to them later if it is known that they gave money to German anti-Nazis."

"But it is not enough," Mary protested.

"Grapes are very healthy," Rita said. "Children always like them because they are sweet."

The children ate what little they had quickly. One boy saved his food, watching it as he ate, with dark questioning eyes. When he had eaten all but five grapes, he fastened both small hands around them, planning to take his food with him. The young woman in charge explained that he must eat his food at the table and she tried gently to loosen his fingers.

For a moment he looked at her as if he did not understand what she was doing. Then he began to cry, squeezing the grapes in his hands and crying loudly so that

77

the other children were frightened. "No," he wept. "No, no. For tomorrow."

The young woman calmed him, promising him more grapes tomorrow, many more, a big bunch for each child, and she told Rita, over her shoulder, as she rocked the child in her arms that this boy was new, he had only come two days ago.

"It took them over a week to get here," she said, "walking at night."

Now the other children who had started crying out of sympathy or fright were quieted too. The ones who had scampered into corners, hiding with their flannel-covered bottoms roundly displayed to the room, were picked up and carried to bed. Every child had been tucked in under his one shredded remnant of blanket. It was still light outdoors. The black-haired young woman talked to Mary in whispers, waiting for the children to sleep before she left them.

"Where are their parents?" Mary asked.

"It is different for everyone. Sometimes the mother is here or the father; some are dead, some are in prison in Germany, some are fighting in Spain, some are looking for a place to live in other countries, some are lost. I do not think there is any child who has two parents that we are sure of. The mother of the little boy who saved his grapes is nineteen and alone now. The father of the girl with black curly hair, the little one who laughs to herself, did you see her at the end of the table, she is too young to talk, well, he is in Spain but we do not know whether he is alive. He is twenty-two. I do not know about the mother. He was very happy to go to Spain. He told me before he left that we would win in Spain and he would have a home for his daughter. So. Well, I do not know. Some are the children of intellectuals." She counted quickly on her fingers, "Three doctors, a lawyer, two engineers, a former naval officer, a government clerk. But in a way," she said shyly, "we are all their parents."

Rita stood by a cot, looking down. The child slept, burrowed into the pillow, with fair hair matted on her forehead and the soft eyelashes making a shadow on her cheeks. Mary thought, maybe we could give her that, since you can see from her shoulders and her back how sternly she is keeping herself from touching the child; maybe we could go quietly away and leave her alone here, with what she'll never have.

"Shall we go into the next room?" she said softly.

The woman moved to call Rita and Mary said, "No."

"She has no children?"

"No."

"It is better to have none," the young woman said, as if she had thought it often, "than to see them hungry. Or cold. Or without a home. Or sick from long journeys and no place to sleep. And where shall we take them when they drive us from here? It is better to have none."

"Let her stay a moment," Mary whispered, "even so."

They closed the door behind them without noise. The older children, shapeless and plump in their pyjamas, crowded together at one end of this room, whispering and clearing their throats and very pleased.

"Oh, yes," the young woman said. "Now they sing. In the evenings they sing before supper."

The room was growing shadowy but there were no

79

lights. On the center table, two candles stuck in bottles would give them light to eat later. Now across the long room, Mary saw them dimly, the hair cut in bangs, the pigtails, the cropped heads, the silky floating hair that would have been the pride of the mother, dark hair and fair and brown and silver blond and red, all the small bodies pressed close in a semi-circle, waiting as children wait to open a present.

A man, who must have been kneeling or sitting on a low stool, surrounded by the children, spoke now: *"So, ein, zwei, drei . . ."*

The voices came up together, delicate as light, and fresh, spreading through the room.

> *"Es kommt ein Vogel geflogen,*
> *Setzt sich nieder auf mein Fuss,*
> *Hat ein Brieflein im Schnabel,*
> *Bring von der Mutter einen Gruss."*

They lifted their faces to sing the old simple song about the bird who brought a letter from Mother, singing it in the child voices that are the same everywhere, and the young woman beside Mary smiled with pride and pleasure that they sang so well. Mary Douglas did not know how long they sang, until the room was dark perhaps, she could not see them, blinded with tears and blind with despair for them. They sang now, with joyful soaring voices, a song about spring.

The road was made of patent leather and the trees were made of oilcloth and the lights of the car cut through a mist of rain that blew in glass streamers across the black shining road and the gleaming black trees.

They did not talk.

Rita, by herself, remembered the child's face (why that one from so many, why that rumpled yellow head when there were many others, as blonde, as light, and as tangled?). I am homesick for Germany, she thought, and for my own people. I must not think of this, she told herself, it is weak, it is sentimental.

Long ago she had known that this world made no special provision for her having children. There is no time, she thought, no money; as if you would need time or money. You needed a country; you needed land, you plant a child to grow. She knew also that she would be without courage if she had a child, she would be crazy with fear for it. No one wants the children either, she thought. They will just grow up, won't they, and be more Jews, more Communists, or just more penniless foreigners? My God, she thought, what will they do when the grapes run out? How soon now? And who would carry the children and where; you would carry them until you dropped, but where and where and where?

Now, she said to herself, think. Do not be a fool. But think of what, think of the map, oh the map, she knew the map. We are surrounded here by Germany, Austria, Hungary, Roumania, and Poland. On the map, you can cover it all with two hands spread out. Indeed? Roumania. Only Roumania. They don't like Jews either, she thought. They cannot afford to encourage refugees. They don't like Communists. They don't like penniless aliens. We must get the children out. Aren't they hated too? Aren't they our children? There are no roads, she thought (always remembering the child's face; I would carry her everywhere): there is no free and open road to walk along.

She put her hand over her eyes. Stop it, she told herself, there are thousands of children, fool, as homeless as these, with the food running out, or finished. But she had taken that one child, for herself, as it slept. I must not, she thought, I cannot allow myself so much love.

Mary Douglas watched the raindrops on the windowpane beside her, bouncing off, splitting and flying out into the darkness. She was glad to keep her face turned away. I've spent enough time on this already, she thought; I should see some big executives, coal and sugar and textiles and God knows what not, and find out how this has hit them; there are politicians to interview too, with quotable sentences; and some high army men; and perhaps even literary celebrities. I've got to get a story, articles, the rounded picture as they say, complete bird's-eye view of tragedy and defeat by our foreign correspondent Miss X. That's what I'm here for. I must not do this any more, I must not waste my employer's money. Who wants to know that I have now twice in my life seen something no one will ever read about by me, because I am not paid for that and besides, in a world hurrying between large disasters, there is no time for these trifles. So who will care that I have twice heard children sing?

No propaganda, they would say. We want the inside story. Make it clear, make it colorful, make it lively. If I knew how, I would write a lament. I would tell how I heard the children sing once in Spain, in Barcelona,

82

that cold and blowing March when the bombers came over faster than wind, so that it would all happen in three unending minutes, but if you saw them they were hanging in the sky not moving, slow and easy, taking their time, you'd think, not worried about anything. But usually the planes were higher than you could see or hear, and suddenly the streets beneath them fountained up, in a deep round echoing underground all-over-the-sky roaring that seemed never to finish, and the windows bent inward and the furniture shook on the floor and in the stillness afterwards you would hear one voice, wild and thin and alone, crying out sharply, and then silence. I heard the children at school, between air raids, sitting obediently on small red painted chairs around a low piano; between air raids. The teacher struck chords on the piano and the children stood and lifted their faces to the dangerous sky and sang as softly and sweetly as you will ever hear an old song about being a good child, and sleep now, sleep well. I heard them again today. It is all the same. So who wants to know that, and I better get to work.

Be careful, Mary Douglas told herself, you're only a working journalist. It is better not to see too much, if no one will listen to you.

6

MARY DOUGLAS was glad to go home with Rita, only hoping that having one extra person to eat her food would not mean a meal less for Rita tomorrow. She did not feel bright and dispassionate, as would be required for dinner with the other journalists; and she was too sad to eat alone. She told Rita to direct the taxi; it was after seven now, and they would go straight to her house.

Mary paid and followed Rita into a courtyard, lit by one electric light in a wall bracket. Rita led her up four flights of stairs, and took out her key. Mary knew Rita was smiling: to have a door, to have a key, to have a water-tight place to come to at dark.

An unshaded bulb hung from the ceiling and lit the room. It was small and the windows were high in the wall, the walls were whitewashed plaster and the floor was made of uncarpeted, unvarnished, but very scrubbed boards. Mary did not see the room clearly until later because a man had been reading at the round table under the hard light, and he rose to greet them. Rita went to him, slipped her hand through his arm, and faced Mary, standing side by side with him, joined and proud, and said, "This is Peter."

Mary was surprised when she saw him. She had not

known what sort of man Rita would love, and perhaps she had been a little afraid to see.

Peter shook hands with her (oh, fine hands, she thought, long and dry and holding your hand hard but quickly) and said Rita had spoken of her and he was was happy to meet a friend. And all the time Mary looked at him, and Rita watched her face with frank, possessive, pleased eyes. Then Mary thought: the poor man, no need to inspect him this way; and she turned to Rita saying: what a lovely home it is.

Peter was tall, with a narrow light body, and he carried his shoulders as if he were tired. He had blond hair, not truly yellow, but more the color of sand or dust, and it curved up and back from his forehead, without a part, ridged by running his fingers through it while he read. He had a small face, gentle, like a Rilke story, with almond-shaped, grayish, thinking eyes. His voice was low and modest, and as they stood discussing the treasures in Rita's home, he put his arm around Rita's shoulders and Mary saw that he loved Rita very much.

She wished that she had bought wine for this supper, she wanted to celebrate the two of them and their being together, and she was so happy about them that she spoke almost incomprehensible German. I wonder if I could say to Rita: in this pitiful destroyed city, it is the happiest thing I ever imagined to see you two in your home. But that would embarrass Peter and she must behave herself.

They stood together in the middle of the floor and Rita pointed out the red bookcase and said that Peter had built it from two packing boxes and she had

85

painted it; and she showed the bed cover which was a little faded and strange, and explained that it was the reverse side of two old banners which she had sewed together. They had been carried in some parade months ago, and on the other side they said, "The United Bakers Local 180 Pledges Allegiance to the Republic," and the other one said, "Pioneers, Troop 40—Hail Democracy," and they all laughed. The table they had bought (Rita told this wonderingly) and the chairs had been loaned them from the Socialist Club on the next block where they had too many.

"We also have a kitchen," Rita boasted, and opened a door into a windowless closet where three pots and a frying pan hung neatly on the wall and a double oil burner stove stood on a table, and a small wooden box, with a screen door, held their food.

"It's a lovely home," Mary said again, and envied it.

"Now I will make some dinner. You talk with Peter."

But Mary felt suddenly shy, and offered instead to set the table. She watched them in the kitchen, and knew how they loved to prepare the meals together, every moment grateful to live as others did, as ordinary married people, with a saucepan and a tablecloth and a roof and each other. She thought, very cheerful now: what a pleasure to see happy people again.

At dinner Rita started to speak of their day and Mary stopped her.

"No," she said. "Peter knows all about it and we've been miserable enough for one day, so let's talk about something else. Let's talk about housekeeping," she said. "Let's talk about how the price of food has gone

86

up, and how expensive laundry is, and the quality of milk."

"Do you know about these things?" Peter asked, smiling.

"No," Mary said, "but I always wanted to."

"You must get married," Rita said comfortably, like a solid matron.

"Darling," Mary laughed, "you're wonderful."

"But why don't you?" Rita insisted. "You could."

It hadn't seemed necessary or perhaps they were afraid to change anything: they were doing so wonderfully. What difference would it make, Mary wondered, marriage is for living in one place, and tennis with the neighbors on Sunday afternoon. We aren't like that, we'll never be settled. Maybe marriage was also for absence: if she were married she could now say, "My husband John thinks . . ." She looked at Rita and Peter, and practiced saying it silently, with delight, "My husband John contends . . . my husband John opines . . ."

"How do you mean 'could'?" Mary asked. It was nice to talk about.

"Well," Rita began and suddenly she looked less happy, darker and afraid.

Peter turned towards her anxiously.

"Schatzlein, isn't everything fine now?" he said. "So we will not worry this evening?"

They had forgotten Mary for this moment, and sat there, her hand flat under his on the checked tablecloth, looking at each other. Mary saw then how desperately they had built their home, how fast and yet how carefully, knowing how happy they could be and how happy they were: but always knowing there was

87

no time for them. She loved the blonde child, Mary thought suddenly, because it looked like Peter. Oh, let them keep it, she thought, let them stay together no matter how they have to live or where they have to go: at least let them stay together.

They're just like us, Mary thought. They love each other the same way. Only they are smaller and with no luck. We have the jobs and the passports: we can always get on trains and meet each other, we can talk about how it will be when we're old and we can make plans for next year. She could imagine John sitting where Peter was, this could be their home, she could be Rita: in another country, perhaps, and in danger for other reasons. The reasons didn't matter. If you were always and naturally on the side of the oppressed, you would always and naturally have reasons for danger. Sometimes it was one system that oppressed and sometimes it was another. The names of the systems might finally be interchangeable. In another time, a long ago time, Rita and Peter might have been Christians when they should have been Romans, or Protestants when they should have been Catholics. They were bound to be the hunted.

Peter took his hand away. "Mary will marry when she finds a good American anti-Fascist," he said, "and have beautiful blond anti-Fascist children and live in a big rich anti-Fascist country, and always be happy."

"Yes," Rita said, "that is the way it will be."

"And you will come to live with me and teach the children lovely anti-Fascist German," Mary said.

"Of course," Peter answered. "It is what we always planned to do."

They washed the dishes and made plans. Rita would have to work at the Solidarität tomorrow, then Mary would go to Kladnow alone and they could perhaps, the three of them, meet for dinner on Friday. Would they dine with her? She knew a really good restaurant, quiet and in the basement and run by friends. It would be all right to go there. So they would meet? And Rita was an angel to have taken her around today and she didn't know how to thank her. And their home was lovely, lovely, and it had been a delicious dinner. No, she could get back to the hotel alone, she would call a taxi at the corner. And good night, Peter and good night, Rita, *Kinder,* she said suddenly (who was younger than either of them), darlings . . .

She did not call the taxi at once. The rain had left the city sweet-smelling and warm, and she walked down the badly lighted street in a direction she thought must lead towards the Wenceslaus Square. She walked slowly, thinking that no one had yet found a system to regiment a man and a woman, no one had yet discovered how to corrupt the good hearts, or turn love into a silly slogan, or make what a man and woman gave each other cheap or small or cowardly. We will win in the end, she thought. There are still men and women alive in the world.

"Are you tired, Schatzy?" Peter said.

"A little bit."

"I will put you to bed." He lifted her and her head tilted back against his shoulder and she thought how comfortable she was in his arms, how lucky, how lucky, and she could have wept with gladness to belong to him, forgetting everything that had happened before him, and whatever came next. He carried her towards the bed.

"Peter! We must fold the cover first. It will wrinkle."

He put her down on a chair, and said, "Wait, now." He folded the two banners so that the white lettering was outside, scraps of words showing. The bed cover made them laugh every night. The parades had been very nice and cheerful and without point, and the banners were like the parades. It was always a wonderful period of history when they or their friends were allowed to walk down streets carrying flags; that was all finished now.

"Now, hup. One, two, three." He swung her from the chair and dropped her on the bed, so that she bounced, and then he leaned over and kissed her.

"Peter, Peter."

"Little one, you are just tired," he said.

He undid her shoes and balanced them in his hand before putting them under the bed. He rolled down her stockings and told her to raise her arms, while he pulled off her dress.

"Peter, you'll tear it. Oh, Peter, stop it. I'll do it myself," she said, laughing. She knelt on the bed and wriggled out of the sleeves and he lifted the dress from her head.

"You are a picture," he said, with pleasure. "You wear so many clothes."

This is what I have, he thought. She sat on the bed, dark and shy and happy to be fussed over and cared for and teased.

"You laugh at my petticoat?"

"I love your petticoat," he said.

"And you love me?"

He stood back from her, and shook his head in wonder that he could love anything so much, that he dared, and he was afraid to lose her, he could not endure the thought that he would ever return (to some room in any city) and not see her, with bare feet sitting cross-legged on a bed, the small tidy brown body hidden under a stiff white petticoat.

"*Liebling,*" he said.

"Peter, put your arms around me." She knew they would have to leave their room and she was homesick for it already. But I'll make us a home wherever we are, she thought, and we can always have a new joke to take the place of the banners.

"Now," he said, "where is your nightgown?"

She pulled the nightgown from under the pillows. It was too big for her, and he played with her, tumbling her about the bed, imprisoned in the nightgown as if she were sewed into a balloon, and she laughed and pleaded with him to pull it over her head, she couldn't breathe, and at last he let her bring her arms and head through. Her black straight hair was rumpled and seeing her, so gay and breathless and innocent, he thought with hatred of the people who had felt righteous in hurting her.

He undressed quickly and turned off the light and lay down beside her. She moved, digging herself deeper into the bed, and murmured with pleasure.

"Good evening, Peter," she said.

"Hello, my sweetheart."

"Peter, I'm so happy."

He patted her and she curled up against him. Their bodies were loving and quiet together. The nights were good if they only lay, close beside each other, or he sleeping with his hand warm on her breast. You could not forget what you had seen all day, even at night; the body was as heavy as the mind. They did not speak of it or worry about it. They knew they would find each other as they had before. But they knew a man and woman could be tired and caressing and at peace; nothing was lost, nothing was spoiled.

"All day I was ashamed to be so happy," she said, "seeing the poor people."

"No," Peter said, "you do not need to be ashamed. You have a right to be happy."

"No more than they do, Peter. And I looked at them, and thought: I have everything. And I felt ashamed."

Everything, he said to himself, ai, everything until tomorrow or the next day or next week.

"You must not, silly. It would not be better for them if you were unhappy."

"What did you do today?"

"Just work, nothing much." He would not tell her of the two strangers in plain clothes who had come to the office of his newspaper and asked questions. He would not tell her how, when he left, the one who smelled Gestapo worst had said, smiling (really smiling: you could kill them for that, you had always wanted to kill them for that), "It will be a privilege to see you in Germany again."

"It was all right," he said.

"Did you like Mary?" she asked sleepily.

"Yes. She is a good woman, and she has fine legs. I think she is not politically developed."

"Of course, she has never been in prison," Rita said, teasing him, "but she is very kind."

"Go to sleep, little one, there is much work tomorrow."

"Are you sleepy?"

"No."

"Then I'm not either."

"But let's not talk." He meant: If we talk, we will think. Let us not think. It is night now and until tomorrow there is nothing we can do, so let us not think. Because if you thought, you could only go over what you knew: I am responsible for the people who work with me and I cannot save them. They come to me all day long and ask for help to escape but how am I to open a frontier, how am I to buy them safety in the rich safe countries?

After a while she breathed evenly and softly and he moved his arm from under her head and straightened out her body, careful not to wake her, and tried to keep relaxed and still, but he could not sleep. They will be pleased to see us in Germany, he thought. They are waiting for us in Germany. Naturally. Everything is in card indexes. Nothing is ever forgotten. Nothing is over. Only death closes those files. It would not be a quick death, not a simple death. There was always the before part. Always there was the questioning so that you might bring them more deaths. Always there was the hope you might break first and scream out the names that would bring them more deaths. So that the many others, who were not yet known by name, could

93

be listed in those files and tracked until they were caught.

I cannot even save Rita, he thought. She has been a name on those lists for a long time.

In fourteen days, the official order had stated, the German and Austrian refugees were to leave Czechoslovakia. There are no frontiers open. And the refugees from the Sudetenland itself, the new ones, coming into Prague with wild eyes and stunned exhausted faces, were given twenty-four hours to return to the homes they had just fled.

Do those who are responsible sleep well these nights, he thought, are they rested and fresh in the morning, can they smile and accept the thanks and compliments of their admirers? More than likely, more than likely, he told himself; don't be a fool, these are old-fashioned unsuccessful ideas. He knew the Czech government only existed with permission from Germany: the Czechs themselves, broken and ruined and heartsick, had turned bitter and he understood that too. It was not their fault; none of this was their fault.

No one will have us at any price; and we have four more days to disappear. Anybody can die for a cause, knowing what he does and fighting. But not this way, not this way.

If I do not sleep at all, I will be even more useless tomorrow. We must fight, he thought, but the words sounded helpless and false to him, spoken in silence in his mind. Fight where? Fight how? They did not let us fight.

The weakest would kill themselves, the weakest or those who were too tired and had already suffered more than they could in one life. The others would go underground and hide. Each man would be alone again. How could you ask them, the destroyed and driven, the lonely and empty-handed, to fight what free nations and trained armies refused to fight? But they must find a way, or each man must find his own way, and go on fighting.

Sleep, he told himself. He lay for a moment, too tired to think, and Rita stirred beside him. He touched her arm, for comfort, in his loneliness, but not to waken her. If he waited now, or if he could sleep a little, it would come back to him. He must be careful and guard his faith. That was why they made you a leader, because you could hope longer, because you would never admit that any retreat was final.

This cannot be the end, he thought.

It was raining again, and he could hear the rain smacking on the cobbles of the court, and the sky turned grayer, before the gray whiteness of dawn. I will sleep now, he thought, and tomorrow I will do my work: I can do nothing more. They will not expect miracles of me, they will know I do what I can, they will not blame me.

Suddenly Rita pulled away from him and screamed. "No, no," she choked, and beat at the air with her fists. He could see in the gray light that her eyes were closed.

"Cowards!" she said, and her hands fell flat on the sheets, and her body twisted and went stiff. Her eyes were still closed.

Peter took her in his arms and kissed her eyes and

her hair, and rocked her gently, waiting with pity for her eyes to open and for her to come back to him.

She woke now, and stared around her as at a strange room, and lay a moment not even sure of him. Then she held to him, crying, "Peter, Peter."

"What is it, beloved?" he asked, but he knew the shape of the dream, it was always the same one.

She told him uncertainly. "I was running through the streets—first it was Prague—everybody turned and stared at me but if they stared at me that showed the others who I was and I begged them as I ran not to look at me—please don't look at me—then it was Berlin and I went into the bakery at the corner of my father's street and begged them to hide me but they said no, no, and waved their arms and were afraid and said go away from here, and waved their arms at me—then I ran and all the doors closed in my face—then I ran down a long corridor and I never saw what was behind me and I came into the room."

The room: the dreams always ended here.

"They were standing there in their uniforms and smiling and smiling and there was a big light in the ceiling and they looked at me and laughed and then I saw what was behind them."

"No," he said. "Do not speak of it, Rita. Little one, it is all right now; we are here in our bed, it is all right now."

"I'm afraid," she whispered.

He tightened his arms around her.

"I'm afraid for you," she said.

"No. You must not be."

She touched his hair, and laid her cheek against his

chest, which was hard and warm, and she could hear his heart.

"Peter, I would rather they caught me than that they caught you, but I hope I die before they catch me again."

"They will not catch us," he said, trying to make his voice right.

"You would not lie to me, Peter?"

"I would not lie to you," he said, and lied to her with all his heart. "We will leave for France before it is too late, but there is still time. We will leave for France together."

"You promise me?"

"I promise you," he said softly.

"If they caught you, I would not live," she said.

"We are going to live, Rita," he said. "Go to sleep now, my dearest."

She moved her head to kiss his shoulder. There were his arms around her, strong and good and faithful arms. We are going to live. He would not lie to her. The sky was white now, and beyond their window and beyond the steeples of Saint Clement, Saint Salvador, and Saint Francis, beyond the river and the Charles Bridge, the sky was turning pale green and gold. She slept without dreaming.

7

THE old blind woman said, "Come and sit here with me, my chickies." She knew by their feel and their sound that they must be small and fluffy.

The two children crossed the courtyard towards her. They held their tin soup cups in front of them and walked with care on the cobbles.

"Oh, dummy," said the little boy.

"You pushed me," the girl said.

"You are a cow," he said. "I spilled nothing. Now you sit down by the grandmother and I will get our bread. I must do everything here. I expect I will have to chew for you."

"You will not," she said indignantly.

The old woman sat on a stone curb that rimmed the courtyard. The sun came down across her back and warmed through her black sweater and her shawl. She had not thought she would ever be warm again, after the night when she walked from her village alone to the highroad and joined the moving, whispering, groping crowds who were fleeing towards Prague (as blind as I am, she had thought with panic; nobody knows where they're going).

For a few miles a man's hand guided her, then he would swing off, without sound, crossing into the fields to hurry faster than the long, slow, burdened line could move. He would have touched someone's shoulder before he left, handing on the old woman to the care of the next one. She rode in a cart (whose cart? all the voices were new to her), and something of metal cut into her and, touching it, not wanting to be curious or troublesome in the stranger's cart, but only hoping to find out what it was so that she could rest her body comfortably, she felt that it was a sewing machine, and she found a way to lean her back against the iron legs. Later, a woman had taken her hand, but the woman walked more and more slowly and her breath came out of her like water from a pump, and at last she said, "I cannot, I cannot, but who will carry the child?" The old woman had not known the other was carrying a child; on this journey, everything she used instead of sight was gone from her. But she had said serenely (because she knew she was going to die tonight, so she was unhurried and indifferent), "We will wait here until you can breathe again, and then I will carry the child."

That was how they walked later, and she knew it must be dawn, for the wind came up and people walked faster. Now that she had the child in her arms she walked more easily, or with more desire to go on. She had forgotten, if she ever knew, what villages lay behind her home towards Prague. The child is very good, she thought, it does not cry. The child was too quiet and suddenly she was afraid and stopped, with her blind face turned uselessly in the direction of the hills of home, and pulled back the blanket and let her soft, light fingers move over the child's face. The eyes were shut, but she laid her finger against the temple and felt

99

a pulse. The mother said in a quick sharp voice, "What is the matter with the child?"

"It was so quiet," the blind woman mumbled, in apology for worrying anyone, for stopping when everyone must walk if their hearts beat until they burst, if their backs cracked and splintered, if their tongues were rock dry, and walk and walk and never stop.

"She is sick," the mother said. "Give her to me. Give her to me, I will see if she will nurse now. I dared not wait for her to be well again."

Then that woman was lost, sitting at the roadside probably with the cold-faced, too-quiet baby, and someone else guided her and then they came to a town and she felt the cobbles of the street, the curbing, the air held in between the buildings; and she heard all the noise of their feet, their carts, their horses, their dogs, the two canaries singing in a cage, the pots rattling on a wheelbarrow, and she stumbled with deadly weariness and was frightened to be with so many strangers in a place she would never recognize.

Now they were here. Here was a courtyard where you could sit in the sun, a room hot from the stoves where women cooked and gave out food, another room with mattresses on the floor. Someone would hand her the cup of soup and the bread, then she would wait in the sun and the hours went by, full of sounds she could not remember or identify, and then there would be more soup and bread, and when night came, someone would lead her into the room with the mattresses and show her where to lie. She did not like to ask questions or worry anyone, and she knew she was too old to be useful or to understand any of this (except the Germans, she knew the Germans were behind them, in the hills of home).

The children, the ones who seemed to her as light and downy and quick as newborn chickens, were alone too. She listened for them and never heard the same grown-up voice calling them or helping them or loving them or scolding them. She asked them to eat with her, in the sun on her narrow ridge of stone. She spread her shawl for them to sit on, so that they should not catch cold, and they called her grandmother and talked with her as they ate, recounting the problems and wonders of this new life, when suddenly, aged five and six, they found themselves alone with more people than they had ever seen, in a city whose name they did not know.

They came from a village near Most and had lost their mother somehow the first night, and had wept in the morning, not seeing her, and run among all the long dark grown-up legs and pulled at all the skirts that looked familiar and finally they lay down by the side of the road and went to sleep. A man put them on top of a mattress on a cart, and there was a parrot in a cage hanging to a pole quite near them, and they had a fine ride and enjoyed themselves. At night in this new city they remembered their mother and were frightened and sad and cried to each other, lying under an old army coat on a sack filled with straw. But in the daytime they walked about together, busy and excited, and ate their soup with the old woman who they thought was probably grandmother and was nice and had given them six pennies, two pennies a day, for candy.

There was much news this morning and the little

girl began, "Many people came last night. I heard the lady in the kitchen say they were going away later because there is no more place in this village."

"So?" the old woman said.

"And many children too, but they didn't want to play. They were hungry. There was a baby."

The little boy came back and handed her a piece of dry bread.

"Say 'thank you,'" he told her.

"Thank you. The baby was very very little. The mother wore a red skirt."

"The baby was dead," the little boy announced. "I told you that before. You never remember. You will stay forever in the same class at school."

"I know it was dead," the girl said. "I said it was very little and it was."

The old woman shook her head and drank some of the clear, thin soup.

"There was an old man with pieces of teeth left in his mouth, and a woman with something burned on her at the bottom of her neck and a man with a white cloth and a lot of blood on his head," the boy said proudly. "I saw them all. Elsi did not see them. But I did. And all the big people were standing around them and talking and talking and some were crying, and then they went away."

"You should not see these things," the old woman mumbled. "They should not let you."

"Oh, we see many things," Elsi said, dipping her bread into the soup cup. "Yesterday we saw four big boxes to put the dead in the ground."

"I tried to get the soldiers who were here yesterday

to give me a ride on a horse. But they were in a hurry and they did not laugh. Anyhow, Frantisek is going to give me lessons."

"Who is Frantisek?" the old woman asked. She would like to know who her children saw, she would like to hear their voices to know whether they were good people.

"He is a friend of mine," the little boy said importantly.

"Karel," the girl said, "he is a friend of mine too. He will give me lessons."

"Maybe," Karel said. "But I think you are too little."

"Where does he come from?" the old woman asked.

"He is from Chomutov. He is quite old, I think he is seventeen. His mother was too sick to go away. He polishes his shoes every morning and walks to the stream out beyond the village to wash. He says he is going to be an engineer but now the Germans have his school."

"Good-by, grandmother," Elsi said. "Come on, Karel, let's see if those children in the schoolhouse will play with us now."

"You should take a nap," the old woman said. "You will not grow if you run about all day. You should lie down and sleep and have a little time to grow."

"Oh, no," they both said.

"Nothing is like home here," Karel added. "We do not have to wash our ears and Elsi's feet are dirty."

If it would not be a nuisance, the old woman thought, she would like to find one of the young women in the kitchen, and ask her please to see that the children were clean and took a nap. This was no way for children to be. They would be sick next. But she stayed where she was. The women were doing their best surely, so many to feed, so many mattresses to make, those who were already sick needed care. She thought, the children must grow up as they can now, it is not like before.

Karel and Elsi ran along the street past the police station and the post office, playing a game, hiding behind the trees, to jump out at each other with shrill and excited "boohs," until they came to the German school. Karel was lordly with schools because he went to one, at home, but Elsi was shy, and he led her down the hall and up the stairs to the class-rooms on the first floor where the Sudeten German refugees lived. He had been here before and there was a girl with yellow curls and a pink dress who lived in one of the rooms and he would not mind seeing her again.

They did not knock at the door but went into a large room with blackboards at one end. Now the school desks had been pushed to the center of the room, and bicycles were leaned against the walls. Drying clothes hung from the handlebars and from the desks, stockings and shirts and underpants and handkerchiefs; and mattresses were rolled up and stacked like logs in corners. Women sat at the desks talking to each other, or sat silent, with limp, tired faces. It was cold out of the sun. The men gathered around the teacher's table, waiting for the day to pass. The yellow-haired girl was there, sitting on the table, leaning against her father, a big man with the dark hair of his chest curling up over his open shirt. He had his arm around the child, holding her. He was talking with another man about

Canada. He was a blacksmith; he knew he could always find work, if he could first find a country.

Now another man joined them. Karel whistled softly at the door but the little girl in pink did not hear him. The children did not understand German, but they waited, watching the grownups. Karel pinched Elsi and whispered, "It is like the ones in our house."

It was like the ones in their house and in the Sokol House, and even like the ones in the basement of the Old Folks Home where some refugees were sleeping. It was always the same. They had never seen such a thing before, and the first time they saw it, they ran away, feeling ashamed and sick the way you do if you eat too much very quickly at night. Now they had seen it several times and they could look at it, but it still made them feel strange. They had talked it over together, but found no way to explain it.

The other man came up to the father of the girl in pink and began to talk. First he talked quietly, like singing, Karel thought, and the others looked at him, as if he were sick. Then he talked faster and the women came closer around the table and one of them wiped her eyes with her apron and another put her face in her hands, though this did not seem to have anything to do with the man who was talking, but to be something of their own. The man was talking now in a loud, angry voice, waving his arms and shouting, but the other men did not become angry or try to hit him or get out of the way of his arms. They looked at him, talking, as if he had hurt himself and they were sorry for him. He was talking and the men were sitting there not saying anything, and the women were wiping their faces, and then it happened: his voice stopped in the middle, as if you had broken a stick, and his shoulders moved in jerks, and a terrible noise came out of him, not like coughing and not the way women or children cry, but a terrible noise that must have hurt him to make, and he put his arm across his face and turned away. The men still looked at him and one woman touched his arm, as if she wanted to pat him but didn't know how.

Never, until they came to this city, had they heard a man making such sounds. Now it happened all the time. It was crying, they knew that, but they had not known men did it before.

"Come on, Elsi," Karel whispered. "She won't play with us now."

They walked down the hall on tiptoe and when they got outside, Karel leaned against a tree, as he had seen Frantisek do, crossing his feet in front of him, and said, "Everybody cries in this place."

He was very worried about it. He knew it was not right. He did not know what they were crying about, but it was not his fault, he had not been wicked in any way.

"I don't," Elsi said proudly.

"You," he said, and looked at her sternly because she was telling a lie. "You cry every night. Every single night. You cry for Mamma. You wake me up. Don't you know you oughtn't to tell lies? God will punish you."

"That's different," she mumbled. She hadn't meant to tell a lie and now she felt sad. Crying for Mamma was not like the big people crying in the daytime where everybody could see them.

"Well, come on anyhow," Karel said more kindly. "Maybe we can find some children in the Sokol House to play with. I wish we were home," he sighed. "I'm tired of this place. There's nothing to do. If we were home I could go out in the woods with Tiso and Ludovic and look for rabbits."

She walked behind him, sniffling a little. She had her doll at home, and she missed it, and she had nothing to play with either, but if she spoke of her doll, Karel would only say she was a baby. She walked behind, scuffing her feet, until she found a new game to play, hopping over the cracks in the pavement.

8

THE distant woods waved like high ferns under a rain-dark sky. In every hollow, a small lake gleamed black as the sky was, and smooth. The fields stretched between the curves of the land, evenly laid out in potatoes and sugar beets. The earth was clodded and rich and carefully furrowed. Peasants worked in the fields, bending in that slow uncomfortable way, straight down and sideways, to weed and tend the low green plants. The villages all looked new, the pale color of cement, and as you came to them you saw, rising over the housetops and the neighboring hills, the square practical towers of their churches.

They had passed the last line of defense north of Prague, a heavy barrier made of steel spools wound with barbed wire, each spool about five feet high. The spools lay in an unbroken black spiky line over the fields, but they had been cut to leave the highway open. The Germans had the first line of fortifications, that improved model of the Maginot which stretched along the Bohemian frontier, and the second line of defense, which was a crafty use in depth of strong points: concealed machine gun posts made of reinforced concrete and looking closeup like round black warts on the earth, deep concrete trenches dominating heights, artillery emplacements so hidden that all you would ever see was the quick emerging and recoiling gun barrel.

Having seen, in the past two years, how fortified positions could resist, Mary Douglas thought now, it wouldn't have been so easy for the Germans to get all that, if they'd had to fight for it; and she guessed some of the awful in-eating bitterness of the Czechs, who knew just how hard it would have been.

Now on an empty stretch of road, they passed soldiers, in twos and threes, with unbuttoned coats and dusty shoes and dusty faces, walking aimlessly from town to town. They did not raise their heads as the car passed, and walked with the shame and the weariness of a retreat.

The driver asked her if she wanted to stop, when they came to Slany, and she said no, we'll go on to the frontier. The driver honked and slowed the car to avoid two children, both blond and plump, who were walking one behind the other as confidently as if they were walking across the fields. They jumped back and stared at the car with frightened faces. Mary looked at them out of the back window and thought what an enchanting pair they made, with their round fluffy yellow heads and round cheeks, and the soiled pinafore of the girl, the little boy's stockings falling down. She thought their mother must be quite foolish with pride at having produced two such children. (Karel said to Elsi, "Well, hold my hand then. I was looking, I saw it coming.")

The refugees no longer moved in the daytime, crowding and clogging the roads as far as you could see. Now they passed the frontier at night. It was like war now, the frontier was closed and dangerous; flight was forbidden, those who were caught on the other side of the barbed wire were prisoners and must escape like prisoners. To go home to your own country and your own people was a crime, and they waited for night. But here there were stragglers, moving farther inland, having found that the villages nearest to the frontier were full and food was scarce and there was no work or hope of work. They walked south, looking for a home again.

The land was open here and bare and the people looked bent and small under the sky, and they walked as if they were pushing against a current, their bodies bending and straining forward. First there was a man pulling a two-wheeled cart, and beside him walked his woman and behind, painfully, their eyes on the cart, keeping up with it, trying not to be lost and left behind, came the old people, the man walking with a stick, the woman shading her eyes, her face soft and folded with age, but gaunt with weariness. The cart was piled high with mattresses and blankets, the pots tied on behind clinked cheerfully. The younger woman opened her worn black leather purse and took out a large piece of dry bread. She did not stop walking. She carved off a strip of the bread with a clasp knife and handed it to the man. He shook his head; he could not pull the cart with one hand, they must keep walking.

Farther on was a woman carrying a suitcase on her head; her children walked beside her, the youngest holding onto the blowing edge of her apron for support, the others stumbling and thirsty-looking and incurious. The faces were all hard and staring ahead; the eyes saw only the long white cement road.

(They knew now that you would have to go a great distance from home to be safe; but was there work ahead, or a house to live in? Where they came from the land was all taken up, always had been, from father to son as long as anyone could remember. Everyone had the same house too, there were no empty houses for strangers in their village.)

Then they passed six people, resting by the side of the road, their bodies cramped even as they sat, as if they were too tired and stiff ever to move or lie easily again. They carried nothing except small bundles wrapped in brown paper or cloth. One of them looked at his worn-out shoes.

The road went on, a wide flat concrete strip, climbing a hill past a clump of trees and a white farmhouse, and curved and lost itself beyond. There was nothing wrong with the road, there was no sign up, there was nothing to tell you: but the road was condemned. The country had come to an end.

"What is it?" Mary asked the chauffeur.

"That is Germany now," he said, and pointed ahead.

"I don't understand."

He looked at her. "Nobody does. But if we drive on, after a while we will meet the German soldiers."

"But isn't there a frontier post or something, how do you know where you are?"

"Sometimes there is. Not here. I will turn off on this side road."

They drove over a dirt road, bumping in the ruts. Deep ditches lined it, and cultivated fields. Then up ahead, they saw a group of people standing in the road.

"What are they doing?" Mary asked. "What is happening here?"

"They are looking," the chauffeur said.

He stopped the car behind the people and she walked to join them. There were about twenty of them, some seemed to be peasants from the neighborhood, in their work clothes, but there were city people too. No one talked. They stood in the road and stared at a piece of barbed wire that was pegged into the ground over the road and cut short on either side.

"That's the frontier," the chauffeur explained.

She looked at it with absolute unbelief. You did not simply peg up fifty feet of barbed wire and proclaim a new rule; you did not drive people from their homes or jail them or shoot them, confiscate property and deny their language and the old forms of life, and then lay down fifty feet of barbed wire to prove it. The people beside her were looking at the barbed wire with the same shocked, unbelieving faces. Why here? Why not farther ahead or farther behind? The land on the other side belonged to the land on this side; it had the same shape. The fields had been planted by one man, and now he had sown in two countries. Oh, no, she told herself, I don't believe it. Why don't we lift the pegs ourselves and move the silly frontier backwards into that newly stolen piece of Germany?

Then she saw the soldier. He had been leaning against a tree, on his side of the wire, green-clad and silent, and she had not seen him. He was dark, good-looking, and very young. Twenty, she thought. The

Czechs watched him, not saying anything, not moving, their faces blank and polite. The boy shouldered his rifle and began to do sentry-go but it was too embarrassing, and he leaned on his rifle and tried to stare the Czechs down. But the Czechs were not insolent or afraid, they were only amazed that men could do what these men had done. Underneath, behind the expressions he had learned from his masters and heroes, the soldier's face was ashamed and shy and uneasy. He knew that this was no way for the conquering German army to seem or behave, and he overlaid his face with an arrogant, boastful smile. He stood there, shaping his mouth into a smile that became a sneer, and the Czechs examined him quietly. The silence was too much for him and he called out, "Why don't you come on over here then?" like a small boy, bullying.

No one answered. Mary Douglas stared at him, fascinated like the others, unbelieving. But he was true, he stood six feet in his field-gray uniform, with his square steel helmet and heavy boots and his rifle; he was part of the army that had overrun the land, and behind him lay Czechoslovakia, that piece fitting into this piece reasonably, as the shape of the land demanded, but now it was called Germany and he was on guard.

"Come on over here," he said again, to no one in particular, laughing to give himself confidence.

A peasant who had been near the wire, looking at the crazily divided fields, sighed to himself, with unhurried contempt.

"Ah, the fool," he said, not loud, not for the soldier

or anyone, but just speaking his thoughts, "the poor stupid young fool."

The soldier flushed with anger and said, "Come over here and say that."

The peasant answered him, "With a rifle you are very brave. You are all very brave with a rifle. We have none now. Do you want me to say it again?"

Mary Douglas wondered whether the soldier would shoot. No one would punish him; he would simply have protected the honor of the Fatherland and shot down an enemy of the Reich. He might even get a promotion; and surely the Czech government was in no position to raise a fuss because one old peasant was shot by a German soldier in the line of duty. They all waited, the old man waiting too, perfectly ready, but keeping his contempt, and keeping it very surely and proudly, as a man who is used to making up his mind. The people watched the soldier with unwavering, not hating, but cool, and mocking eyes.

A woman said, in the silence, "He does what he is ordered. He cannot know what he does and he is not allowed to know. Leave him."

The peasants and the city people turned slowly and started walking back along the dirt road towards the highway. The soldier looked after them, with hate in his eyes now, because they had shamed him. If there were three of them they would start shooting, Mary thought, but it is too risky for one alone. And she thought, his own father is probably someone like the old peasant, a poor man, a farmer or a worker. And the land is exactly the same, on the other side of the barbed wire.

There were soldiers on the road, more hurried now at nightfall, thumbing a ride. They did not look like soldiers going home or soldiers going on leave. They had the shabby, bowed look of the unemployed who travel from one place to another, expecting no work when they arrive.

She told the driver to stop the car and they waited for a plump middle-aged man, a corporal, who ran towards the car banging his suitcase against his legs. He had pink cheeks and very clean pince-nez, and was out of breath. She did not speak to him, supposing he would know only Czech, but after he had his breath again he began to talk to her in German. He said he was going home to Mikovice and if she would drop him at Olsany, he would be very grateful.

"There are no railroads, and the buses have been taken for the army. We must get home as we can. So I stopped you," he said, embarrassed at doing something not fitting for a man of forty who was a corporal in the army and a bank clerk in private life.

Mary said, "Naturally."

"Many of the soldiers," he went on, "do not know whether their homes are still in Czechoslovakia or whether they are now in Germany. Also those who came from the Sudetenland do not know where their wives and children are."

"Yes," she said. "It is very bad."

"We were alone," the corporal said, and his breath seemed to have gone from him again, so that he choked over the words. "The others will see for themselves when the time comes. When it is Alsace Lorraine he wants or colonies, or the Corridor. But we could do

115

nothing. Ach," he said, and took a handkerchief from his pocket and wiped his face. "Well, I am going home."

He said it as if it were the last thing a man could do when all was lost, as if in going home he admitted that the army would never need him again, and he was helpless. Mary, thinking to cheer him, said, "You have a family waiting for you?"

"My wife," he said. "And my son. I am sorry for my son now."

They passed a long clanking line of troop trucks. There were soldiers in the trucks, with faded flowers in their caps, or sticking from the barrels of their rifles, but there was no singing and no calling to girls along the road. Behind the troop trucks came motorized field artillery, the blunt noses of the guns covered in khaki canvas, pointing back towards Germany.

The corporal said softly to himself, "For nothing, for nothing."

Later they overtook a procession of horses, more than two hundred of them, unsaddled, being herded back by cavalry to the farmers who had given them to the army. Nearing Slany, with the sky now purple blue and square lighted windows in the farmhouses, they passed eight tanks, rolling one behind the other, with loud, deadly, blind precision.

Night seemed to be the signal, so that suddenly all the dark roads swarmed with this powerful broken army. They came inland from the flat frontier of the Austrian plain at Mikulov; they converged on Prague from the Silesian border at Opava, where they could have held along the hills and in the fields sowed with camouflaged machine guns. They were returning in force from their intricate steel and concrete underground defenses in the Bohemian Forest and the Erzegebirge. You could hear them before you saw the shapes in the settling night. The anti-tank guns were reed-long and slender, and the barrels of the .75's looked in the dark like chopped-off tree trunks. They were passed by six ambulances, the crosses showing up clearly in the headlights of their car. An open khaki-colored staff car, with a high commanding triple-note horn, swung out and speeded ahead of them towards the city. Then there were more horses, then two troop trucks, one almost empty, then a company of soldiers marching in rank.

"Where are they going?" Mary asked.

"They are leaving the front."

Why didn't they fight? she thought. Why didn't they fight if they had to do it alone, no matter what came of it. If you fight and are defeated, you still have that behind you: it is not shameful to be brave and to be too few. And to die? She thought: one must never be generous with other people's lives. But what of it: this way of buying life was too costly, the people would not want a life so expensive it would be no good to them. They had arms, she thought, they had an army; to have a war at all is so stupid that no reasonable decent person can accept it without loathing. But when it gets this bad, when you have only a choice between fighting or this. It is easy to be brave after the event, she thought, and I never imagined it was jolly to be a soldier, and from what I have seen of war I cannot recommend it, but if it were my country, I would want to fight or wait in my house for the bombs, or take it however it came to me. She thought: they can destroy men other ways than with high explosive. When they have destroyed the men, with this peace, they have destroyed the women too. There are worse things than war.

The corporal touched her arm. "Here, please," he said.

She knocked on the glass for the chauffeur to stop, and the corporal shook hands with her and said, "Heartfelt thanks," and got out of the car. He stepped back, and spoke as if he were making a promise to himself. "We will fight the next time, as we did in the last war, in every country. It will be bitter because we have no friends, but we will fight to win back our republic. This time it is a failure, but it is not the end."

He saluted her proudly, not looking at all absurd with his pince-nez and his bank clerk shoulders and his pink cheeks. He seemed suddenly to remember his army with confidence, knowing that to be betrayed is different from being defeated. He and all the others would keep alive by themselves, in secret as long as need be, and one day they would be an army again.

"You will see," he said. "It is not the end."

Mary Douglas watched him a moment, walking with his suitcase still bumping against his legs, down the sideroad in the direction of his home. Probably, for once, women were not glad to welcome their men back from the wars.

The high old car ran smoothly in the night. The trees made a darker regular shadow along the road, against the flat black sky. She tried, leaning back and closing her eyes, to put in order what she had seen, heard, and what she had known before. She wanted to place her knowledge in paragraphs (a good opening sentence? she thought), so that it would be easy to handle when she came to write it. But it did not fit in paragraphs and she could not see it, plain and informative, colorful but unimpassioned, on a page. There was no beginning, no middle, no end.

The little man lying so badly and apologetically in the police station, and his shaking hands; Rita, smiling at the wonders of her home, the new Rita, tender and defenseless because of Peter; and Peter, with the gentle Rilke face; the tough young ones in the Truhlarska street, handsome and hard and cheerful, with all their bravery behind them, waiting; the ones with the stony faces and the crazy eyes in that crumbling house beside the river; the children singing; the army looming up on the night road, from the front to nowhere, the men as silent as the night itself, and the loud trucks, the huge noise of the tanks, the swift whispering of the tires of the anti-tank guns on the cement road; the refugees that you passed in the villages, like people escaping a flood, with the water, rising and spreading behind them; the lonely ones on the roads, walking as if they carried great weights or pulled on heavy ropes, bowed and numb with weariness, hunger, not knowing where to go, only walking inland; the fifty feet of barbed wire pegged across the road and the German soldier, wearing an expression he had seen in pictures, the arrogant smile he knew he ought to wear, and the silent people watching, not believing: where shall I begin, everything is as important as everything else, she thought, and what is the end?

She thought: there will have to be a terrible justice,

119

blowing over the world, to avenge all the needless suffering. Thus far, she had seen the innocent punished and insulted, pursued and destroyed; and when they tried to protect themselves, their enemies were swift, unanimous and relentless. Simple men were ignorant enough still to fight against each other instead of fighting side by side. She had seen only the triumph of the lie and the victory of the liars. It will take a long time to change this, she thought, we learn very little, we learn very slowly. She was afraid she would be reporting disaster and defeat her whole life.

I'm not getting anywhere, she thought. What I need is an opening sentence, not a conclusion.

9

AT five o'clock Peter got up in the cold dark, closed the window, and dressed. His clothes hung on one of the Socialist Club folding chairs and he found them easily. He did not wash. Rita was sleeping with her arms around the pillow. He opened the door of the apartment, holding his shoes in his left hand, and walked quietly down the stairs, guiding himself by touching the wall. When he reached the courtyard, he sat down on the steps and put on his shoes, tiptoed through the passage that led to the street door, slid the bolt, and waited. He looked up and down the dark street.

The milkman would not be by for another hour: the garbage was picked up at seven. There were no policemen here on this back street near the river, and the nightwatchman had gone home, since it was technically morning. A few streets farther to his right, people would be moving in the Rathaus Square, and farther still, the farmers would be arranging their stands in the fruit market. But the Wenceslaus Square was the best place at this hour: the women who cleaned out stores and office buildings would be walking to work, the men who lived in the worker's suburbs would be changing street cars here on their way to the factories, and he could get a cup of coffee at one of the Automats that stayed open day and night, and he would not be noticed. He walked close to the buildings until he reached the corner of Jilska Street, then turned right towards the center of the new town. He walked fast for six blocks, and then slowed down. Good, he thought. The two men had been following him since Monday, but he had shaken them off every night.

Last night, he took a bus out to the Vinohrady section, walked aimlessly until he found a café and stopped in for a beer. Then he climbed on a street car and changed twice before he got off at the Palacky Bridge. From the Bridge, he walked along the river until he came to Narodni Street, as if he had nothing to do and was enjoying the good weather and the view of the sleek dark water, with the lights splashing on it. As he was now close to home, he took another street car in the opposite direction as far as the Powder Tower, at the entrance of the old town. The street car was crowded at the end of the day and he got off unnoticed and joined the stream of people moving along this intersection of five streets. He made a wide semi-circle through the old Ghetto, skirting the Rathaus, to reach home.

He raged at this loss of time, and he was tired so that the two hours he spent making sure he had no escort seemed more than two hours. But he had not been followed. He was not going to lead them to Rita, if he could help it.

Six o'clock. No one will ever know about time the way we do, he thought. He figured it out, automatically: half an hour for coffee, then the waitress would begin to wonder why he didn't move. At this hour people drank their coffee and ate their rolls and hurried to work. He could waste another hour on buses and street cars, with intermittent stops. If it were only later, he could go to watch a newsreel, but the movie houses would not open until ten. He could drop in at a café near the Wilson Station, and use another twenty minutes or so there. At eight o'clock, he must be at his office.

They could not pick him up at the office, with so many people around. On Saturday, they could turn him over to the Prague police, denouncing him as a German refugee who was overstaying the time limit. I must be careful until Saturday, he thought, but if they planned to get me sooner, they could have taken me any day this week. If they are waiting and following me, it is because they want to hand me over to the police. The police would put him on a train, as a routine enforcement of the law which obliged refugees to leave Czechoslovakia on certain dates. After I am on the train, Peter thought.

He paid for his coffee and went out into the Wenceslaus Square. It had started to rain. Fine, he said to himself. Rain was good. People huddled under umbrellas, turned up their coat collars and pulled their hats down on their foreheads, and hurried, hunched and bent against the rain, trying to keep dry. Everyone seemed to be hiding. You could not see so well and people thought of spoiling their clothes or catching cold, and moved blindly and quickly. The windows of cafés, shops, taxis, street cars, were filmed and smoky and you could not look in or out. He thought: I hope it rains for six days.

Peter turned up his collar and walked to the cement runway in the center of the street and waved at a street car. He sat down in the middle of the car and turned his face to the window. Now, he thought, don't get sleepy or careless. Only two more hours of this. He would be at the office to get his instructions at eight. There was work to do.

The rain had cleared and a clean wind blew between the hard gray houses. Rita smelled the sunlight and felt the wind slapping and pulling at her on street corners and she thought: how lovely, it's almost North Sea weather. I should have taken a street car, she thought, seeing the jeweler's clock on the corner. Peter should have waked me at eight before he left. Ach, she said aloud, and put her hands on her skirt that had ballooned up in the wind. She let the wind catch her and blow her along. She felt her cheeks getting cold, and the stiff long strands of her hair came loose from under the beret and whipped against her face. She laughed with pleasure and a fat woman, carrying a market bag on her arm, turned and smiled as she passed. Run, run, Rita told herself, and now the wind blew her skirt tight behind her legs and cupped it in, and picked up the loose cloth in front so that it spread in a serge fan before her. Ten o'clock, she thought; Ludwig will be angry.

She leaned a moment against the stone arch of the entrance to get her breath, and then crossed the narrow court with the grimy office windows opening on to it, ran up the dark unclean wooden stairs and pushed open the frosted glass door that was marked *Solidarität,* in five-inch red letters. The waiting room was almost empty, but usually in the middle of the morning you could not elbow your way through the tired shabby bewildered people who came here every day for help. She opened the door to the inner office and stood still, the coolness drying from her cheeks, and stared at this room as if she had never seen it before.

The office was too small and it had always been a chaos of desks, chairs, filing cases, piled papers, stuffed wastebaskets, cigarette smoke, twisted telephone lines. She knew how it looked and how it felt; but today it was torn up and splitting apart. For two days, three days (but days meant nothing any more, there was no time at all, and yet everything seemed to have been going on for months, so that you realized with wonder and disbelief that it was only Wednesday), she had felt this coming. And now she saw it.

Men and women worked at the desks with a fixed violent concentration and speed. Open that file: how many people at the Visocany? Eighty? We could send about ten more. They have shut the Visocany: the refugees have been sent back to Germany. Here's the list of eating places: can they feed another fifty at the Pankrac? They haven't enough to eat now, there is no money, it will have to close in a day or two. The Studentenheim? I don't think so, you can telephone and see. We will have to get the people farther south into Slovakia. What are you thinking of? You know what is happening there.

She crossed to the corner desk and put her hand on the shoulder of the man working there.

"Ludwig."

He looked up. "Rita. Good. You are late. Wait a minute."

He was sorting papers, moving his lips as he read them. He frowned at the typewritten sheet in his hand, and placed it on a pile at the left of his desk.

"Cleaning up," he said flatly.

"Yes."

"You see how it is?"

She nodded. She had seen it before in Berlin.

"The Central Committee met early this morning," he said. "We have been too optimistic up to now. Now we must work fast. We are going underground."

They looked at each other; they both knew what it meant. They had lived that way before.

"Sit down," Ludwig said, and reached out to pull a chair to the desk. "I know how bad it is."

She took in her breath very carefully, little by little.

"So," she said. "Again."

"Again."

She sat still, trying to keep her mind clear and attentive. She held her hands, gripped between her knees, and the room seemed to her as quiet as if they had already crept away from it. We are not ready, she thought, this is not a thing that can be improvised.

"The League Commissioner came last night but none of us has been able to see him yet," Ludwig said. "Those responsible will go on trying, of course. The Party has been declared illegal in Slovakia. Some escaped and some have been caught. We cannot wait too long."

"No," she said. Now hurry, if it has come to this, hurry, hurry. There is not enough time. There is no time at all. If it has gone this far, we can wait for nothing.

"I am cleaning up this office," Ludwig said. "It goes very well. I have sent out five comrades to organize our refugee homes. It must be done today: all of it. I prefer to send those who have experience in this. You take the Truhlarska street and report here when you are through. Listen carefully."

She reached into her bag for a pencil and stopped. The old habits came back. Now you would carry your orders in your head, and the people you instructed would memorize too. It had come to this again. Behind her attention, steadily, wearily, she thought: we were safe here, it was a free country, everyone was safe.

"The refugee homes are dangerous," Ludwig said. "Anyone can find out where they are. Also there are too many comrades concentrated in each home; sixty is the smallest number in any one center. If one of the sixty is arrested, and is not as strong as necessary, he could be forced to tell the names of all the others."

"Yes," she said. In Germany, there were five comrades in each cell. She knew what they did if they caught you, to make you talk. If you were healthy, it took them longer. If you would not talk, it took them longer still: but few people lived to remember what had been done to them.

"So. There are eighty in the Truhlarska. Hans is in charge. Since there is so little time, and so little money,

127

we will have to break up into groups of ten. Hans will divide them, and tell each one individually what group he is in. The group numbers are M eight through sixteen. They are not to talk this over among themselves; the less they know the better."

"Good," Rita said.

"Hans then has eight groups of ten comrades. He will appoint one to be organizer in each group. You will get their names for me, and their group numbers. They must leave the Truhlarska tomorrow morning. I will give you some money which Hans will split into eight parts. Each organizer is responsible for getting money to the members of his group. But they must not live together. We have no list of private homes where they would be safe. It is terrible," he said angrily, to himself. "How can we have been so confident? And there is, of course, not enough money."

She did not answer him. They had been using their money since the summer, not saving it because there were people hungry, people homeless, more refugees streaming in than they had ever planned to help. She knew that without money they would be caught in a few weeks.

"The group organizers will report to Hans. In the first weeks, they should report if possible twice a week, so that we can check how it is going. Later, perhaps it will be safer to meet less often. Of course he must meet them in different places and at different times: he is not to see any one of the eighty except the seven group organizers."

She went over this quickly in her mind, repeating

it to memorize it. He waited until she nodded, sure that she had the orders straight.

"Hans will have charge of one group himself. He will report directly to me. The first time will be next Monday at ten o'clock at the flower market. He will see me walking around, and will know whether he is to speak to me then, or wait, or follow. I do not yet know who will be the contact man for money, possibly I will, possibly someone else. The Central Committee has not told me."

"That is all?"

"No. They are of course to burn any lists of names and addresses that they have, or any pamphlets or documents. They are to destroy any personal identification they may have in their clothes, or in books. They are to wait there in the Truhlarska until tomorrow morning. Someone will come to tell them by nine o'clock tomorrow morning. We are waiting that long, to see whether the League Commissioner can do anything. The man who runs the house, what is his name?"

"Schultze," Rita said.

"Had better close the house and leave too. He will not be safe. In all cases he would be arrested for questioning, as soon as the Gestapo could get around to it. The Czech police are not doing anything more than they have to, but the Gestapo is very busy. I think no one will be arrested for a week or two except on sight if they are seen by Gestapo and suspected and taken in for questioning. Therefore the comrades should not talk German on the streets. I think it will take a full month before the Gestapo is systematic about arrests.

But it is dangerous anyhow and then there are those who are well known. Worse for them."

Worse for them, she echoed, less time for them. In the day they can be recognized, at night the streets are too lonely.

"That is all?"

"Yes. I do not need to tell you how to do it." He smiled at her wearily and bitterly. "You remember very well. But see that there is no panic. Bernheim and Leidermann and Becker are in some danger in that house. I know they are wanted. You can tell them privately."

"Have you seen Peter?" she asked timidly. She was ashamed to do this. It was not worthy of Peter. Their lives were only two, it was a vanity to give them importance. But she could not help it; she only wanted to know that he had been seen.

"He's all right," Ludwig said. All right, he thought, except that he is among the first twenty on the Gestapo list. Well, so was he, Ludwig, and they had always known it, and they would have to take care of themselves when they could. There was work to do. Peter would be in his office now, cleaning it up. They had word (we know so much about them, Ludwig thought, it stands to reason they know a great deal about us) that the newspaper was to be suppressed tonight.

The paper was a weekly with a limited circulation among German-speaking refugees. They used the presses at night, with special crews, to print much of the literature that was smuggled across the German frontier. The underground workers who carried these leaflets reported to Peter, and used him as a contact man between them.

A mistake, Ludwig thought, correcting errors in his mind, to remember, never to make them again. We have forgotten what it is to be illegal. It was bad, he noted, ever to link a newspaper with the underground work; the connection was too obvious.

Peter's work today would have to be fast and final. Ludwig did not tell Rita this. It was not her responsibility. Each one must fulfill his assignment: the less each one knew the safer for all.

I must hurry, she thought, but she could not hurry. She knew them all and she knew how they looked when they were listening. She knew how Jacob rubbed his chin and turned his eyes down, how Katy stood with her weight on one leg and her head sideways, she knew the patient puzzled eyes of Schultze, the bright green eyes of Thomas who was always thinking a sentence ahead of what he heard, she remembered the three shy tall brothers from Cologne who glanced at each other to see whether all three had understood the same. I will have to make the news easier, she thought, I will have to find some good way to say it. (Return to the old way of life, the hiding, the waiting, the dangerous tricks to get food, the sly and desperate signals to each other, the night fear, the money running out, the memory of the punishment for those who are caught, keeping alive, keeping together, breathing carefully, hoping no one will look at you.) I cannot make it easy, Rita thought.

The streets seemed very crowded and all the people were walking against her, hurried and angular, and she pressed forward, thinking: I should not be so tired. I have work to do.

We must live again as we have forgotten how to live. The Czechs are as homeless as we are; whatever happens to us now will happen to them too, slower, later. To be hunted without reason, to be forced beyond the law for no crime: how will we learn again when we never believed in this defeat?

And where is Peter, she thought, her own fear seeping through. But that would come later. Now, before she reached the Truhlarska street, she had to hold in her despair and manufacture some faith for herself so that she could give it to the others.

She rang the doorbell under the brass name plate. SCHULTZE, Rita spelled it out. Better take the plate down and change the name. It would be a bad name to have in a few days. The girl Sofie opened the door; she looked thin and sick and her face was without color.

"What is the matter?" Rita asked.

"Thomas," Sofie whispered.

They were all in the dining-room, quiet, listening to Katy. Seeing their faces, Rita thought, I will not have to tell them anything; it has come to this, and that is all there is to it, she thought. But she was sick in her heart for them. Even in exile, always too poor, always deprived of what they wanted and needed, not able to work, or learn, always pushing deep back what dreams they might have for themselves, or what hopes, they had been careful of each other, and laughed, and kept their faith. Only they are very young, Rita thought, loving them, and this is the second time, and between the first

132

time and the second time they have had no chance to live.

So now, these who had always talked loudly and laughingly together and had made their small mean refuge into a cheerful place (as cheerful, she had thought, as a camp in the Black Forest in summer, or a ski shelter in Bavaria, as cheerful as if they had chosen it for themselves) sat and stood in the small dining-room with the flaking paint and the maps tacked on the wall, and listened to Katy in silence.

She was telling them again, this time very coldly and clearly, about Thomas, the boy with green eyes, whom she loved, and why he was not there and would not be back.

"We had been together and then I walked off to look in a shop window," she said, "and he waited near the curb, but looking out to the street away from me. They must have come along then, and not seen me, and later Thomas did not look at me or turn his head. I saw them take his arm and start to pull him along the street and first he jerked back, but then he saw it was no use. There were not enough people around to hide him if he broke away, and there was no side street close by. There were two policemen just ahead. They could have cried, Thief, or anything, if he got loose. He knew they had him."

Rita watched Sofie. She is too young, Rita thought, understanding Sofie's eyes, but fearing them. Terror could be dangerous to them all. They would have to take care of Sofie. Now, listening to Katy, Rita studied their faces harshly, to measure them and plan for them. She would have to judge how they would be in two weeks, how they would hold up after two months (if they were still free). She was responsible for this house; nothing must go wrong from carelessness or sentiment.

Katy could not manage her voice; she had forced it low, to keep it under control.

"I don't know," she said helplessly, looking around the circle of faces. "Then once, at a street crossing, he pulled back (did I tell you?) and they twisted his arm up behind and you could see his shoulders jerk, and his head turned a little sideways and his face was screwed up and white. They hurt him."

Rita felt this as they all did, coldly, in their throats, and beating behind their eyes. To be picked up on the street and forced to walk with two men whom you had never seen before: they all knew it, they had seen it. They had themselves been held and led by two strangers with unrevealing faces. It was not easier to know. The girl, Sofie, pressed her knuckles against her mouth.

"But where did they take him?" Sofie whispered. "What will they do to him?"

The men looked at her slowly, all turning. No one answered. Each one could guess, but you could not be sure. (She is too young, Rita thought. She should never have come to this house. There are safer places.)

Sofie stared at them.

"Why don't you tell me?" she cried out. "You lie to me. Why don't you tell me? I must know. I must know! It is horrible never to know anything!"

Hans said, "Be quiet. We would tell you if we knew. We have no way of knowing yet. It is not like a thing that is done under the law. There is no law in this country that allows the Gestapo to work here. How can we know?"

"I followed," Katy said. She was talking to Rita. "I know the address."

"What was it?" Rita asked.

"A private house. It looked like a private house. It is across the Manes Bridge on the other side of the river. The street is behind Saint Thomas' Church. It is an old house with a big doorway. Number 4 Valdstyn. I think there is a garden in back."

"I do not believe it would be headquarters," Jacob said. "I do not think they would pick people up in the daytime and take them openly to their headquarters."

"You cannot be sure," Hans said.

"I waited two hours," Katy went on, "walking around and standing in doorways. Maybe they saw me. I did not see anyone come out."

Better not to know, Rita thought; better for Katy. Whatever she imagines happening inside that house is easier to bear than truly knowing. She did not dare touch Katy or speak to her gently, knowing Katy could not now endure kindness. She would have to go over this morning by herself, day after day and all the nights, seeing it and remembering and wondering and never knowing, until such time as she could sink into quietness and think of her man as dead. They could not help her, and they knew Thomas would not come back. Rita thought: it is going very fast now.

"We must organize so that this will not happen again," she said, speaking to them all. "I have instructions from Ludwig. I will go over them first with Hans alone, and later we will discuss them together. Please

135

do not go out now. Is everyone coming to lunch today?"

Hans looked around the room. "By two o'clock every-one should be here," he said.

"Katy," Rita said, "you check everyone who comes in. Keep count so that we know how many are here, and who is missing." She would give Katy as much work as possible, to carry her through this day.

She went into a far small room with Hans and shut the door behind her. They sat down on two packing boxes and she repeated what Ludwig had told her, ex-plaining the reasons; though he needed no explanation. Thomas was gone. It had begun again. She made Hans say over what she had told him twice, to be certain that he understood it and remembered it.

"Put Katy with Sofie in the same group," Rita said. "I am worried about Sofie. She is too young and she is new to this. Katy is very reliable and can take care of her. I think they should even live together, though all the others must separate. You can explain it to Katy alone. Also, now, it will be better for Katy to have a responsibility and not be by herself."

"You do not trust Sofie?"

"It is not that. You saw her yourself. She is fright-ened."

He shook his head. "You can understand it."

"Naturally. But it is dangerous. We cannot take chances."

Hans said, "For a week she has been trying to find out about her parents. This is the first time she was ever away from her village. She has heard nothing. She is afraid for them."

"Yes."

136

"And, Rita, it is so stupid."

"What is?"

"She is in danger because of picnics."

Rita laughed. "What are you saying?" she asked. "What kind of picnics?"

"You know she is from Chodov, up near Carlsbad?"

"I knew she was from the Sudetenland."

"Well, they were mostly Henleinists around there. In Chodov, though, it must have been comic. The whole thing. I am not sure in Chodov anybody understood anything."

She thought: this is not wasting time. It is better to learn everything about Sofie.

"In that village there were two youth organizations, the Nazi one and the Communist one. Sofie's father is a worker, I forget what he does, maybe he worked on the trains. She joined the Communist Youth organization. First the Henleinists were stronger, because of the marching and the singing and the meetings and the flags, so all the little puppies in Chodov got some white stockings and became Nazis. Then Sofie proposed to have picnics, and she was given that work. She organized good picnics, with sausage and cheese and beer, and they have a place to swim near there and in the summer it was very popular. So all the young fatheads left the Henleinists and went on her picnics and soon the older Henlein people decided she was dangerous." Hans shrugged his shoulders. The Henleinists were solemn idiots and he had laughed at them for years. Still, there was nothing to laugh at now. "I tell you this," he said apologetically, because he knew he was using time, "so you will see she has no preparation."

"Then just before the Nazis entered," Hans went on, "a Socialist who was a friend of her father came to her house at night and told them that Sofie must leave, as she was on the Henlein list for revenge; they were going to shoot her; seriously, if you can believe it. Sofie never slept outside her own house before. She walked to the nearest railway station and just got the last train because some Czech soldiers helped her and she came here, and she is homesick and she doesn't know what has happened to her family. After she had been here about three days someone spoke of the parents of a boy they knew in Eger who had escaped, but they put his parents in a concentration camp instead of him. You see how it is."

"I did not mean anything against her, Hans. Only she is too young; she has had no experience; and she is afraid. Naturally. But with Katy to help her, it will be all right. Now we must talk to the others."

The four larger rooms of the apartment were crowded. Those who did not sleep here usually came for their meals in shifts, ate quickly and left, to make space for the others. Now they had rolled the mattresses against the walls and were standing as people stand in a railway station, awkward and restless.

"There are eleven missing," Katy reported. "They may be eating some place else. Probably they will come in the afternoon."

"You have their names?" Rita asked.

Katy nodded.

"Then Hans can tell them later. Now . . ." She looked around and saw that the windows on the court had been closed and the door was closed. She gestured

to them to crowd into two rooms so that she could speak
without raising her voice. Hans had taken the list from
Katy and stood beside her. Rita explained again the
division into groups, how it would work, and why they
were waiting until tomorrow to leave this house.
Schultze, wearing always the limp cap and the bedroom
slippers, leaned against the front door and listened to
her. He watched his children with sadness, wondering
how they would manage now, alone, each one alone
without him to help them. He thought: it is worse to
be young.

Rita asked if they understood or had any questions
to ask; did they agree with these plans? No one spoke
and Hans said, "You will all wait, please. Schultze, can
you feed everybody now? I will speak to each one
alone, in the little room. Gertrude," he pointed to a
fair tall girl, "you first."

Gertrude followed him back through the apartment.
Rita looked at her watch. It was almost two o'clock but
it would be better to wait here and be sure it had been
properly arranged, before going back to the office. Gertrude returned and called for Jacob. One followed another; Hans worked fast. Rita took a cup of soup and
a piece of bread from Schultze and thanked him. She
was standing by Katy, not talking. The rooms were very
quiet. These are good people, Rita thought, they are
without panic. A man beckoned to Katy and she gave
her soup cup to Rita to hold and went to Hans' room.
When she came out she looked around and asked someone, "Where is Sofie?"

"Sofie!" Jacob called.

Rita did not see her in this room.

"Have you seen Sofie?" she heard Katy asking in the next room.

"Not here."

"Sofie!" a voice called, farther back in the apartment.

"Schultze," Katy said, "is Sofie in the kitchen?"

Schultze stuck his head out the kitchen door and said, "No, nobody."

The girls were beginning to look puzzled, the men stern. Where could she have gone? Why would she leave when they had orders to stay here? Where did she go? Hans looked quickly at Rita, questioning her; his mouth was tight shut and his eyes were angry. He had been sorry for Sofie; he was sorry for her because her voice was light and high like a child's, and she was bored like a child too—bored with doing nothing, with waiting. She had been, of all those in this place, the one they allowed to complain (like a baby who wants candy, he thought, or whimpers with stomach-ache). They had all cared for her and petted her; they all knew the story of her picnics, and were delighted by it, unable to be serious about anything as small, gay, ignorant and harmless as Sofie. But now she had disappeared. This was no time to go away without a word. You could only think one thing. Rita had said Sofie was afraid, and she had said fear was dangerous.

"If we don't find her, or she doesn't come back," Rita said to Hans, "you better leave here tonight. You understand?"

He understood. He felt ashamed too; ashamed for Sofie if she had done this thing. And he was angry, thinking how easily she could endanger far better people than herself, braver ones, more useful ones, people who would be needed.

Katy said, "Rita, I know she'll come back."

It will be a fine day for Katy, Rita thought, if first she loses her lover and then her friend turns out to be an informer.

"Possibly," Rita said. "Hans, go on with your work. It will be wise to get it done now, quickly."

Rita waited, with her eye on her watch. It was three o'clock. She would have liked to ask Ludwig's advice but the feeling in the apartment had changed since Sofie disappeared. They were nervous now, and suspicious. She would have to decide this for herself. If she is not back by four, Rita thought, I will tell them to leave this place at once and not return. If later, things change, they can always come back. It is better to be too careful. If she does not come back we may expect the police.

Then Hans came into the room and took Rita into a corner.

"We cannot open the bathroom door. It is locked. No one answers."

"Break it open," Rita said. "But make as little noise as possible. Ask Schultze if he has tools."

At the first noise of splitting wood, the others crowded into the narrow dark corridor that led back through the apartment. The bathroom door opened onto this hallway, at the far end. Rita told them to stay in the front rooms, and pushed past them to join Hans.

Hans had a small hatchet that Schultze used to chop kindling for the kitchen fire. The door was solid wood and the lock was strong.

"Idiocy," Hans said angrily. "If it is Sofie, she has lost her mind. The door will look very bad. I don't like it anyhow."

Two men, helping him, put their shoulders to the door. Jacob and Katy were standing with Rita. The corridor behind them was empty. The wood splintered away from the lock and the two men stumbled into the bathroom. It was lighted by a sooty skylight and they could not see well.

"Turn on the light," Hans said.

One of the men slipped, before the light went on, and said, "Ach," with disgust, and then he pushed back, out of the room.

The electric light bulb hung from the ceiling. It was a high room, with an old-fashioned marble washstand, a big toilet with a square bowl, painted with flowers, and a tub standing on feet made of iron claws. The walls were cream-colored, grown brownish with age and soot, and the floor was scratched blue and white tiles. The razor gleamed in the light, in the center of the floor.

Sofie had fallen backwards, so that her head was in shadow between the toilet and the bathtub, and her legs had buckled under her strangely. She was grayish-white and looked shriveled and her lips were blue. She had cut her wrists and held her hands over the washbowl, letting the blood drip neatly, and then she had fainted and the blood lay in puddles, dry now on the tiles, spotting her green leather jacket with brown sticky spots. She did not look young at all. Her eyes were closed.

"My razor," Hans said.

142

Katy cried out, and then put her arms over her head, to hide from it, and bowed her body and wept like choking.

"To do such a thing," Jacob said, with horror in his voice.

Rita thought: this should not have been. We failed her. We did not know how weak she was, and we failed her. She heard too much from the others about prison and concentration camp: she was too afraid. And too alone, she thought, and worrying about her family, and alone here. We must have seemed hard and careless to her, or she would have talked to someone and we could have stopped her. It is our fault, she thought.

One of the men, who had broken in the door, leaned against the wall of the corridor and looked sick. The other stared at Sofie's body and at his shoes, which had blood on them, and did not move.

"The poor little one," Hans said. "The poor stupid little one."

We should have known, Rita thought. This is wicked and terrible, we should have seen it before it happened.

Hans said, "Rita, now we will have the police here."

She shook herself and turned away. There are still the others, she thought, I should have known. Ludwig sent me here. This was part of my work.

"Everyone must leave," Rita said. "Is there a place in the basement where the mattresses can be stored?"

"Yes," Jacob said.

"Is there a furnace?"

"Yes," Jacob said with wonder.

"To burn all the papers immediately, to get rid of everything." Rita explained.

"But Sofie?" Katy said. She looked ill now. Rita put her arm around Katy's shoulder.

"The apartment must be emptied at once of everything that shows how many people lived here. Everyone must leave. Have they all their instructions now, Hans?"

"Nearly everyone," he said. "In fifteen minutes more."

"You attend to that. Jacob, get Schultze, and take whoever you need and begin carrying the mattresses and the packing cases and the extra cups and all those things down to the cellar. Shut the door here."

Rita led Katy down the hall. "Katy," she said, "you were always kind to her and always helped her. But now we must think of the others. We will have to declare this to the police. But first the apartment must be cleaned out and everyone must leave. Only one person must stay here. We will send Schultze to the police, and he will say that a refugee, a friend of his daughter, who was staying with him, killed herself in his apartment. He will say that she was staying here with another girl."

Rita stopped. It was easy enough to invent the lie and you would have to tell it before you could see how well it worked. But who would stay? The police would take the one who stayed for questioning. Schultze was all right; he had lived in Prague for twenty years. He would be released. But if the friend of Sofie were a refugee, she would be expelled. She might of course only be given a warning, and then she could disappear. But if they watched her, or simply put her on the train, as the law now obliged them to? Whoever stayed took that risk. I'll do it myself, she thought, it is my fault: and I must pay for it. She would send Katy to Peter, to explain; Katy could report to Ludwig. She would stay here and take her chances.

Katy said, "I am Sofie's friend. Schultze will tell the police that I am waiting in the apartment."

"Schultze could not handle it alone?" Rita said.

"He would need a witness that it was suicide."

"Of course. No, Katy. This is not your job."

Katy took Rita's arm and held it so hard that Rita stiffened with pain. "You will not tell me what to do," Katy said. "I am going to stay. Today they got Thomas. Do you think I care so much now? Besides, I was her friend. And you have work to do and you have Peter. I will do what I say I will do. You will not get me out of here."

"Quiet."

"I am not crazy. I am not excited. I know what I am going to do."

"You know, don't you," Rita asked, "what it means for you if the police decide to put you on the train, as they do now with refugees?"

"I know that. You don't have to tell me."

"As I am responsible for this house . . ." Rita began obstinately.

"As you are responsible for this house," Katy said, "you get everyone out and get the things stored in the cellar and report to Ludwig and go on with your work. You are being sentimental. I tell you I am staying."

"All right," Rita said. It would be useless to argue with Katy. What she said was true. No one needed Katy now. "By law, as a German refugee, you have two

145

more days in Prague. So possibly the police will only warn you and tell you to report back on Friday."

"Certainly."

"I will get you something hot to drink."

"Leave me alone," Katy said, "and hurry to empty this place."

There were only twenty people left in the front rooms. Hans had told them to go quietly, by twos. He had finished instructing them, and now ten men were filing up and down the stairs to the cellar, like laden ants, carrying away the extra chairs, the mattresses, books, maps, plates and cups, towels and packing boxes. Schultze directed them, looking bewildered and old. He showed them what things to remove, and stood beside them shaking his head, as if he could not believe what was happening.

Hans said to Rita, "I will go down in the cellar and burn anything that should be burned. Here is the list. Will you give it to Ludwig? All I know now is the names of the seven group organizers and the meeting places I have given them. Ludwig will have the only complete list."

"Yes," she said.

Katy sat on a chair by the window and closed her eyes. Rita went into the kitchen and heated some coffee and brought it to her, but Katy turned her head away without speaking. Rita stood by the windows watching the street. People still left the house, but well and quietly, you could scarcely notice their going.

Schultze had taken a broom and was sweeping one of the dismantled rooms.

"It will look very bare," he said to Rita.

146

"You are a poor man," she said. "They will not expect you to have fine furniture."

"I am to go to the police station and say that a friend of my daughter came here as a refugee and killed herself while I was having a beer in the kitchen?"

"Yes."

"The little Sofie," he said. "I did not know she was so sad."

"She was afraid," Rita said. "She was afraid of what would happen to her if she were caught. She had heard so much from the others. She did not think she could bear it. Jacob's concentration camp, Thomas' prison, Katy's prison, the way they tortured Hans. She was afraid to live."

"I would be afraid not to live," Schultze said.

"I, too," Rita said softly. So lonely, she thought, so little and so lonely; in that dingy, dark bathroom, and holding her hands neatly over the washbasin like a well-brought-up little girl who does not want to make a mess and cause trouble.

Hans came back; the four of them were alone now.

"Everything is stored and the door is locked. There is no reason for them to search down there. I have burned everything and waited to rake the ashes. Everyone has gone and everyone has instructions except four who did not come. I have sent Johann out to find them and tell them what to do. If he can find them. So. I will go now. Katy is staying with Schultze?"

"Yes," Rita said.

"She is not known to the police here; I think they will only warn her about leaving in two days."

"I hope so," Rita said.

147

"You better come too. Schultze, are you ready?"

"In a minute. I must make it a little cleaner."

"You go, Hans. I'll follow later," Rita said.

Katy had not spoken. At the door Hans turned to Rita and said, "You must not take this for yourself."

She looked at him and he saw her face twisting up to hold in the tears.

"She can't have wanted to die," Rita said. "She didn't know what else to do."

"It is done now. And you have work to do." He took her hand. "Good-by, Rita, in case I do not see you for a time."

She held his hand suddenly tight and drew him back and looked at him. In case I do not see you for a time. They would not see each other any more, or only by chance, and possibly it would be dangerous to recognize him then. It was breaking up all around her, she would lose her friends too; she had not thought of that before. All the others were gone, and he was leaving, and each one would be alone again.

"Good-by," she said. "Be very careful. Good luck. And good-by."

She watched him go down the stairs and came back to the room. Schultze was in the kitchen. She put her hand on Katy's shoulder, and said, "Will you speak to me, Katy? I am going now."

Katy stood up and put her arms around Rita and kissed her. "Good-by," she said. "You are a good woman. I was not angry. I have been sitting here thinking about Thomas and how we went swimming last summer in the Vlatava and how cool the water was and

148

how his back got too sunburned. I have had no time before. So good-by."

Schultze came out of the kitchen and sat down on one of the chairs and leaned his elbows on the table. He pushed his cap back a little and scratched his head and sighed. "It is all clean now, so I can go and fetch the police."

He waited for Rita to say something, he would have liked her to think for him, because he was too tired and everything happened too fast, and he felt old and uncertain. But before, he had taken care of them all, and they could not manage without him.

"Now there is no home for the children," he said, talking to himself. "And no home for me."

"I must go now, Schultze," Rita said. "You have been very good to us. We will never forget you. And thank you, for everybody."

He shook his head. "You are going too, Rita?"

"Yes."

"Everybody is gone?"

"Yes."

"You are staying with me, Katy?"

Katy nodded.

"Shall we have a good cup of coffee then before I go to the police station? There is no hurry about the little Sofie now. It is too late. We could sit here, the two of us, and I could smoke my pipe and we could have a cup of coffee?"

"Yes, Schultze, please."

"I wish I had some butter. I would make you a butter bread. That is good with coffee."

"Just the coffee will be fine," Katy said.

The street lamps were coming on. Rita could not say anything more to them. She closed the front door softly behind her. Katy was staring out the window, not seeing the street, the bright windows across the way, the dark-dressed silent hurrying people, or the blue-lighted street cars. Schultze built up the fire and put on the coffeepot. There is no hurry now, he thought, it has all happened.

Rita walked close to the walls, in the shadow of the houses. She stopped before she came to the corner where the street lamps shone down on the curb. In the next block there were shop windows lighting the pavement. She stopped and wiped her eyes and cheeks and took a deep breath and pulled back her shoulders. She looked all right, so that no one stared at her, but she walked very slowly.

She felt that she had walked through the city for hours, holding her coat tight shut at the neck because she was shivering with cold, stumbling and then taking care to lift her feet (though her shoes seemed made of iron, they would not bend), waiting forever at street crossings because she was suddenly nervous and undecided and the lights of the passing cars blinded her.

First to the office. "Ludwig, Sofie killed herself."

"Where? When?"

"There at the house this afternoon."

Silence.

"It is my fault," Rita said.

"Don't say stupid things," he answered quickly and sharply. "I am sorry it happened. Is everything arranged?"

"Yes."

Now where? All the streets looked the same; Rita shivered with cold. She walked from habit to Peter's office and stood on the opposite side of the street, heavy and numb, and looked up at the dark windows. She turned and walked away, and much later thought: that is closed and shut up and finished too. Everything whispered to an end, everyone sneaked off and hid, the windows were darkened and where they had worked and lived it would be silent now. She did not recognize this street and told herself: go home. But at home, she would be alone, she did not want to be alone.

The desk clerk at the hotel kept her waiting; she looked like a beggar. He was about to tell her to leave without asking her what she wanted. Her eyes were vacant and humble, she carried her head forward in the weary, pitiful way of those who wander into hotels or cafés to ask for pennies.

"Is Fräulein Douglas here?" Rita asked.

The desk clerk looked at her again. Miss Douglas was a journalist, the journalists saw many strange people.

"She is not back yet; she has been gone all day," he said shortly, and smiled at a gentleman with a flourishing, well-tended mustache who asked for his key and his mail.

Go home, Rita told herself. She walked blindly up the wrong street, not hurrying, and corrected herself and set off again in the right direction. She was not aware now of walking and she was not thinking. She only knew she was tired.

She rested twice on the stairs, climbing to the room. When she came to the door she thought she heard something moving behind it, so she waited on the dark landing, holding her key in her hand. No light came from the crack under the door. If there had been a noise, it would not be Peter. She leaned her head against the door and listened and heard nothing. She turned the key noisily in the lock and pushed the door open. She switched on the light, her breath coming too quickly, and the apartment was empty. Then she was ashamed and at the same time felt herself shaking and jangled, ready for sick helpless tears. She shut the door and stood in the middle of the floor with clenched hands, talking to herself harshly and hatingly, to control this panic and this fatigue.

I'll set the table and get dinner, Rita thought. That will give me something to do until he comes. She moved slowly from the kitchen closet carrying one plate at a time, slowly and carefully she peeled the potatoes and dropped them into the boiling water. It was eight-thirty. She folded the bed cover and placed the two pillows against the wall and sat back, with her legs stretching across the bed, and tried to read. But after she had gone over the same page six times, not seeing the words, she went to the drawer for the socks that needed mending. If she could not stop thinking, she could at least keep her hands busy.

At ten she decided to eat, because the food would be wasted. She sat and looked at the plate of stew and boiled potatoes and listened for Peter, listening so hard that she thought she must be able to hear the people on the first floor talking, or undressing for bed. The stew hardened into a grayish blob on the plate and the potatoes caked and looked dry and mealy. She cleared off the table and washed the plates. When Peter comes, she thought, I will make him a sandwich; this food is ruined. When Peter comes.

She opened the window to have the street noises for company, because the house was too quiet and in her room the steady loud ticking of the alarm clock began to make the muscles in her face jump and her head ached with the effort of not hearing the minutes pass. It was cold outside and standing by the window, looking over the roofs, and out across the river that she could not see to the dark climbing mass of the Hradcany, she felt for a moment drifting and vague and rested. Then her shoulders became stiff with cold, and her legs seemed to give under her. If Peter were here, she thought, he would undress me and put me to bed and spoil me and I wouldn't be tired at all. Sofie looked so old; she was seventeen and she looked old and shriveled. The ones who die violently always look tired, she thought. She had seen a woman in her prison who died after being too long in the basement cells; she had not been beaten, but perhaps what went on in her brain before she died was the violence. She had seen her brother on the floor under the bright light. She had seen . . .

"Peter!" she called out in the empty room.

She buried her face in the pillows on the bed because she could feel the sobs in her rising and sharpening, until she did not know whether she was crying or screaming. Peter, don't leave me! Peter, come home, come home, come home!

Are they all dead in this house, she thought, has no one a radio, don't they have friends in to visit at night, don't they ever talk or move furniture or make a noise?

She began to walk the room, circling the table and counting her steps. Her feet clicked on the bare boards. Then it was midnight and the sound of the bells came through the window, clear and serene. Peter, she thought, Peter, what have they done to you?

The two strangers came up to Thomas on the street and each one took hold of an arm and led him, between them, not saying anything, to a house no one knew. She thought: I will go out and look for him. But what if he comes while I am gone, five minutes after I have gone? I can leave a note. How would I know whether he was there or not? I could not knock at the door and say: Is Peter here?

She began to walk again, but she no longer counted, and she bumped into the folding chairs and once, wavering and blinded with tears, she knocked against the sharp corner of the bookcase. She came to rest finally on the bed and lay flat on her back, emptied out and numb with the crying and the waiting and the fear. She did not take off her clothes, but rolled over and put her arms around a pillow, and hugged it close against her. The room was very cold but she did not notice. She talked softly, to Peter, with her lips brushing the stiff cold cloth of the pillow slip.

"Geliebter," she said, "you must be safe. I need you. I love you. Peter, please come home."

When at last she slept, she slept smiling, dreaming that her head was on Peter's shoulder, as on other nights, when you slept safe and loved, and woke happy in your own home.

10

MARY walked past the two doormen, and the two potted yew trees, into the marble lobby. It was a much better hotel than the one the journalists lived in; you could tell by the deep blue, thick, allover carpeting and the cut glass chandeliers and the expensive quiet. She saw Thane and Tom Lambert and Luther sitting at a small table in the salon. They looked tidy and bored and were drinking scotch and soda in a dispirited way, not talking. She stopped in front of one of the long hall mirrors and fastened two hooks at the side of her dress that she had missed in her hurry, and wiped the corner of her mouth with her little finger: the lipstick had smeared.

She went over to the table and put her hand on Tom's shoulder.

"Hi," she said.

They stood up, and Thane reached over for a chair from the table beside them.

"Have a drink," Thane said.

"You got my note all right?" Tom asked.

"Yes, thanks for leaving it. I'll have a scotch and soda, please."

"Well," Luther said, "well, well, well."

"Is something the matter?" Mary asked.

"No, turn your head that way, to the right, so I can get the effect. What are you trying to do, coming in here this way? Trying to break our hearts?"

"I've been wondering where you were keeping yourself," Tom Lambert said. "Friends in town, eh?"

"I did it all for you," Mary said.

"You know," Thane said, studying her, "you're wasting yourself in this business. If I were a woman and looked like you, I'd marry for money. It's only sensible."

"I value your advice," Mary said.

"Don't get sore."

"Sore?"

"We're going to have a party tonight," Tom announced.

"We can try anyhow," Luther said.

"It's just what I need," Mary said. "Let's go somewhere and dance."

"Where have you been, Mary? What's the idea of hiding?"

"I've been working."

"You mean to say you can find something to write about?" Thane asked.

"I don't know if it's good. But there's plenty to see."

"I don't see there's a thing happening," Thane said. "The whole country's stone dead. If they don't take me out of here pretty soon, I'm resigning."

"Me," Tom said. "I'm going to become a rummy. There's nothing else to do. I always wanted to be a rummy."

"You ought to get a bottle," Luther said, "if you are going to be a rummy. A rummy always has a bottle."

"I don't want to be a vulgar rummy," Tom said. "Not a bottle rummy. I just want to be dissolute."

"It's too late for you to be dissolute, darling," Mary told him. "You're typed as an earnest but puzzled young liberal journalist."

"God," Thane said wearily. "Don't be bright on us."

"I'm going to be a dissolute, unpuzzled rummy," Tom said. "Watch me."

"Well," Thane said, "drink up and let's go eat. It's time now. We killed that last half hour okay."

"But when does it start?" Mary asked.

"It's all over," Tom said.

"What?"

"Sure," Thane said, "we've had our press conference. Brief and to the point as press conferences go. Delighted to meet you, gentlemen, says the Commissioner, and I am returning to London on the noon plane tomorrow."

"Is that all?"

"That's all," Luther said. "And the drinks are foul. It costs twice as much as any place else in town. I'll never put myself out for that old bastard again."

"But isn't he going to do something about the refugees?"

"Listen to her," Thane said. "Oh, Mary."

"No," Tom said. "Nobody is. You ought to know that by now."

"Which is he?" Mary asked.

"The Englishman," Luther said with disgust, not turning around. "You know, the one who looks English."

"There are a lot of them over there," she said, "who look English."

"The other three are his aides or secretaries or what not. The younger ones who have such beautiful manners. The old boy in the big chair is the one."

She saw a tall man with gray hair and a gray mustache, leaning back in a chair listening to a man who was talking to him, fiercely, it seemed. The Englishman had his hand over his eyes and he nodded from time to time. Then he smiled politely and rose and shook hands with the man who had been talking, a dark small rumpled man, and this one took the offered hand and looked breathless and dismayed, as if he had been suddenly hit in the stomach. Then he turned and walked out of the room, slowly, with bent shoulders.

"Who was that with him?" Mary asked.

"One of the refugees' representatives. He allowed them an hour to come and tell their stories. He's a busy man," Luther said.

Mary Douglas was so tired that her hand shook, holding the glass, and her face felt as if it were covered with paste, stiff and hard with fatigue. She was perhaps even too tired to go out and eat and drink and forget this city, though that would be all she could do with pleasure. She wanted to rest here for a while longer, the time for two more drinks, and then they would go somewhere and perhaps be cheerful. After all, she thought bitterly, no one pays me to get the horrors over this place; I'm supposed to be a journalist. I'm through work for today. I've worked enough.

How can he receive them here, she thought, in this large muffled room, where they have to talk to him in whispers or have the waiters smiling and nudging each other and the people at other tables turning around to look at them as if they were making a mess on the floor. They're talking to him about life and death; how can he treat them as if they were trying to sell him second hand clothes. Hasn't he any imagination at all, can't he even guess what these people are up against?"

Now, Mary told herself, be reasonable. What are you going to do? Nothing, she thought, nothing at all, as usual. I will sit back and watch it. She put the glass down on the table and wiped her hand. The awful sad hopelessness of the city weighted the air.

"What are you looking so gloomy about?" Thane asked.

"Nothing," she said.

You'll make a fool of yourself, she thought. You'll get thrown out or laughed at. It's none of your business. You have no right to interfere. Nobody asked you to. It won't get you anywhere and you'll just make a scene and look like an ass.

A woman had come in and was talking to the gray-haired man. She sat forward uncomfortably on the chair and twisted her gloved hands together (cotton gloves, Mary Douglas noted), and the soft glowing light of the room shone on her unpowdered nose, and on the loose rough skin of her cheeks. Mary could see what trouble she had with the words and how from time to time, despairingly, she stopped talking and looked around the room as if for help. The gray-haired man waited, with patience, and smiled as if he did not see her and at last without his saying anything she rose, and bowed to him (she stopped in the middle of a sentence, Mary thought,

159

she saw it wasn't any use) and walked from the room. The woman's clothes were very shabby and old-fashioned, and the waiters moved aside for her, disdainfully, as if in coming here she had ventured into a place where she did not belong, and she must be made to feel her intrusion. But the woman did not see them. Mary turned to watch her, and thought that she took a handkerchief from her purse, as soon as she was in the hall, and pushed quickly and blindly through the revolving doors into the dark street.

The gray-haired man beckoned to one of his aides and said something and the young man smiled in the manner of one who responds quickly and exactly to his superiors and Mary, suddenly angry, decided that she was ready to make a fool of herself now.

She opened her bag and felt around for lipstick and powder and worked swiftly at her face, looking critically into the mirror of the bag.

"Ready?" Tom said, rising.

"No."

"Want another drink?"

"No. I'm going over to talk to Lord Balham."

"You won't get anything out of him," Tom said. "He's one of those polite birds who always agrees with you and when you ask him a question he says, 'How interesting.'"

"I don't want a story." She put her powder and her lipstick back in her bag and lighted a cigarette. She had a sickish feeling, from nerves, guessing how ridiculous she was going to look.

"What do you want?" Thane asked, curiously.

What did she want? There were probably a quarter

of a million people in need of help: she wanted the Englishman to help them. It was as simple as that.

"I want him to do something about the refugees."

Thane whistled softly. Luther sat up straight and looked at her in surprise.

"You're going over there and give him a lecture?"

"Something like that."

Luther laughed. "Good for you. Tell him a few hot things for me while you're about it. Tell him not to call out the press unless he's got something to say. What the hell does he think we are, a bunch of bellboys, just to ring for us and send us away."

"Are you going to make a plea for suffering humanity?" Thane asked, smiling.

Mary felt almost dizzy now; she could see it in advance: the Englishman's polite wondering greeting, the expression of bored attention as he listened to her, perhaps the eyes flickering with irritation, then a few cold but civil words to put her in her place, after which she would walk humbly back to this table and try to make a joke of it. But it wasn't a joke and they would know it, and they could tell it as a fine story for months to come.

"I'm going to make a fool of myself," she said seriously. "And you will all have a swell laugh, and I won't be able to think it's funny at all. And it's none of my business as I'm the first to admit, but there's nobody here who can do anything about it and I've got to try."

Tom said, seriously too, "Go ahead and try. Maybe you can get away with it. Anyhow it's okay to try." He looked at Thane. They were all dopes, Thane decided, but if they were so godawful earnest about this refugee thing there was no sense laughing at them. Journalists shouldn't get moral and partisan and it made him uncomfortable. This was their show, he might as well go out and pick up a tart for company and leave them to stew around for mankind's sake. The Englishman would just kick Mary out anyhow, and then they'd have to spend the evening assuring her it didn't matter.

"Have a good time, children," he said. "I'm hungry. I'll meet you later at the hotel bar and you can tell me how it turns out. So long."

"Don't wait for me," Mary said to Tom and Luther. "There's no reason for you to get mixed up in my righteousness."

"If it came off," Luther said, "maybe we'd have something to send."

She found that the room was full of people, all watching her. She felt awkward and her throat was dry. She was holding a cigarette and decided it looked too casual, but she couldn't see an ashtray handy. The three young men with beautiful manners fell back before her veil and her fur coat, and she introduced herself to the tall gray Englishman.

"Do sit down, Miss Douglas," said Lord Balham.

Now what, she thought, where do I begin? If it's as bad as this for me, what must it have been for those others?

"I want to know why you're not doing anything about the refugees," she said.

Lord Balham looked astonished and one of the

162

young men came closer, ready to remove this lady courteously in case she should become tiresome.

"May I ask why?" Lord Balham inquired.

"I haven't any authority to ask," she said. "I'm a journalist. But I have seen the refugees, and you haven't." That's a fine way, Mary told herself, I'm not going to get anywhere making him angry.

She talked very fast, to say it all before she was interrupted. She told him of the house by the river and the rigid waiting people. She told him of the children eating grapes and dry bread. She spoke of the little man who had harmed nobody, and how he had searched through his pockets for a train ticket to safety, when he had no ticket and there was no safety. She described Rita to him, and what she had come from and how she had built a life again. First, as she talked, she thought: this has to succeed, lay it on, lay on the charm, lay on the tears, anything, anything. But later, she forgot the room, and Tom and Luther watching her, and the young men hovering about ready to lead her out politely, and she forgot who this Englishman was, or who she was: what she remembered was the homeless people, and how little time was left for them.

When she stopped, she felt that she had been shouting in a cave with echoes. She knew she ought to smile, winningly if possible, to wipe out the impression she had given of accusation and command, but she could not smile. She waited, shaken with weariness, for her dismissal, and dreaded crossing the room again. She doubted whether Lord Balham had heard her at all; he had shifted his position once, nodded his head several times, and kept his eyes shaded with his hand.

Now he waited, thinking, and no one spoke, and Mary groped around in her bag for a cigarette, to have something to do.

"I do not quite understand you," Lord Balham said.

"No?"

"No. How did you happen to come here to tell me these things?"

"I didn't plan it," she said, quickly. "I came in and saw you, that was all."

"It is a question of conscience, isn't it?"

"Oh," Mary said, and pushed away the cigarette smoke. She was deeply embarrassed, and she was angry. So he wants to make a fool of me that way, she thought. Does he expect a brief autobiographical sketch, taking in my home and childhood, education, hopes, fears and dreams?

"If *you* saw someone beating a horse that couldn't get up, you'd do something about it," she said unpleasantly.

"I was trying to understand you."

"Oh. Well, then. If you'd seen the refugees, you'd know. They're good people," she said, quietly. "They are really good people. There is nothing I can do for them. But I thought at least I could talk to you. It wasn't much to do for people you admire."

There were many things he would not tell her. He would not tell her that he had no faith in his position. He was getting out soon and he was glad because he was an honest man. They had given him the title and the honor and the secretaries, but there was no government behind him. It was a farce to think his office could help anyone, since the countries he collectively represented were unwilling to take in the refugees he was supposed to find shelter for. Now, from pride, he kept up appearances until the job was finished, but he had no power and he knew it. In a period of history when bullying prevailed, he was without force to back threats. What could he do: call on a prime minister or two or three and speak to them in the name of humanity? They would listen with respect and possibly even emotion: and the refugees rotted all over Europe.

"It will not make you any happier if I tell you I have seen this tragedy before?"

"No," she said stubbornly.

The terrible thing, he thought, is that I know I am right. I can do nothing. On the other hand, there are so many comfortable, immediate compensations for disillusionment, as you grow older, that finally you forget the disillusionment altogether. Perhaps to be wisely realistic, deploring cruelty and corruption but admitting in advance one's total helplessness against them, is only a form of laziness. Perhaps I have grown very lazy, whereas I thought I had grown wise.

Mary was waiting for him to speak. She could tell nothing from his face. The face angered her. I cannot endure their serenity and their stylized good-looks, she thought. I want to meet a nervous English upper-class man someday, one who bats his eyes and bites his fingernails and does not have that unshakable, rugged, self-confident profile.

"For the sake of our beliefs," Lord Balham said, smiling, and making the words light, "we will go on trying."

"You will?"

"Yes. But there is very little time. I have a meeting in London tomorrow night. It happens to be extremely important. In any case, the main problem is to find asylum for these refugees and that cannot be done in Prague. What exactly is your proposal for here and now?"

"You see," she began earnestly, "we've got to stop that expulsion order. That's the first thing. It doesn't do any good to find them homes some place else if they're already in concentration camps."

He could not help himself, and he thought, mockingly, with your white hair you should know better. Her excitement caught him; it was the grand and lost feeling of being young, of believing you could move mountains; and immediately, because you so passionately willed it, produce something good where all was evil.

"Yes?"

"The only one who could do that is the Czech Prime Minister," Mary said.

"I have not seen him, and no appointment has been arranged."

She sat back, and said, "No!" thoroughly shocked. So that was how they did it, those crooks who didn't want the news of this disaster to get out, those more than crooks who wanted this peace to seem successful. They work well, she thought.

"But you must."

"I don't know if he would listen to me. There is no reason why he should. He's in an unbearably difficult position. You must see that."

"But he has to receive you. And you could persuade

him. You could explain to him. They're honorable people, the Czechs."

How simply she sees it all, he thought, with amusement but with no unkindness, she thinks truth and justice will prevail because they should prevail.

"Is it just the business of getting an appointment?" Mary asked timidly.

He nodded. He was thinking about that, knowing how a refusal would further damage the prestige of his post, a prestige already so uncertain, so academic, that he dared not risk a rebuff. For himself he did not care at all.

"Look," she said. "If the American Ambassador arranged it, would that be all right? I think the Americans are all right here. It isn't as if they'd sold out the country."

"Like my compatriots."

"Well," she mumbled.

"As you say, it isn't as if they'd sold out the country."

"May I try?" she said. "I could try, you know. It's so important. If you don't see the Prime Minister, nobody will. And if that expulsion order isn't stopped . . . I know the refugees; we have to try everything."

"Good," he said. He nodded to her. He was treating her now easily, like an equal. She was surprised by this, not knowing how in his mind, he had suddenly thought: we are in fact two private citizens, let us see what we can do.

"Do it on your own," he warned. "Do not say I asked you to. You're a journalist, you can work out some way of handling that."

167

"All right."

"But one thing we must remember."

"What is it?" she asked.

"Nobody has helped the Czechs. It's something to think about."

"I'll be back later," she said, "and thank you."

She walked into the hall to the telephone booths. She did not know what she would do, but the telephone seemed the place to start, whatever it was.

The telephone operator, a man in the green uniform of the hotel, asked for her number.

"I don't know it," Mary said.

"May I look it up for you?"

"No. Please give me the book."

She took the book to the shelf under a light, where the Paris and London and Berlin directories were piled, and began to turn the pages, reading the unpronounceable Czech names, idly, following a particularly incredible name to see that the street address was equally difficult, and then saying over to herself the telephone number. Think of something, she told herself, you can't get out of it now. She had lunched with a young man who worked in the Embassy or was it the Consulate, last May. She did not remember his name or anything about him except that his tie had been a pretty material and she thought it probably came from Lanvin's and the material would be good for a dressing gown. That's a help, Mary thought, that makes you an old friend of the Ambassador.

Then she thought: the only person who'd get in trouble would be me, I'd be the impostor or the dangerous lunatic, or just the meddling woman. Whatever

I do is my own affair, she thought, and felt scared and reckless: and what can happen? They can ask me to leave the country, and Lord Balham can snub me, and if word gets back to my office I suppose I could be fired for misusing my connection with the paper. But if it worked, she thought, why, then, it would have worked. And if I get through this part, maybe we can stop the expulsion order for a while anyhow.

All right, she said to herself, are you going to?

She went back to the telephone operator and said: "I want to speak to the Secretary of the Prime Minister, but I can't remember the number. I don't know whether it would be the residence of the Prime Minister or his office."

"It would be best to try the office first," the man said. "I do not know the private number."

"Good."

Then a light came on, over the door of a telephone booth, and the bell inside rang firmly, and the telephone operator nodded to her and gestured towards the booth and she was inside, and had dropped her bag on the floor, but could not stoop to pick it up, and it was hot with the glass doors closed and it smelled of cigar smoke from the last caller, and she took off the receiver and waited two long seconds for her voice to be calm and assured, and then spoke.

A voice was already speaking querulously, in Czech. She hadn't thought of that: if they only spoke Czech she couldn't carry it off.

She asked in German for the secretary of the Prime Minister and waited. She could feel the dampness of her forehead and she could not yet think what she would say. What language will I speak, she wondered; my German isn't fancy enough for this.

A deep, rather hurried voice came over the wire.

"*Monsieur*," she said tentatively. If only the man knew French.

"*Oui, qu'est-ce qu'il y a?*" the voice said, hurried still and a little cross.

She turned her head away for an instant so that he should not hear her breath going out in relief and then, taking it all carefully and slowly, smoothing out her voice so that it was as colorless as possible, she began:

"Here is the secretary to the delegation of his excellence Lord Balham, Special Commissioner for Refugees of the Society of Nations. I am telephoning you on the part of his Lordship to inquire whether it would be possible for his Excellency the Prime Minister to accord a brief interview to Lord Balham tomorrow morning at ten. Lord Balham desires to make his respects to his Excellency, before departing for London. He excuses himself to request this interview at so late an hour, but having only arrived yesterday and having been constantly occupied, he was unable before to telephone. He also excuses himself for this informality but is sure the Prime Minister will understand it, due to the events. . . ."

When she had finished, she waited and there was no answer. Does he guess, she thought, in panic. I said it all right, no mistakes in grammar. Then the voice asked whether she would wait.

"Perfectly," Mary said. "Very good. I will wait."

She thought, I know how people feel when they're

170

passing counterfeit money; and she held the receiver so tightly against her head that it hurt her. What is he up to, she thought, is he having the call traced or whatever they do when they think something's crooked?

At first she could not understand, and said, "I beg your pardon?" but when she realized that the interview was arranged, the Prime Minister had accepted, she started to speak too gaily and corrected herself, saying formally, "A thousand times thanks, Monsieur. I will inform Lord Balham. Lord Balham will be at the Ministry at ten tomorrow. Understood. Again many thanks. Good night, Monsieur."

She hung up the receiver and leaned back against the wall and patted her forehead, underneath the veil, with her finger tips. Soaking. But it worked. It worked, she told herself, looking with amazement at the telephone. You can do anything with a telephone, she thought. If this is the way our superiors usually do business, no wonder it's such a mess.

A waiter stopped her as she returned to the salon and said that the two American gentlemen had left, and would be dining at the Sroubek in case she could join them. "They said also to say to you, Fräulein, 'Good luck.'"

Mary thanked him. The luck was fine thus far. The luck was wonderful. She had forgotten the time and she was not hungry. She felt her cheeks hot, and she wanted to run though the salon to tell Lord Balham the news. We're going to do it, she thought, wait till I see Rita. And if we stop the expulsion order, we'll find them a place to live too. If you start winning, you go on. It's not going to be so ghastly, she thought, and

I was wondering all afternoon what to do about Rita. Now it'll be fine, Rita can stay here for two weeks and in that time we'll get her a passport. It's all going to be fixed up. Of course it won't be easy, she warned herself, but Balham's all right. He'll do it.

There's so much room, Mary told herself, they can't refuse: Canada, South Africa, Morocco, Tunisia, much of the west in America, Alaska, the south, even; they could do with some smart Czechs and Germans. We can work up a press campaign. They allowed this rotten business to happen; let them find homes for the victims.

She saw Lord Balham eating alone, in the circular, false, Empire dining room, where the waiters outnumbered the guests three to one, and the atmosphere was heavy with respectfulness towards the rich food. He's sent his secretaries away, she thought, he's probably sick of them. He's a nice man, nice and good-looking, she decided, cordially. He can't help it if he's English.

"It's arranged," Mary said. She felt that they were old friends by now.

"Won't you have something to eat? You must be starved."

"I'm too excited. Just a scotch and soda, please."

Lord Balham looked across the table at her. It was frivolous as well as a scandal to be having such a good time, he thought, but her excitement was catching, as was her hope. He forgot he had known all this before, how many times, in how many years, and he forgot what the end was. He thought: it can't hurt either of us to feel victorious for a change.

"How did you do it?" he asked. She was enchanted

with him. She was enchanted with herself and the Czech Prime Minister and she couldn't wait to spread the good news. She would find Rita tonight. Rita, she thought, almost shouting with delight. Rita, it's all arranged. You're going to be safe. Darling, you and all the others, safe, do you hear?

She told Lord Balham, being warmed by the whiskey and gay with it (not having eaten since morning), how she had arranged the appointment, and he leaned back and laughed so that the head waiter, who was prepared to respect him as an English milord, was displeased by this loud and jovial behavior.

Then Lord Balham said, "My dear, neither of us is acting like a responsible adult. Nothing is done yet. You've arranged the appointment. Fine. But now we have to convince Sirovy. That's another matter. I don't need to explain it all to you. We mustn't think we've won. You'll be too disappointed," he said, and he meant it, but he was thinking of himself, when he had been her age, and of the huge but always possible hopes he held, and how slowly, year after year, he grew more tired, seeing that he could not make them come true.

"Everything depends on tomorrow," Mary said soberly, but she could not doubt. It was so little to ask, after all. They only wanted a two weeks' stay of an expulsion order. Nothing. The real battle would come when they began looking for homes for the refugees. But only two weeks' grace: nothing. Sirovy couldn't refuse. Nobody could refuse.

"What if Labonne went with you?" she said suddenly.

"You *are* wonderful. Do you want another drink? I don't know him."

"I met him last May."

"Do you think he would?"

"I'll ask him," she said. Nobody could refuse her now. We're fixing everything, Mary thought, it's all going to be fine. All you have to do is know what you want and ask for it.

"I can't wait to tell Rita," she said.

"Rita?"

"A friend of mine, a refugee. But don't you think it would be good if Labonne went with you?"

"Of course it would be." He thought: perhaps she is invincible now. Perhaps it has descended on her somehow, the faith, or the hope, or the not knowing about defeat. Perhaps it is only being young and not wanting anything for herself, and refusing to believe in indifference or wickedness seriously; anyhow, he thought, she has done well thus far, but I don't know how French Generals take to this sort of high excitement.

"I'll go and see him," Mary announced. "Right now. He speaks Czech and that would be useful. And certainly he has more standing than anybody in this country."

She was planning again, with great speed and the same onrushing optimism. Labonne had been the head of the French Military Mission and he had resigned, when his country did not honor its pledges. He had watched the whole contemptible process of betrayal, and he alone (he, almost alone in Europe) had protested, as an individual. He resigned his commission

174

in the French army to be free to help the Czechs. But the war was over, without fighting. He had nothing now. Only, she thought, he wouldn't have done what he did unless he understood all about justice and injustice.

"I know he'll go with you," Mary said, "and then really Sirovy can't refuse. Labonne's like God here, as he ought to be."

"Are you going now?"

"In a minute. May I say something?"

"What is it?"

"It's that I'm very happy now because I think we're going to get what we want and all that's fine. But also, morally," she said it very seriously and waited to see whether he would laugh at her, "I think it is an outrage for the refugees to have to depend on this kind of hectic, unplanned action. It's too casual. It's revolting," she said. "I don't mean to criticize you, but it's not right anyhow."

Lord Balham said, "Historians have often been surprised at how haphazardly the fate of nations is decided."

She felt very silly. I ought never to talk, she thought. Every time I open my mouth, I have cause to regret it.

"Well, then I'll go to see Labonne and let you know. Telephone, shall I?"

"Do."

"*Bon appétit.*"

"You do me good. But again, you're acting on your own initiative. You have no authorization. You understand that."

"Yes. I understand that," she said. "Thank you very much and good night."

Mary Douglas gave the driver a piece of paper with the address written on it. The hotel porter had told her it was quite far, perhaps twenty minutes away.

Now she lay back against the stiff, not too clean, gray-smelling upholstery and closed her eyes. The tiredness came back, since there was nothing to do now and no one to talk to, and the excitement chilled and the hope began to melt. This is all fine and dramatic, she thought, but the people who run the world are smarter than this; they make their plans more carefully, in advance. They know what they intend to do, and why, and they don't rush about, in a state of emotion, appealing to conscience or honor or what-not. The people who planned this defeat knew what they were doing. We cannot tidy up the disaster in one evening. It isn't that sort of disaster.

But you're missing the point, she warned herself. You only want a two weeks' extension of safety for the refugees. It isn't like that. Disaster grinds itself out. In war, they bomb hospitals; in peace, they arrest the citizens. That's the system.

But it's Balham's job to save the refugees. You're not being so fantastic in thinking he can succeed. Nobody stopped to consider the refugees before they made this peace, no one will stop now.

That's a fine way to think, she told herself, you've started on this, kindly have the guts to go on believing in it.

I'm tired, she thought, and I'm hungry, and I'm not

176

Joan of Arc, I'm only a journalist. Nobody asked you to be Joan of Arc. You've made one telephone call. Thousands of people like you, perfectly unimportant but horrified people, are trying to do what they can all over the world. Think of all the committees that bloom after each catastrophe, all simple citizens, collecting pennies and old clothes and bandages and railroad tickets. You're one of the ineffectual army of the men of good will, Mary told herself, you and Balham, just joined up, and maybe we can enlist Labonne. But we must succeed, she thought, only two weeks, that's all we want, only two weeks.

No, she decided, I must think this out straight before I see Labonne. He's French so he'll be logical. The point is that it is not surprising that Balham and I, strangers, should be working together in a frantic, last-minute, amateurish effort to give the refugees two more weeks of safety. It is surprising (disgusting, filthy, heartbreaking) that we should have to do this at all. It is surprising that no official governmental action has been taken for the refugees. It is surprising that innocent by-standers must suddenly rush in and try to do a job too big for them, because the proper authorities ignore the job. That's the logic of it, she told herself, and felt less dismayed. Labonne will see that.

They had come to a dark wide street. Each house was walled in, and the trees, still summer-full and soft and black in the night, rose above the walls and screened the houses. Some of these were lighted and looked square and solid. Gray concrete, she thought, the way everything is, not handsome but large and enduring. It was evidently a street where comfortable people lived. You could not see the house numbers on the garden gates.

The driver asked her in German which house and she said she did not know. He stopped the taxi in the middle of the block and Mary walked close to the walls peering at the numbers, until she saw the one she wanted. She asked the driver to wait and rang the gate bell.

The gate clicked open and she walked up a paved drive to a porte-cochère. The door was open on a stone entry, and Mary Douglas had a confused impression of a waiting soldier, like a sentry, and on the wall above him, two crossed spears and a stuffed animal head so dark and shaggy that she could not decide what it was, and beside him a small table bearing a silver plate and a discreet assortment of calling cards.

She gave the soldier her card, saying that she desired to speak to General Labonne. Then she waited, standing uneasily in the hall, thinking that if the stuffed animal head was a bear it was a very odd bear, and presently the soldier returned and led her up carpeted stairs to a high shut double-door. This he threw open, ceremoniously, and said something in Czech, and Mary found herself in a study or library, with books on low bookshelves, two green shaded student lamps lighted, one placed on a huge bare desk, the other on a table piled with magazines, and she saw three brown leather chairs, framed photographs on the walls, ugly beige net curtains, two bronze standing ashtrays, and then General Labonne came forward and bowed, and said, "Mademoiselle," so that it was a question.

She had forgotten to plan a speech. She said her name and he offered her a chair.

"You do not remember me, Monsieur."

"But of course," he said politely, and Mary knew he didn't.

"I met you last May, at a reception at the home of Madame Vlasska."

"Oh, yes, certainly," General Labonne said, and she saw that meant nothing to him either.

Her weariness slowed her now, so that she did not notice how long she sat, looking at him without speaking. I cannot be clever and tactful and do this the right way, I am too tired, Mary thought. I will just have to tell him and he must decide. But still she did not speak, and he seemed to understand that she was resting and he waited without appearing to wait. He had taken the chair behind the desk and looked even smaller than he had before. Now she saw only his shoulders, neat, straight, and thin, in the plain khaki uniform, his hands that were very small, very fine, veined, not soft, and so delicate that they surprised her, and his head. Mary did not realize how carefully she looked at him, and he did not show that he felt the silence.

She felt suddenly and irrationally serene, and she thought: of course he had to look like this but I had forgotten. She saw a face wide at the eyes and forehead, the forehead as clean and grave as a child's; the eyes behind pince-nez, blue, shy, calm, unwinking and friendly; and a snub nose; and a gentle mouth, under a shaved gray mustache. She thought: they invented him, he's what you think the French are on the days when you love the French and say there are no people like the French. The fine flower of France, she thought, you couldn't see him without thinking patriotically that they will always be the best and most civilized in the world.

"I am come to ask your aid," Mary Douglas said.

The small straight-shouldered man said, "Will you take a little cognac before speaking?"

"Please."

The soldier servant came at once and shut the doors silently behind him.

General Labonne held her card up to the light.

"You are a journalist, Mademoiselle?"

"Yes."

"But you did not come in the night," his eyes laughing, "to the home of an old soldier, to demand an interview?"

"Oh, no," she said quickly.

"I did not think it. Here is your cognac."

She took off her gloves, and pulled her hat back from her forehead, and placed it on the floor by her chair. The servant had drawn up a small table and left the round glass standing beside her.

"Good," General Labonne said. "Tell me."

"It is about the refugees."

"Yes?"

"I do not know how to begin. There is so much of it. But do you know that by order of the government the refugees from the Sudeten territory are forced to return at once to their homes. And also, the refugees from Germany and Austria who have been living in this country for years are to be sent away in a few days."

"Yes?"

"It should not be," Mary said.

"The Czechs are not cruel people," he said. "I have lived here since the war and I admire and love them. They have suffered a great treachery. One should shoot the traitors but I read in the papers that crowds follow them and throw their hats in the air and women offer them flowers and the fools rejoice and thank the traitors for this betrayal. What the Czechs do now, they must do. You will understand that."

"I understand," she said, and she thought, I cannot argue with him. He is too good for that.

"And have you heard that in one Czech village where the Sudeten German refugees were in exile for three days only they demanded at once a German school?" he went on.

"That may be true, Monsieur, but it may also be a thing recounted to discredit the refugees. I had heard it also."

"There is something in the Germans, I do not know what it is. An anger they carry in them, perhaps; they cannot live with other people."

"There are good ones. They have lived tranquilly and usefully in my country."

"Do you see what it is for the Czechs?" he asked. "They say, we have now a mutilated country but let us at least be at home in it, among ourselves, all Czechs. Let us be sure of each other and solid together. The brave allies have spoken of minorities, as has Hitler, the noble Lord Runciman spoke constantly of minori-

181

ties. Then let there be no more minorities. Let there be no persons but our own people."

"We do not ask that the Czechs keep the refugees in a permanent manner. We ask only that the refugees be given time to find safety. We must arrange other domiciles for them. They do not care where. All they ask is a place where they may rest with their families, where they may at least be free and think as they like. It is not too much for the Czechs to protect these people for a while longer, is it? One does not abandon the wounded on the field of battle. One does not shoot prisoners."

"No," the small gray man said slowly. "It is true. Two wrongs do not make a right."

Mary leaned back in the chair and finished the cognac. There was not much more to say but she could not hurry. She would have liked to stay here in this worn, ugly, and comfortable room, resting in the half shadow between the circles of green light, with the night silent outside and the street silent, dark, and safely asleep. He would help, because he could do nothing else. I am sure he is poor, Mary thought, with a face so grave and cleanly shaped and fine, a man would have to be poor. Poor and unrewarded, she added, thinking of him. She remembered reading something in a Paris paper about an acting army officer being beyond his rights in resigning, about disloyalty. He is certain to be treated badly and forgotten, she thought, and he will live in scrimped retirement, and there'll never be a monument to him, one of those bronze martial monuments with a horse, in some French village where they put flowers on the monuments of heroes on the Day of the Dead. But he'll help, she thought, and rested with her glass in her hand: because he doesn't think like other people. He has probably thought simply and clearly all his life about justice and injustice. That makes it hard for a man to live, she told herself; and harder now than ever; and who will thank him?

"Mademoiselle," he said suddenly, and his voice waked her, "what is your project?"

"You have heard that the Commissioner for Refugees of the Society of Nations is in Prague?"

"I have read it."

"Tomorrow he is to speak with the Czech Prime Minister. No one can question your sincerity or your devotion to this country. If you would accompany Lord Balham, the meeting would be a success."

"You are an optimist, my child," he said. "What does this Lord intend to ask?"

"He will ask that the order of expulsion be arrested for two weeks."

"And then?"

"And then, during this two weeks, other refuge will be found for these people."

"It is possible that the Czechs will accept," he said. "They have an old habit of honor. The difficulties you know, but the Czechs are good, only we must not expect them to be saints. Sometimes good men who have been beaten and insulted and lied to can become wicked, in despair. But even if the Czechs agree, I tell you this: the democracies will do nothing. They will help no one. You will see. I have lost confidence."

She had not dared go forward in her thinking, beyond the two weeks. She did not dare now. But perhaps the three democracies would buy safety for these refugees in other countries, in South America, or in their own colonies. It was the only hope. She would have to act as if she still believed in the conscience of their rulers.

"It will be arranged somehow," Mary said. "It must be arranged. We must advance day by day; one can do no more."

"So you also work with the Society of Nations?"

"No," she said. She had wondered when he would ask for her credentials. "It is a curious thing. I have no right to be here truly, or to speak with you of this affair. I am only a simple citizen. But this evening I spoke, by accident, with Lord Balham, to urge him to make another effort for the refugees, and so, since I asked him to help the refugees, I have been trying to help him. It is not protocol. He knows that I have come here, but I am not an official personage. I trust you will not think it an impertinence or be angry with me?"

He smiled, "I am now only a simple citizen also. At what time is the meeting?"

"At ten in the morning. Could you meet Lord Balham at his hotel, the Palace, at nine-thirty and go with him, then?"

"I will do it. But if we are refused do not blame this government. Blame the others, the friends and allies, who permitted this disaster."

She blinked her eyes because she was afraid they were going to fill with tears and the tears would roll stupidly down her cheeks and she would look like a fool. It's because I'm so tired. What can I say to him, she wondered. He just knew, she thought, he knew there was a wrong here, a cruelty, and he did not stop to consider whether it was wise or not for him to be involved; he chose his side without thinking at all, with his heart, very naturally.

Mary said, not daring to look at him, "I cannot thank you, mon Général." She had used the title, as a subordinate in the army uses it.

He smiled at her. "I am glad you came."

"There is one thing I would wish to tell you before I go. You will please forgive me if it seems too personal. If I had not seen you, I would have written you, and it would have been better that way, from a stranger."

"Tell me."

"I wish to tell you," she said gravely, "how much I admire you. But it is more than that. I thank you too. When we heard of your resignation, we took confidence again in human dignity."

"No. You speak too well of me."

"I can only tell you what I feel."

He had lit a cigarette and now he was watching the smoke waver up towards the ceiling. He seemed to talk to himself. "I love this country," he said, "and the people. I have respect for them. I helped them a little to make their army and it was a fine army. What has happened here is worse than war. I suffer for this country and for this people." He leaned forward and now he talked to her as if he must say it aloud to someone else. "But it is for France I suffer most." How beautifully he says "France" she thought: if it's spoken like that, with passion and love, it is a great name.

"It is the shame of France that is unbearable," he said.

She thought: you would have to love very greatly to be so hurt. She would have liked to comfort him, but there was no room for comfort, there would be no easy phrases to console him. And they will never know in France, she thought, that he is the finest France can make, and they will never thank him.

"Forgive me," he said. "I have thought of all this too much."

"What will you do now?"

"I?" he said. "I do not know. My sister lives in the Touraine. She has nice grandchildren. I shall go there for a time. It is a beautiful country, the Touraine."

"Yes."

"Perhaps I will be able to serve again. Later."

She stood up. She had no right to keep him longer. "I thank you for everything," she said. He seemed to know what she meant.

The taxi driver could not understand why the woman looked this way; she looked happy but her eyes were wet. He was glad she had come anyhow: it was a big fare and now he could stop driving for the night.

I've seen enough in the last five years, Mary thought, to make anyone despair. But disaster doesn't harm the really good ones: they carry their goodness through, untouched, and nothing that happens can make them cowardly or calculating. I've seen some fine people in these disaster years. I've seen one tonight. There's that to remember too, when despair sets in.

So now Rita will be safe, Mary thought, and the others will be safe: the innocent will suffer just a little less this time.

The taxi driver opened the door of the car and said, "Here is your hotel, Fräulein," and waked her, tugging lightly at her coat.

11

IT was not a dream that moved or changed and there was only Peter in it, and herself, and nothing happened. They slept, that was all, she with her head almost under his arm, his arm curving up and just touching her hair and the top of her head, her cheek lying against his side, against the soft cool skin of his side that was tight over his ribs but tender. In the dream her right arm was under her, hollowing out a place for itself in the mattress, and her left arm stretched lightly across his chest, light and friendly and binding him to her even in sleep.

She slept in her dream and did not hear the front door open very slowly and slowly shut. She did not hear Peter cross the room, making no sound on the bare boards, and she did not hear the little rustling as he took off his clothes. He pushed her gently closer to the wall, because she lay in the middle of the bed, and slipped under the covers. She did not wake; her hand moved across his naked and cold body and rested on his chest, and her dream folded over him, without interruption or change.

It was four o'clock, clear, without moon or wind, and the dimmed street lights of Prague seemed to burn even lower as the night wore on. The streets were empty. It was too early for the heavy trucks that rattle every city awake, and the last street car had clanged into the depot hours before and the few taxi drivers, who waited before the two late cabarets and the rich curtained houses on side streets in the Mala Strana where you could get girls, had all gone home for want of fares. At this hour you could hear if you were followed. It was a chance to take and Peter thought: it is the last time. I must risk it now because there is no other way.

Now he lay beside her, cold, very tired but tight and listening and afraid to close his eyes, and he was careful not to wake her because he had nothing to say except good-by. Slowly, her warmth and her peace worked in him, not so that he could forget why he had come and how he would have to go before the night ended, but he stopped listening and the tightness went out of him, and he felt her soft beside him, the softness of her breast and leg against his side, and far down, he felt her cold curled feet searching as always for a warm place. He turned and leaned over, looking for her mouth.

The dream melted and blurred; it was as if a feather had been drawn across her mouth, but his lips came back, warm and pressing harder and she raised her face, not awake and not asleep, and quickly he lifted her up to have his arms all around her and held her hard against him. He did not let her go, their mouths were almost touching, and she said, without wonder, because all night he had been beside her in the dream, "Peter, my darling."

The memory of the day and the night was not clear

and tormenting any more to him, only he knew he must hurry, they must have this quickly, now, for always, to have had it before the night ended. She ruffled the hair at the back of his neck with stroking, smooth fingers, and he felt her touch aching through him. She lay close against him, sleep-warm and sleep-scented, and her body molded into his under the pressure of his hand.

He wanted her entirely to share this and to know it had been. "Rita," he whispered, "Rita, open your eyes, look at me."

She woke, and knew he had been away and come back, and saw his eyes bright in the darkness and saw his face. She cried out, like sobbing, and he caught her tight against him. She felt the hardness of his bones, and his weight. She pushed against him and he did not notice. He had always been as careful as if there was something unhealed in her, as if any roughness would be a reminder and sicken her again, and take her back to what she had been, before he came, with his gentleness. He did not hear her breathing. She was not really awake and she was afraid of his fierceness and she thought, this is not us, this is not us two who love each other. This was like dying. This was like the last thing you would do before you died. She thought: he is hating me; what has happened to him? His hands hurt her and she wanted to stop this fury, she wanted to say wait, wait, *why*, Peter? but she had no breath to speak. Then she knew, without thinking or putting it into words. Her body joined him; her hands were as strong as his. For this moment they would be hard and reckless and triumphant like those who always won.

She wanted to cry out with joy but this was not joy, this was anger, this was how they were finally cheating the ones who would destroy them. They would wrench the bitter violent pleasure from this night. No matter what. No matter what afterwards. She had a feeling of terrible speed and burning; they were alone together as they had never been, and for one instant, when the darkness behind her eyelids flared up into the yellow light, she thought: now we are dead.

Then he lay on her heavily, his face hidden in the hollow between her throat and her shoulder, and she tried to quiet her breathing and not think.

"Sleep now, Peter."

"No."

"What is it then?" He would have to tell her in words, though he had already told her.

"I must go in five minutes, in ten minutes."

She did not speak.

"I lied to you, Rita. You must forgive me for that. We cannot leave together."

There was no pain and no surprise; only the cold empty deadness in her mind.

"Now?" she said.

"There were only a few who could not be replaced," he said. "Those have gone. It was not easy. I could not ask for myself, and it would have been refused. I am not the most valuable; there are many others like me. We must do what we can for ourselves later. You forgive me for the lie?"

"My dearest."

"Please, oh, please, Rita, I would have found the passports and the money and the tickets for everybody if I could, but I could not. I beg you to understand."

"No," she said, "it isn't that. I know that. Peter, let me come with you."

"Together we are easier to find."

"Don't leave me, Peter."

He took her in his arms and smoothed her hair and kissed her forehead. He could not save her or protect her, with him she was in greater danger, and he could see ahead the days of her waiting, alone, and he could not face the cruelty of leaving her. But if he said yes, and she crept down the stairs with him into the dark street, he would be leading her into worse than loneliness.

"My little one, my child," he said, "I dare not take you. I love you," he said, because he had thought suddenly, with horror, that she might believe herself abandoned for want of love, that she might have that also to hurt her in the days to come. "You know that, you know that. You must not think."

"You love me," she said, so quietly that he had to lean his head closer to hear, "and I love you." It is all we have, she thought, and now not even that.

"You must go to Mary. She will help you. I know she will help you. She will arrange somehow for you to go to Paris." So now he would send what he loved, what was his, what he should care for and stay with and watch over, to another woman, a stranger, hoping that this woman would do his work for him. He thought, with bitterness, what use is a man to a woman now? I must leave her alone and trust that someone else will do what I cannot do.

"I will stay here," she said. "I will stay in the same city."

"No, Rita, you must not make it any worse. If I know you are safe, I can try harder myself. We will meet in Paris, you know where. Keep in touch with the comrades there, and perhaps I will be able to send word, and as soon as I can I will come to you. Others have done it, on foot across the frontier of Roumania and down to the Black Sea. There are freight boats to Marseilles. It can be done. But not if you are still here. You must promise me."

"If you wish," she said. "I will do what you wish."

"Kiss me. I must go now. It is getting light."

She turned to him and pulled his head down to her and kissed his eyes, his cheeks, his forehead, his mouth, not breathing, choked and shaken with tears, and he tried to go away from her, but she hung to him so that he dragged her up with him, and he stooped and undid her hands and laid her back in the pillows. She put her hands over her eyes, not to see him leaving, and she thought: if I could die now, now, now, and not know he had gone and not say good-by.

He heard her on the bed, holding in her breath, to hold in the noise of her crying, and when he was dressed he came and stood over her a moment, and did not touch her or speak, and then she heard the door creaking shut.

She stumbled across the room after him, meaning to open the door and follow him down the steps, to see him once more or touch him, but she stopped, with her hand on the knob, knowing she would wake the house and he must go like the hunted, without being seen and without being heard. Then she ran to the window and leaned out to watch the street door, and later she saw him slip through and not look up, and walk like a cat, dark and swift, close against the walls of the houses to the corner, where he turned and was gone.

She leaned her face on the windowsill, and much later she raised her head and watched the morning, gold and pale and cloudless, lightening the city.

Mary stood in the sunshine between the two potted yew trees talking to the doorman about the weather and smoking.

"You should go inside and have a cup of coffee," the doorman said. "They have not been gone a half hour."

"There were two gentlemen, weren't there?"

"Yes."

"I'll wait inside. When you see them, rap on the window, will you? Lord Balham will be in a hurry."

"All his baggage is downstairs waiting. But the plane is at noon. I will watch for you," the doorman said, and moved out to the curb to open the door of a taxi.

She ordered coffee in the salon, where no sun came through the long velvet curtains, and the air smelled faded. She poured the coffee and let it cool in the cup and did not touch it, but lighted another cigarette. It was ten-thirty: they must have left here at about a quarter to ten: provided Sirovy received them on time they would have been speaking for half an hour. That was a good sign, or was it?

She heard a car stop and she went to the window and pulled aside the curtains to look, but it was not Lord

Balham. She had not eaten breakfast, and felt shivery and still tired, and with a sick cold fluttering inside her throat. But they can't refuse Labonne, she thought, they can't. Oh, hurry, she thought, let's get it over with. No, it's better for them to be slow, that means Sirovy is listening to them, and making some sort of deal. She went quickly to the window again and saw this time a black Packard town car and as the doorman opened the door he looked over his shoulder and she ran through the salon into the hall and stood outside on the pavement, waiting as Lord Balham and General Labonne stepped from the car.

Lord Balham stopped to give some order to the chauffeur in a fretful hurried voice and General Labonne waited politely beside him, looking tiny and elegant in dark blue civilian clothes. Then they crossed the pavement and saw Mary in the doorway, and Lord Balham said, "Good morning," but Mary felt in his voice that it was different now; he was the League Commissioner and she was an American journalist. Last night they had been equals and friends, plotting together with hope. It was morning now. General Labonne, shy and formal, took her hand and bowed.

Lord Balham swept them with him into the hall, still hurried, looking about for his luggage, and said to Mary, "He wouldn't listen to us."

"Oh," she said, and stood still.

"We did all the possible, Mademoiselle," General Labonne said in French.

"He refused?" Mary said. "He didn't? He couldn't!"

"Yes, he did," Lord Balham said.

She saw that he was thinking now, angrily, of his

position, of the damaged prestige, of this fresh proof that his office was powerless and insignificant.

"Rather brusque about it too, I thought. Wouldn't hear of it. So there we are. I'll be back in a moment. Pardonnez-moi, mon Général."

She waited in the salon with General Labonne.

"There is nothing to do?" she asked.

"I fear not. You cannot blame General Sirovy. He is not a bad man. I have known him for years. He does what he must now. Lord Balham and I said everything, but it was useless."

"Only two weeks," she said.

"I think there is much pressure from Germany, and much bitterness here in the country. I am sad as you are, Mademoiselle, very sad."

"I did not think he would refuse," she said helplessly.

"I did not think this country would be betrayed by France," he said. "I could not believe that either. We live to see many things."

"Well," Lord Balham said, coming back to them, screwing the cap on a fountain pen, patting sidepockets to see that tickets, passport and checkbook were in place, "it is a rotten shame. You've been awfully good about it. I can't thank you enough. You'll look me up in London the next time you come, won't you? *Je vous remercie sincerement, mon Général, et je regrette que notre visite n'a pas reussi. Je m'excuse d'être si pressé mais j'ai donné rendez-vous à l'aéroport, et il faut que je me depèche.*"

"*Naturellement. Mais il n'y a rien à me remercier, je vous assure. Et bon voyage.*"

They shook hands rapidly and confusedly and the black Packard pulled to the curb, luggage was stowed alongside the chauffeur, Lord Balham turned to wave at them from the back window and Mary, watching him, thought: we will all leave, we can leave, nothing happens to us.

"Thank you," she said to General Labonne. "Thank you truly."

"Do not make me ashamed. I have done nothing. If you will permit me, because I am old, I would like to say something to you."

"Yes?"

"There is never one injustice alone, but always many others which follow naturally. If you live, you will see many more and worse. But you must not become bitter. And if you live long enough, you will see it change."

"I will take care and live a long time."

"There are good men."

"There are not enough of them, then," she said.

"Yes, but they are like us. Sad and making failures. For the moment. Now, can I take you where you are going?"

"No, thank you, I'll walk. I live near here. And I hope I'll see you sometime again."

"We will meet. I wish you good luck."

"If things keep up this way, we'll meet in a concentration camp."

He laughed, as if the idea delighted him. "Perhaps we will," he said. *"Vous êtes une brave fille.* If we do, I hope we will conserve our good humor all the same. I know very little but one thing I believe is still true.

The French will fight before they go to concentration camps and the Americans too. Perhaps for nothing else, and perhaps too late. So let us say, we may meet in a concentration camp, but we will meet at the war first."

"In that case," she said, *"Vive la guerre!"*

His car had waited for him, the soldier chauffeur holding the door open and smiling at the conversation which he did not understand but smiling because the General laughed and his voice was gay and brisk again.

"What an idea," General Labonne said, shaking his head and chuckling. *"Vive la guerre.* Women are terrible. Good luck to you, Mademoiselle. Perhaps we will win the next time."

But now there was no small, porcelain-perfect Frenchman to talk to in that language which always led you, happily and easily, into laughter. Now there were only the wide, gray streets of Prague, and the October sun, and the high clear October sky, and nothing to do, except leave, safely in a plane, nothing to do now except gather together quickly a few odds and ends of information for the articles, pack, see the boys once more, and find Rita. Find Rita and tell her what they had tried and how they had failed. It would not be a happy meeting. And tell her good-by and leave her too. No. She would not leave her. I'll get her out, Mary thought. I can take care of Rita anyhow. I didn't believe it. It isn't possible. Are we never going to win?

The desk clerk said that there were three people waiting to see Miss Douglas; their names are written down here: not Rita, but perhaps she would come later; well, she would receive the visitors in her room, would he send up the gentleman in about five minutes and she would telephone down for the other two, as soon as the gentleman left. No word from Mr. Lambert? All right. And no telegrams? Then the gentleman in about five minutes.

The maid had cleaned her room and she sat down on the faintly grimy blue satin coverlet of the bed and wondered what to do with five whole minutes. I might have known it, she reasoned, it would have been too good to be true, but she had gone ahead, in her mind, to the meeting with Rita, saying in imagination, "It's all right, Rita, there's two more weeks, we can manage in that time to find a safe place for you all." Only that was a fairy story and that was not the way things worked and in fact, as before, you sat still and watched history roll on like a rock crusher.

I'm getting out, she decided, there is nothing more to do here.

She picked up the telephone and called the concierge.

"Will you reserve a place on the morning plane tomorrow for Paris? You can send up a boy for my passport to take over to the airline office. Thank you."

How do you get people out of a country, she wondered, now that traveling is a crime? She would go to the American Consulate, before lunch, and ask. Probably a question of money more than anything else. Five hundred dollars, a thousand, some sort of guarantee? Have to find Rita and see whether she has any kind of passport at all.

"Come in," she said, and turned to see a middle-aged man with an uneven black mustache, a black shiny suit, and worn laced high shoes, standing just beside her door, evidently uneasy to be calling on a strange woman in her bedroom.

"Yes?" she said.

"I am a friend from Richard Sommers," he said.

That's odd, she thought, Dick's in England.

"You have some word from him?" she asked.

He fumbled in his pockets. "I have been to the four great hotels questioning for you. Here I find you. Richard have not write the hotel, only the name."

Wait and see, she thought, no need to get nasty with him unless he can't prove he knows Richard.

The man opened a scratched, bulging leather wallet and took out a small sheet of notepaper.

"See."

She read, "A colleague of mine named Mary Douglas is in Prague, collecting material for articles. I do not know which of the big hotels, you will have to go around and inquire. I am sorry you have lost your job—she may be able to help you, or at least you can see her and perhaps we can work something out." It was in Dick's handwriting and signed.

"What can I do for you?"

"Fräulein," the man said, coming closer and speaking in a whisper. "I must go from the country."

She stared at him in amazement.

"There are many people who must go."

"You do not understand."

"Yes, I do."

"We must need foreign exchange and passports."

Good God, she thought, what next.

"But look," she said helplessly, "I don't know anything at all about illegal work. You've come to the wrong person."

He began to mumble apologies. She could see he wanted to leave, but he was looking at the telephone. He thinks I'll warn them downstairs to stop him, she thought, this is getting crazier by the minute.

"I mean I can't help you with that," she explained. "I'm not going to denounce you; don't be a fool. The thing is I haven't the faintest idea how you get a false passport or how to smuggle in foreign exchange. I have less than a hundred dollars myself, and you can't cash checks for dollars in Prague. And about passports, God, man, I've never fooled with that sort of thing."

"*Natürlich.* I excuse me."

"Wait a minute."

She reread Dick Sommers' letter. Dick must be out of his head too, or else he hadn't known what this man wanted.

"You're one jump ahead," she said.

"*Bitte?* I cannot understand so good."

"Now listen. Dick wants a report. He didn't expect me to get you out of the country. He wants to know what you need, and how many of you there are." I hope he doesn't tell me, she thought, I know enough about this place already. The more you know, the worse the responsibility; and if everything falls through and there's bad trouble, they can always blame the outsider for carelessness or talking away secrets.

"I gather this is quite a thing. There are several of you?"

"Yes."

"The mail is censored coming in?"

"Some yes, some no. It can always be."

"That explains it. Dick being so mysterious. But that's what he means surely. He knows me very well; he knows I can't handle anything like this. Have you been in touch with him?"

"To write: I have lost my job, many of our friends too. We must look other places. The situation is bad here."

"How long can you stay here?"

He shrugged. "Nobody knows. Maybe tomorrow, maybe two weeks. But soon they get us."

She thought: carrying a letter would be dangerous, for him more than for me, in case I am searched at the airport. So now I will have to listen and get this straight in my head and get in touch with Dick, directly, from Paris.

"You better tell me, after all. I will telephone Dick from Paris. It's the only thing I can think of. I think a letter would be too risky, though if you prefer you can write one, and I'll take it out for you. Whatever you want."

"No letter," he said. "They send a letter to Paris and three are arrested here. I do not know how."

"Fun," she said.

"*Bitte?*"

"Nothing," she said, thinking: this is all mad, this is all unreal, all of us acting like spies or escaping criminals, all of us with the back hairs standing up, spooked, and goofy, and nothing you can ever see to be afraid of.

"All right, do you want to tell me?"

"Fräulein, I tell you because Richard write me. So. He knows my name and where he can send me a man to find me. That I will not say to you. Is not needing. But say to him there are eleven now. Many more naturally but for us in the radio work eleven."

"Like the *Freiheitssender?*" she asked, and it became clearer to her.

"Like this, something. He is understanding. Good technicians all eleven, also known to Gestapo. And without passports and without foreign exchange. Some man of us must be sended here at once, tell him at once immediately, *schnell*, with those things. If I am not found, then tell him his man must look for Gustav. He know that too. Tell him the work is stopped."

"Stopped?"

"There is nothing more now from here to Germany. It is too dangerous. Not for the comrades who are working only, but the Gestapo must not learn our methods. Und was good work too. But now, anyhow, it is different. Now they see in Germany once more again victory for Hitler. In September was big discontent in Germany and solidarity with us. Now again comes discouragement. No one can fight Hitler, not even England, they are thinking. We have lost much in the propaganda against Hitler."

"I can see that," she said.

"Well, now I go. *Gute reise.* Please to call Richard quickly." He smiled and looked like somebody else, younger and unworried and she could see that when he was doing his work, he must be a sure, reliable, determined man. "Now I go downstairs and whistle at the one who follow me. He wait just a little back, now in the passage up the street. He follow since a week but now it is *komisch.* I come to a hotel where is full of Fascists and he wait and cannot understanding it. Gestapo is like hunting dogs and when they get you is all ended; but just following many times I see them *dumm* like cows. So. *Salut.* And much thanks."

She shook hands with him and watched him open the door, and look both ways down the dim, carpeted corridor, and then go.

She stood behind the closed door, thinking not with laughter but with a kind of light-headed dismay, that being a respectable American bourgeoise did not prepare you properly for the things you saw and heard these days.

The knock at the door was briskly professional and a bellboy entered first to take her passport for the concierge and then a woman came in and said that she was Frau Markheim, and Mary offered her a chair and cigarettes.

The woman spoke rapidly and nervously, making apologies for coming to see her in this manner, for intruding, for perhaps interrupting her at her work, and as she talked Mary tried to place her but was confused by the pink varnished fingernails and elegant silver fox cape and the small hat that was at least a copy of an Agnès model. The woman was blonde with the too rigidly marceled hair that is fashionable in central Europe, wearing rouge only because rouge is respectable, and she seemed about thirty-five or thirty-eight years old. Not a refugee anyhow, Mary thought, and not German.

"I must explain you, Miss Douglas," the woman said. She had put out her newly lit cigarette and was opening and shutting the amber clasp of her bag. "My husband is a doctor and a friend of Doctor Niels in Paris."

"Oh," Mary said.

"They have for many years been associated and when we go to Paris we stay with Doctor and Madame Niels and in the winter we often met at Sils Maria for the winter sports."

"Yes?"

"So Doctor Niels telephoned your hotel in Paris and ask your address here and wrote us and my husband suggest I come to see you because the telephone. You see. One no longer knows about the telephone."

"I'm delighted you came," Mary said. Doctor Niels was a throat specialist in Paris and she had visited him only a few days before coming to Prague, and met him several times in the last few years at rather stiff French dinner parties.

"Doctor Niels must arrange to help us from this country," Frau Markheim said. "We have Czech passports but we are not allowed to leave. I am a Swede, but my husband is a Czech citizen. We have lived here fifteen years. My husband is a Jew," she said.

Mary did not know what to say; there seemed no answer to make.

"It has already started here," the woman said, speaking now with passion. "In this country, where was always before culture and democracy. Already the insults to Jews and the broken shop windows. And in the Sudetenland where we have friends too, also distinguished doctors, has started the suicides. And here too. And here too. Three we know and one a very old man and a fine scientist. They have killed themselves, with the

205

disgust and the despair. Already the patients are afraid to come to my husband and already at the University the German professors, and the ones in the Laboratory who were always Henleinist are saying they will no longer work with Jews."

They leave nothing undone, Mary thought, they never even vary their pattern.

"I am afraid for my husband," the woman said. "I am afraid to see him so black in the mind, saying to me, 'Ilsa, there is no civilization left, there is nothing left for decent people to live in.' We must go away to France. He is older than I, my husband, he is fifty-three. And he says now, 'I am tired of it, I am sick of it, I do not care to bother with it any more.' "

"I will do what I can," Mary said. "What is it you want?"

"You will see Doctor Niels for me and you will tell him? We have money here but we cannot take it out. We are not allowed to leave now; no one may go. We have money also in Paris but we cannot touch it from here. But we are not political, you see it, only medicine does my husband all these years. But now he is a Jew and soon there will be no medicine. Doctor Niels is very important; he can arrange with the French Embassy here to grant a visa, to make a pressure for the passport, and he can buy the plane tickets in Paris for us."

"Do you want me to take a letter?"

"No, please. Now are letters opened and if the name is seen then perhaps there is trouble for my husband."

She's got it too, Mary thought.

"I'll get in touch with Doctor Niels in Paris and tell

him. He should communicate with you through the French Embassy, is that it?"

"Yes, if you will be so good," the woman said, the anxious face loosening, and her eyes full of tears. "If you will help me in this way. I do not know you and it is awful to come to a stranger and say all the troubles, but I do not know what to do and I am afraid even to leave my husband alone for an hour now. He is ashamed to live. He says he has lost his country and he has lost his hope in mankind. He says a Jew can cure people and make them well, but when the ones you have cured telephone to say they are sorry they cannot come back again, since the changes in politics, then he says he is sick of it. A doctor must also love people if he is to help them and Europe is too ugly, one can love nothing."

"You want to go home, don't you?"

"Yes," the woman said.

"I'm leaving tomorrow and I'll be in Paris tomorrow night and I'll call Doctor Niels at once. Don't worry about it. Just take care of your husband and talk to him about Sils Maria."

"You know it?"

"I went there two years ago," Mary said. "It's one of the loveliest places in the world."

It had been very cold at night and the feather bed was a perpetual problem and one morning John spilled his entire cup of coffee with whipped cream on it, and she worked for hours trying to tidy up the mess because a feather bed was an important possession and you weren't supposed to ruin them. They admired the green lake that was so green it looked as if it had been dyed with a chemical, and they ate at least five meals a day and laughed all the time because that was almost the beginning of their life together and I anyhow, she thought, was probably laughing with wonder that anything so fine should happen to me.

"We were so happy there," Frau Markheim said.

"We were too."

Frau Markheim stopped, puzzled, and Mary blushed to have been telling secrets and bent her head waiting for the other woman to go on.

"Even last winter we were there," Frau Markheim said. She had her own trouble; she was not noticing the color in the girl's face and the way she was trying to keep her mouth from curving into an inexplicable smile.

"And so happy and we could not dream the things that have happened since. Even now, I cannot think it is true. I cannot believe it. But yesterday afternoon at five o'clock they telephone and say old Doctor Abrams take an overdose of morphine, after lunch. At lunch he is eating with his wife and two sons and the grand-children, and laughing and telling stories about when he was a student in Wurzburg, and telling big stories to make them laugh about all the foolish things he do when he start out for practice medicine, and then he spoke of his father, and he was too a doctor and his grandfather also, and always they lived here in Prague, no one can know how long, and always poor because of so many patients without paying. He was with pink cheeks and a little white beard, and always kindly with everybody and so much loved and worked all his life with people usually not paying him. So he made fun at lunch and then went to his study for a little sleep like every day, now he is old, and at four-thirty they come and he is dead. This is true," she said, suddenly pounding on the desk beside her, forgetting Mary, and this visit to a stranger, this begging of help from a woman she had never seen. "This is true."

Mary went over and put her arm around the woman's shoulder. She did not look like a woman who had any experience in suffering. Mary could imagine her as the pride of her husband, always young in his eyes, and blonde and chic, probably charming his elderly colleagues and being the confidante of the younger doctors. (Inviting the internes to tea, Mary thought, and listening sympathetically as they told of their ambitions, and perhaps flirting a little with them and always being flattered when she saw admiration for her waved yellow hair and her smart clothes.)

The woman took Mary's hand and to Mary's painful surprise, kissed it.

"You will help us then. You are good. God will bless you."

"But it's nothing," Mary said miserably. "Just a telephone call. You'd better go back to your husband now."

"Yes, yes," the woman said, and picked up her gloves and looked around to see if she had left anything. "I must hurry now. I must hurry. I hope there has been nothing in my absence." She turned at the door and smiled, "Maybe we shall meet some day at Sils Maria, when we are all happier."

"Yes," Mary said. "Next winter."

Mary would have liked to take her hat and coat and

walk down the stairs and through the lobby without being seen; I don't think I'm up to many more visitors, she thought. There was the Consulate anyhow, about Rita, and then a whole series of fast dreary interviews to accomplish: the man who knew about railroads and what had happened to them since the invasion, and the one who would tell her about coal, and another one who she had learned was an authority on paper and textiles. I have to do it, she thought wearily. I've got to get the facts about the break-up of their economy. But it seemed to her that a country's economy could be lying in little broken pieces and if the people were still free, they would live and build up a homeland again.

She told the telephone girl to find her other visitor, and she straightened up the room and combed her hair and prepared to be cordial but brisk. It was getting late.

She listened to the woman, without speaking. Then she said, "But why come to me?"

"There is no one else."

"Is it as important as you say?"

The woman did not know how to answer this question; it seemed to her ignorant. She wondered if she had come to the wrong place.

"They are the facts," she said slowly. "No one else has them. Is that important?"

"Yes, of course," Mary said impatiently. "I'm getting mixed-up, that's all. How big is it?"

The woman spread her hands. "So long, so thick," she said, measuring in the air.

"But that's huge," Mary said. "It will be very hard to manage."

"I can perhaps cut down some."

"You'll have to."

The woman waited. Mary looked at her, without seeing her. She was not thinking of the risk, she was thinking of the chances of succeeding. On the whole, she decided she stood a fairly good chance of getting away with it. The woman, in her own mind, was making the same calculations.

"If I can't get the stuff out, don't blame me," Mary said.

"But naturally not."

"I just wanted to be sure of that."

"You will do it?"

"I'll try anyhow. Come around here tomorrow morning at nine and bring it. I'm leaving on the noon plane. And take care of yourself."

"You are taking care of me," the woman smiled. "As soon as those papers go, I am all right. It is my only worry."

"I can see how it might be. You look dead tired."

The woman patted her hair self-consciously; it was stringy and out of curl. Her make-up had been put on yesterday, anyhow. She said, trying not to sound apologetic, "I look disgusting, but I have been too nervous to notice."

"Get a rest," Mary said. "You haven't seen Rita lately, have you?"

"No."

"She was supposed to dine with me tonight. I thought she'd telephone this morning. Probably she's busy. I guess she'll come around or send a message this afternoon."

"I haven't seen anybody," the woman said. "You're in a hurry?"

She stood up. "I will now go to the cinema," she grinned at Mary. "Everybody goes. It is the best place so far when they are looking for you. It will be over of course when the Gestapo thinks of it. I do not like the pictures, so I go where the chairs are comfortable and I sleep a little. I have been to the same one five times, but the chairs are good. And it is dark and crowded and there are many exits."

"It's crazy," Mary said flatly.

"Everything is crazy," the woman agreed. "Only it is difficult to laugh about it."

Rita slept like drowning, sinking deep into a furry thick dark stillness. When she woke, she was lying flat on her back, the way she had been at dawn, after she came back from the open window, and her arms and legs were heavy as logs and without feeling. She opened her eyes and stared at the ceiling, which was bright with afternoon sun, and she made an effort to understand where she was. She closed her eyes and lay, not sleeping, feeling only the weight of her body and the blanket that seemed to strap her into the bed. With her eyes closed, she could see little circles of light, and little glowing points that jumped across the darkness, and burned and changed into wavering lines. If she kept very still, she could watch these small irregular fireworks. Then they faded into blackness and she slept again, as if she had been drugged, a dead, black, un-resisting down plunge into nothingness.

The bed dipped on one side, and she woke and saw dimly a man's elbow, near her, and felt him sitting sideways to her facing the room. She flung her arm across her eyes and pulled back in the bed.

"It is four o'clock, Rita," Schultze said gently.

"I'm sick," she said, trembling with a chill. There was a sharp digging pain in the back of her head; it hurt her to keep her eyes open, and she was sweating.

Schultze went into the kitchen for a glass of water, and gave it to her. She held the glass in both hands, un-steadily, and drank it. He put his hand on her fore-head. It was very hot.

"Ach," he said, "you have fever."

"I must see Mary," she said, sitting up in bed. "He told me. Go to Mary. Meet me in Paris."

Schultze could hardly understand her. She was mum-bling to herself.

"I'm cold," she said. "Why is it so cold here?"

Schultze brought her coat and wrapped it around her shoulders. He did not know how to talk to her, she was too sick.

"Schultze," she said, looking at him with surprise, as if this were the first time she had really seen him. "What are you doing here?"

"I came to see you."

"Oh," she said wisely. She did not understand at all. There was a hammer beating hard on her left temple, one-two-three, one-two-three, maybe if she leaned back against the pillows it would not strike so hard. Schultze helped her. Better, now; not a beat, just a steady throb-

213

bing. She was very cold and pulled the covers up and tightened the coat around her shoulders. She felt so sick that the room seemed to be washing around, swaying and floating, and she could not remember what it was she had been thinking, something she must do, but there was no hurry, she couldn't do it now anyhow, she would remember and do it some other time.

"Wie gehts?" she said and smiled at Schultze, who was nice to her and kind and quiet and big and looked like a good brown bear.

"Gut," he said, patting her shoulder. But he would have to tell her now, because he was not sure he could come back here; only she probably wouldn't understand. Perhaps he could write a note and she would find it, when she was better. But no, he must not leave her like this.

He found some dish towels and soaked them in cold water from the kitchen tap, wrung them out so that they would not drip, and he laid them on Rita's forehead, telling her, "Close your eyes. You will feel better in a little while."

The cloth was cool over her eyes and took away some of the red burning inside that hurt her. I can stay an hour, Schultze thought, maybe her head will clear; she must have the influenza; perhaps she took cold in the night. He changed the towels. The apartment was quiet except for the loud tinny ticking of the alarm clock on the bookcase.

Schultze thought she was asleep, and sat down on a chair to wait.

"Are you here, Schultze?" she asked.

"Doch, kindchen."

214

"I am not so cold."

"That is good."

"Please give me water."

Her mouth was sticky and rough; she drank the water and asked for more. Then she sneezed and laughed.

"Good," Schultze said with relief. "Now it goes into a nice little cold. A nice little winter cold."

He touched her forehead again; it seemed cooler, but perhaps that was only because of the towels.

"How do you feel?"

"Fine," she said. She felt fine and sick and not in a hurry. If she lay here with her eyes closed, and felt the pain flow through her head, and felt her body running with heat and cold, but all gently, all easily, and if she did not think, she could just be sick and comfortable, and if she did not think at all, Schultze was her father taking care of her and she was sick, and it was a winter afternoon, and soon they would be putting on the lamps in the street, the man coming around with the long pole that he thrust up inside the globes, and then the short gas candle would glow first green, then blue and then white, and soon they would bring her clear hot noodle soup, hot and light and easy to swallow, the noodles very soft, melting, a little salty, and the soup good and hot but not greasy, and then she would sleep. And tomorrow she would be all right, and wake, and it would be a sharp winter day, blue, with a fast icy wind coming off the snow mountains and blowing the ladies' skirts as they marketed in the Rathaus Square.

"Rita," Schultze said softly.

"Yes, my good old bear," she said, smiling with closed eyes.

"Are you awake?"

"Yes," she answered unhappily. She did not want to wake. She wanted to lie here and enjoy feeling her head grow cool and feeling her body gradually warm all over, resting now so lightly under the blankets. She curled up her toes and rubbed one foot on the other; they were getting warm too.

"I am very comfortable," she said. "Can I go to sleep?"

It is cruel, he thought, if she could sleep now and if I could stay and take care of her, she would be well tomorrow. He had money in his pocket from Ludwig, and instructions to move her to a hotel. He was also supposed to tell her. It would not be safe for her to wait in this apartment another night. But if she gets up now, with the fever, she may get pneumonia, he thought; what is best to do? If only she were not so sick, she would decide for herself; she had always been a good one to decide; she was a clever sensible girl. But now she was sick and like a child and he would have to do everything. How can I tell her when she is like this, he thought.

"Let us talk a little," he said mildly.

"All right," she said. Everything seemed pleasant like a game.

"Would you like to hear about Katy?"

Now it was not like a game, and being sick was not a loose, confused, free swimming and floating between day and night. Now she would have to listen and understand. She frowned and the pain zig-zagged through her head so that tears came to her eyes. She pushed herself with her elbow to sit up and watch Schultze, and she held her fingers tight against her temples to press down the beating blood.

"Tell me."

"They did not keep her," Schultze said, glad to be able to bring good news too. "They asked her some questions and told her she would be required to leave Prague in two days, that is today really, and they let her go."

"Oh," Rita said. There had been such a tightness in the throat that now, relieved, she felt almost nauseated and the room flickered before her eyes.

"Where is she?"

"I do not know," Schultze said. "Like the others, hiding."

"But she's all right, she's free anyhow?"

"Yes. And she did a good work too."

"Always."

"No, but this specially. You remember when they took Thomas?" He was coming to the bad place and he went slowly, watching her face. If she was too sick, he would not tell her. Let someone else tell her. Why should she know anyhow? What could she do?

"I remember."

"You remember she followed and she saw the house?"

"Number 4 Valdstyn," Rita said.

"You remember the address?"

"So do you."

"Yes," he said.

"Well?" Rita asked. She was getting ready to hear whatever he would say.

"Well, Ludwig put someone to watch this house ever since Thomas was taken. That way," Schultze paused and swallowed and tried to make his voice business-like, "they could see who else was caught. Of course, there may be other houses we do not know, but anyhow it was smart to watch this one."

"Yes," she said. Her voice was flat and quiet and he did not look at her.

"They have seen a big closed black car at night several times. Men come out of the house and seem to be carrying something but it is hard to tell in the dark. Ludwig thinks they may take people from the house and drive up to the Sudetenland, and leave them in concentration camps there—at Eger or Carlsbad, perhaps—or else he thinks they may take them across the frontier in this closed car, and send them by train to Munich, for—" he stopped again and looked at the floor, "for more questioning," he said.

"Who has been seen?" she asked.

"Different ones," he said, and now it was too close. He could not do it. Let someone else do it. "Rita, I have some money for you from Ludwig. He wants you to go to a hotel, the one that belongs to Frau Holz. He says for you to try to go to Paris as soon as you can, you will be more use there. Everybody has now permission to leave. There are very few who are supposed to stay. Of course there is not enough money for you to go, but Ludwig says maybe if you have friends?"

Ludwig had said the same thing to him, Schultze, very kindly, and he had listened politely and soberly

and said, *"Gut."* And that was the end of it. He knew
Ludwig was not leaving. Ludwig would stay in order
to go on with the work, whenever that was possible.
Besides, Ludwig had no more means of escaping than
he, Schultze. Where were they going to find friends
who could smuggle in foreign money, lots of foreign
money, so that they could buy their way out of the
country? It did not happen this way. Some had gone,
the truly important ones, the ones with brains, who
were too valuable to risk or lose. But he was only a
working man, and Ludwig, though he was younger and
had more education and was far more useful than
Schultze could ever be, was not valuable enough to be
protected. There were many others to replace him.
When Schultze had said, *"Gut,"* they understood each
other perfectly and felt no rancor. Besides, there was
a pride in them which neither would have recognized
as pride; they would not run away or try to run away.
Here was where they belonged. Schultze had said, timidly, to Ludwig, "I don't think I'll go anywhere, Ludwig," as if there were any place to go, Ludwig had
thought, and loved Schultze for saying it that way,
"there'll always be some comrades here for me to take
care of, you know. I think I'll just stay here and see
what happens."

"We are not officers," Ludwig had said. Schultze did
not understand this. Ludwig was educated, he sometimes said things as if he were talking to himself, which
other people did not understand.

"We are troops," Ludwig added. He thought: to
fight, and if we win, good, and if we are defeated, to
be killed or captured. He thought this without bitter-

ness, and he was not a romantic man. Long ago, he had made a choice of the way he planned to live, and there was no going back. Seeing him on the street, with his pointed stringy face, the thick glasses, the bent bookkeeper shoulders, no one would have guessed that he had trained himself coldly until he was incapable of despair or fear, and that he had forgotten his own identity, his own life, as he had almost forgotten his last name.

Schultze was thinking of Ludwig, thinking simply, *"Guter kerl,"* when Rita spoke again.

"Who did they see going into that house?" she asked.

"Different ones," he said again, uneasily. "Some you do not know. Ludwig told me but I do not remember the names. A few of ours, but also many others. Some of the Socialists, he said. Only the highest leaders have gone from Prague. Some Jews, people who write, I think he told me. A few of the Czechs even. At night, quite a lot of people."

"Schultze," she said sharply, "why does Ludwig want me to go to a hotel?"

"Well, it is not good to stay here. Someone may know that Peter lived here."

"How do you know he has gone? He only left last night."

Schultze stared at her. He had told her without meaning to. He could never do anything right. He was furiously angry with himself and afraid.

She cried out, "Tell me! Tell me why you came here!"

"Rita," he said very humbly, because he saw now that it was no use, he did not know how to lie, "Lud-

wig told me to come and get you and take you to Frau
Holz. He said you would be safe there for a while. She
is a friend. He said you should leave the country if you
could. He said there is no use to wait here any longer
and there is work you can do in Paris. He said that at
six this morning the comrade who was watching outside the house saw them take Peter in. He was on the
same side of the street as the door, and he saw them
drag Peter from a closed car and take him in. They
held him up between them. He said Peter had a bruise
and some blood on his forehead. Now I have told you,"
Schultze said. "You must leave this house. It is dangerous. It is not that Peter would talk but somehow they
might find out and then they would come here, to see
if he had left anything."

He had been talking to Rita and she had been looking at him but he did not think she heard. Her face
was flat, white and empty and her open eyes did not
fix on anything so that they looked blind. She did not
speak and Schultze waited for her to say something, or
move, or cry. But she did nothing.

"You heard me?" Schultze asked. "You heard what
I was saying?"

Still she did not answer.

"I will pack some things for you," Schultze said.
"We can take a street car."

Now he was very frightened.

"Get up, Rita," he said. "I will help you. Say something."

"You can pack," she said.

He found a cardboard suitcase standing on the top
shelf in the kitchen closet. He took it down and dusted

it off without thinking, and opened a cupboard, and took out the two dresses he saw there, but left a suit of men's clothes. He found stockings and underwear in a drawer and scooped them up and looked around for the other things, toothbrush, hairbrush, what else would she have? When he had piled everything in, the suitcase was not full. He put the few bills from Ludwig in the purse he saw lying on the bookcase. The clothes she had worn yesterday lay neatly over the back of a chair.

"Can you get up?" he asked. "Or are you weak from the fever?"

"I will come later," she said.

"No."

"I will come later. Take the suitcase and leave it there."

"Do you know where it is, Frau Holz's hotel? It is beyond the Masaryk station."

"I know."

"I would rather go with you. If you like I will wait outside the door while you dress."

"I will come later. Good-by, Schultze."

"Good-by," he said. He did not know what to do. As she did not speak or look at him, he waited a moment, nervously, and then picked up the suitcase and went softly from the room. He stopped outside the door but could not hear her. She must be alone for a time, he thought, I will come back in an hour to make sure she has left. He took out a large crumpled handkerchief and wiped his forehead, pushing up his cap. Then he walked heavily down the stairs; the suitcase was so light that it swung like a paper sack in his hand.

When it was dark she got up. She turned on the lights, and washed carefully and dressed and combed her hair, from habit, not noticing what she was doing. She stood in the middle of the room and steadied herself, holding on to the back of a chair. Her head was so painful that she could not move her eyes but had to turn her whole head, and she was sweating again and felt her dress clammy against her, under her coat, and her legs quivered, so that she had difficulty keeping her balance. She had not eaten for a long time but she did not feel hunger, and she did not feel the fever and the sickness. She had dressed herself and now she was ready to go. She looked at her home, and at all the things they had brought together and been proud of; she looked at each piece of furniture separately and turned her head to see the pots hanging on the wall of the kitchen closet.

Then she opened the door and walked out onto the landing. She held the stair rail tight because it was hard to walk, she was afraid she might fall from weakness. She left the light on and left the door wide open behind her. It was not her home any more. Let anyone come in.

Mary Douglas pulled out the folding chair and put her feet on it, laid her hat beside her on the seat and lit a cigarette.

"Hotel Universal," she told the driver.

She ran her hand over her face. Like a hag, she thought, I've certainly worked for my money. There ought to be a message from Rita at the hotel now. She raised herself to look at her watch as they passed a street lamp: six o'clock. Have I worked, she thought. Towards the end, she hadn't even understood what she heard, but only written down, in wobbling letters, anything that sounded instructive. She remembered statistics as you remember telephone numbers, but they meant nothing to her. She felt very tired but everything was in order now. Sixty-three per cent of the textile industry lost; 40% of the chemical industry lost; 40% of the metallurgical industry lost; 10% of the soft coal lost. The railroad man had been very curious, very interesting and curious. That was earlier in the afternoon when she was still noticing. She thought: he's something I haven't seen before. He was small, neat, undistinguished, speaking English with an American accent, and childishly proud of all the snappy American gadgets on his desk: but, she thought, he'll get on all right, even with the Nazis. Smart little man, what he wants to do is manage railroads, he doesn't care whose railroads.

So, she thought, nothing more except pick up my passport, pay my bill, pack and get hold of Rita. That young man at the Consulate was a pal. Visitors' visas, he opined, were obtainable with a round trip steamship ticket, a guarantee, and some money in the bank. A thousand dollars, maybe, she thought. If Rita had no passport it would be tougher; but with money she could surely buy a fake passport; they must be for sale, you always heard people whispering about them. Two thousand maybe. If necessary she would borrow. Getting Rita out made it less shameful to leave. Pretty shameful all the same. I can't do anything. Paris. Oh, Paris.

She saw her face in the wall mirror to the left of the door as she entered the hotel. I'll have to do something about that, she thought. She turned to the desk and was waiting to ask for her key and messages when she heard her name.

"Hey, Mary," Tom Lambert said, and half ran, half skipped toward her, from the telephone booth by the elevators, holding a glass in his hand. "Spilled," he said with disgust. "All over me. Nobody answers telephones anyhow. Come on and have a drink."

"I can't, darling. I'm in a hurry."

"You got to. Farewell. Everybody's going. You can't be like that, Mary. Come on." He held her arm, with great strength and determination, and led her down the hallway past the showcases of diamond bracelets and crocodile bags and loud expensive silk pyjamas for men, into the bar.

They were standing at the bar, standing and leaning, or hooked uncertainly onto the bar stools, or wandering between the bar and the tables. They were making a lot of noise. The barman wore that expression of indulgence, wonder, and detachment which is usual when good paying customers are making asses of themselves.

"Gentlemen," said Tompkins in a commanding voice, "I give you Eli Whitney."

"Don't know him," Luther said, "and won't drink to him."

"Don't know Eli Whitney?" Tompkins said, scandalized. "The man who invented cotton gin? Don't know old Eli? My God, boy!"

"Eli Whitney," Thane said. "Drink up."

"Vive la France," Berthold said in a reasonable tone of voice.

"I like that," Thane said, "I like that. *Vive l'Amerique* as far as that goes."

"Vive l'Angleterre," said a tall one Mary didn't know; he wore a tweed coat and gray flannels so he was surely English.

"Not so," Tom said. "No *vive l'Angleterre* for me."

"L'Angleterre of Shakespeare," Luther pleaded. "Merrie old Angleterre. Be a sport."

"Okay," Tom grumbled.

"What's up?" Mary inquired generally.

"Why, Mary," Thane said. "I didn't even see you. Gentlemen, I give you Mary."

"You do?" Tom said suspiciously.

"A manner of speaking," Thane said. "But not if you don't want to."

"Anatole," Luther said, and leaned over to the barman, "we're leaving, Anatole, we're having a little celebration because we are going away at last."

"Yes, indeed," the barman said.

"Call me Colonel," Luther said.

"Where are you leaving to?" Mary asked.

Tom said, "Everybody's leaving, even Louis Berthold of la belle France."

"It's all over here, Madam," Thane said gravely. "It's all over. The funeral is finally terminated. I'm going to Rio. Want to come along?"

"Delighted."

"On the other hand, Lambert is going to Russia. How would you like that?"

"Too cold," she said.

"Also shooty-shooty," Thane said, moving his trigger finger. "Much shooty-shooty. In Rio, champagne and laughter."

"Go on," Mary said. "Tompkins?"

"England," Tompkins said. "An island. Gentlemen, I give you old Tom."

"Old Tom," Luther sighed. "He's dead too."

"*Vive la France,*" Berthold said pleasantly.

"That's all he knows. He's going to Paris on his way to Palestine. He said he had an infected tooth or something so he had to see his dentist first. Dentist," Tom Lambert said.

"I'll see you in Paris, Louis," Mary said.

"*Chère amie,*" Berthold said. "*Chère amie et madame, mes hommages.*" He walked fairly fast but not too straight in the direction of the men's room.

"Not polite," Luther said.

"It isn't a question of polite," Tom said. "There are times."

"All right," Luther said. "Not another word."

"So you're all going," Mary said.

"We're all going," Luther answered. "No more Czechs, no more story. All finished."

"It's sad," Mary said. "Well, until the next time."

"Hey, you haven't finished your drink."

"I have to go, sweetie." She patted Tom's arm. "There's someone waiting for me. I'll see you all later."

She heard Tompkins, as she left, asking querulously, "Where's Eli Whitney?"

"Haven't seen him," Thane said.

"He was here a minute ago."

"Maybe he went to the gents'," Tom suggested.

227

"Well, if we can't find Eli, let's drink to Old Tom," Tompkins said.

"Or Gordon."

"By God, yes," Thane said. "A compromise candidate. Gentlemen, I give you Gordon."

Someone pushed over a stool and a glass broke. There was a good deal of noise and laughter. They were evidently very happy to be leaving Prague.

She thought, I'll give her another hour and then I'll go out and look for her. Very odd. Rita wasn't like that. But first a bath, a lovely, hot bath. How I look. This trade is ruining me.

She lay in the tub and watched herself turn pink from the hot water. The mirror above the washbowl was steamed over. If it were Paris, she thought crossly, I'd have bathsalts. You couldn't buy them every place you went. Not if you wanted ever to get out of this business. And you can't ever carry anything in those damn planes because of the charge for extra weight. She put her elbows on the bottom of the tub and held herself up so that she floated, with only her toes and the tips of her breasts showing above the water. Then she let herself sink and turned on the hot water tap with her feet. She reached behind her and yanked a bathtowel from the rack and fixed it as a pillow. The ends of her hair hung in the water but she did not care. Now, she thought, what else do I need? This is nice. This is really nice and pleasant and homelike.

Then she saw the bellcord beside the tub. I'm going to pull it, she thought, and who knows what will appear? The only time she had ever dealt with one of those tubside bells was in Morocco, years ago, visiting some grand people. Must have been the food, she thought, absolute poison. That time she had started to faint in the tub and had grabbed the first thing she could reach to hold herself up, and it was late at night, and a huge Senegalese servant appeared in answer to the bell, polite and undismayed, and picked her, fainting, from the bath. Afterwards, she remembered, people were awfully cool to me as if I made a practice of doing such things.

She pulled the cord. It will be white, anyhow, she thought; they don't have tall black men in Prague. The maid knocked at the glass door of the bathroom and came in. She looked at Mary without friendliness.

Mary smiled at her but the woman did not smile back. She doesn't approve, Mary thought, and the hell with her.

"Would you bring me my cigarettes?" she said. "And order me a double dry Martini and bring it here?"

The woman nodded to show that she had understood. She did not like foreigners. She knew plenty about foreigners. If you worked in a hotel full of riffraff for twelve years, you could tell a few things. And now, at a time like this, at a time when her country was suffering, they drank and carried on and lay in tubs and smoked and guzzled liquor, as if nothing mattered. Not only immoral, the maid thought, going down the hall, but heartless.

So then Mary lay against her bathtowel pillow and smoked and drank the Martini which made her feel very jolly, and thought what a wonderful comfortable life she had. Only I ought to be in a sunken alabaster job, she thought, and a neat little Javanese maid (Javanese? well, why not?) should be holding up a vast and handsome white satin peignoir—the maid with her eyes properly averted—and I would slip my rosy (rosy? certainly!) feet into swansdown whatnots, and then I think I would just have a hearty dinner on a tray. Her old, mussed foulard bathrobe, pocked with cigarette burns and never anything to look at even new, hung by a hook on the bathroom door, and her flat leather traveling slippers lay like crushed cabbage leaves under the washbowl. Got to get out, she thought, got to leave that maid and that peignoir and the alabaster and all and get hold of Rita. But she would take Rita to a wonderful restaurant and feed her well and tell her the good news. What about Peter? she thought. And then she thought, I will borrow money. I'll get Peter out too. You can do anything with money, or so it seemed. Anyhow you could try.

She went very quickly through the lobby to the street. It was no time to get involved with the boys. Any other night, it would have been fun: a nice long drinking evening, and everybody jolly about leaving and talking about the next place they were going to.

The end of a story was the best part of it. If you didn't have to do it on foot or in a truck, she thought, as long as there still were American passports and planes. But there's more to it, this time, she thought. Though a journalist couldn't afford to get worked up over the various treachery and suffering he saw, any more than a surgeon could take the pain of his patients personally. Wouldn't be able to work, she decided; old Thane is probably very sound. Yet how could you be cool about it and indifferent; you'd be in the same fix yourself if you didn't have a passport and money in the bank. Besides, she thought, you've got to have opinions. You can't help it. Thane said there was no right and wrong; it was both adolescent and unprofessional to pass judgment. But there is, she thought, there is right and wrong. You bet your life there is.

Still, if I get back in time, I might try to catch up with them. She felt cheerful to be leaving. Thane was happy to leave because there wasn't any story (a goddam funeral, he kept saying) and because Prague bored him. Tompkins usually didn't care where he was, but he was a kind man as well as fat, and he did not enjoy seeing unhappy people. He's really a kind old sweetie, Mary thought, without a brain in his head, and he could write his dispatches in his sleep; he just remembers about that opening sentence and putting everything in it and then he lets his hands wander over the typewriter. But Luther and Tom had opinions, though they were more discreet about concealing them, and they hated what went on here. Louis Berthold had opinions too, but he probably had flashy Sulka dressing gowns also; he sort of showed his opinions off, they were his ornaments: still, even he was fairly well shaken up about all this. It has been a gloomy assignment, she thought, not that they exactly make history in order to keep us amused.

"*Ja, hier,*" she said to the taxi driver. It did look dark. She had forgotten what a deep narrow street it was, the houses shuttered and black as if it were night for bombardment.

Mary asked the driver to wait, and explained to the

concierge, who was eating dinner and came out with his napkin around his neck, that she wanted to see Fräulein Salus, and she knew where the apartment was.

Nearing the top of the last flight, she saw the light coming out of the open door and called to Rita. Probably she just came home, Mary thought. There was no answer. Mary stepped inside the open door. She saw the unmade bed, the bureau drawers pulled out and empty, she saw the full bookcase, the pots hanging on the kitchen wall and she heard the alarm clock ticking so loudly that you thought it would break. She was afraid.

She ran down the steps and into the concierge's room. There was a moment when none of them talked; the wife with a soup ladle in her hand, the concierge half rising and sitting, starting to wipe his mouth with the large spotted napkin, and Mary, breathless, unable to speak.

"Have you seen Fräulein Salus?"

"Not today."

"She is not home. The door is open and the light is on."

The wife made a clucking sound of irritation. To go out and leave on the light was careless and wasteful.

"She probably went out to buy something for supper," the concierge said reasonably. "She will be right back."

"No," Mary whispered. The wife stared at her. They had not seen that room. They had not seen how absolutely that room had been abandoned.

"But naturally," the concierge said. His soup was getting cold. "Come back later."

She forgot to thank them or say good-night.

Why wasn't the driver starting the car, she thought, and remembered she had given him no directions. Where would Rita be? She could try the place on Truhlarska Street, where Rita sometimes ate. She did not know the number but she would recognize it. They drove slowly up and down that block twice and then Mary, confused by the darkness and by the similarity of the heavy gray stone fronts of the houses, got out. She found a woman who seemed to be the concierge or janitress and asked for Schultze. Was that the name; surely she had seen that name on a brass plate attached to the door.

"*Ja, ja,*" the woman said. But Schultze had gone away, yesterday it was, or maybe the day before, to visit his daughter in the country. The apartment was empty. No one had come to see him for several days. The woman did not know who Mary was, but Schultze was an old friend. She shut the door on Mary. These days anybody who asked questions was unwelcome.

Mary thought the room was like a dead place; it was as if it had been burned out. Rita's not going back there. The office was the only other address she knew. She discussed this with the driver; he seemed to know where she wanted to go, she only remembered vaguely that the Solidarität was somewhere near the Wilson Station. But when they were outside the building the driver pointed up to the windows; they were all dark.

"There is no one here now," he said. He knew more about it than that. He knew the office was closed. He had a cousin who worked in a chemical plant at Aussig; this cousin was a refugee now. He had been helped by the Solidarität. The Solidarität was closed; wasn't he hiding his own cousin right now when there was scarcely room for him and the wife and the three boys at home?

"Where now?" the driver asked.

"Wait." But where could she go; where could Rita be? I must find her, I must find her. I can get her out. They can't catch her, they can't do anything to her. I can get her a visa in four or five days. It's not too late. Not unless they had already shipped her back to Germany. My God, she said to herself.

"From what station do the people go back to the Sudetenland?" she asked the driver.

It was a funny question; why should she care? "The Wilson Station mostly," he said. If she was going to stare at the poor people, he thought, just for a sightseeing trip, like a tourist.

"I must find someone," Mary said desperately. "Quickly. Is it very big?"

"Big enough."

"I'll go there anyhow. *Schnell. Schnell.*"

Maybe they keep them waiting a long time, she thought, or maybe there's a special room for them or maybe someone in charge will know the names of people who have been sent back. This is crazy, she thought, I'll never find her this way. But where can I look? Oh, Rita, she said to herself, I only knew this morning that it was hopeless. I'd have gone to the Consulate sooner but I thought we could get it all arranged for everybody. I shouldn't have waited. It's my fault. I should have told her days ago and fixed it up and had it ready for her, in any case. I shouldn't have waited so long.

She probably thought I wasn't doing anything. But why didn't she telephone or come? I was doing what I could. But you failed, didn't you? It was silly even to think you could manage what no one else had managed. Vanity, and the vanity of the amateur. I should have told her long ago that I'd get her out no matter what. I failed all the way in everything. I couldn't pull off the big thing and now I have failed Rita. But I'm a journalist, she thought, I'm only supposed to write, I'm only supposed to tell what happens, I'm not supposed to do things. Oh, and not for friends, not supposed to take care of your friends either; go on, find some better excuses.

"This is the main entrance," the driver said.

The great room was dimly lighted. Shadows fell strangely on the faces of a family who sat, stiff and exhausted, on the long yellow wooden bench that stretched down one side of the room. There were eight of them and they sat in a row, not letting their backs rest against the seat, with their feet placed flat on the floor, and each one held something in his lap, a cloth bundle, a wicker suitcase, a roll of blankets, a black market bag. They looked as if they had been there a long time. People pressed around the ticket windows on the left; the lights were very bad, the people seemed to be a smear against the wall, shapeless and dark, now and again an arm would reach over the lumpy outline of the smear, and drop money beneath the wicket and pick up a small colored piece of cardboard. The newsstand was doing no business; you thought the magazines and newspapers were probably of last month. A big sad woman sat behind the counter and knitted.

When you put a penny in the machine to get a ticket to go out on the platform a red light came on inside and a little bell rang. There were many people walking through this room to the train shed outside, others waited beside their luggage, some leaned against the wall, some walked back and forth in the uneasy before-leaving manner of people unused to travel. They all looked as if their feet and backs were tired. The light made everyone seem old and yellow.

Rita was not here.

Mary bought her platform ticket and went outside. In the train shed, the light was so blue and flickering that it seemed to come from torches. There was smoke from the locomotives, blowing up into the black steel girders of the open ceiling. The walls were smoke-grimed cement, the floor was cement. It was very crowded. The trains leaving and those with steam up to start made a steady under-roar, the blue-coated officials who called trains cried out in weird varying impersonal voices, through everything came the hum and scratch of talk, and sometimes the high up-curling wail of a child crying, or a loud greeting from one man you could not see to another, lost also in the smoke, the crowds, the piled bedding, the battered suitcases.

It looked like a camp too. Alongside the iron netting by an exit, out of the push of walking people, one group sat and lay on the cement floor, with bluish-gray faces in the blue light, some eating and some sleeping, as if they had lived here for weeks. Along the wall to the left, between the open doorways, people squatted, with their feet close under them so as not to be stepped on; one man lay along the wall and slept with his cap

236

pulled over his eyes; one woman, crosslegged, nursed her child. None of these people watched the station or the trains, or seemed to notice where they were; one place was like another place, they had been without rest for a long time now. The smoke scratched in your throat and made you cough, and people had reddened watering eyes from the smoke, the coal dust, and from not sleeping.

The open doorways gave onto the offices of station officials, the telegraph office, the post office, and inside two doors you saw white-tiled small square rooms, one was the milk bar and the other was a first-aid station. The milk bar was almost empty, brilliant white and comfortable-looking in this ugly gray place: people did not have money for a soft fresh roll and a glass of clean cold milk. In their blankets, mixed up with their clothes, anywhere, secreted, they kept long tough loaves of bread and hard sausages. They would take these out and cut off pieces and eat, when they were hungry. There was no time anymore, no order. No one had washed or lain in a bed or worked. There was nothing to do except wait.

I'll never find her, Mary thought.

Then out of the loud confusion one voice came clear. It started close to her. She saw a soldier with his tunic unbuttoned at the neck; one of the red regimental tags had been torn loose on the side of the collar. He was young and hatless. He still held his rifle with the bayonet fixed. He was crying out, furiously, to no one in particular, with his left hand clenched and raised high in anger. He looked very handsome and crazy. The people moved a little back from him though some of them seemed to come alive hearing him, and shook their heads agreeing or approving, but others pulled out of his way and sank back into their own closed, limp lives. Light came out of the milk bar and shone on the young soldier's face; he was sweating. One of the station officials came up to him and spoke, kindly, it seemed.

The boy did not appear to listen; he was staring around the station. Then suddenly he threw his rifle down on the cement platform, and kicked it. He turned and walked out of the gate, by the iron netting fence. No one stopped him.

"What was that?" Mary asked one of the men in blue coats, who was standing by her.

"He came to look for his mother. He heard they were sending her back to the Sudetenland. He said I am a Czech soldier, I was in the army, I was ready to fight. Now I get out of the army and I cannot find my mother. Do they think my mother will be safe in our village? he said. Do they care? he said. Then he threw down his rifle."

"I see," Mary said.

She walked back towards the ticket room. A child bumped against her legs and she stooped to catch it. The mother came and took the child's arm, yanking it up. She slapped the child, not hard, and the child began to cry. The mother wore a black shawl, and walked as if she hurt all over from sitting there on the cement floor. She looked as if she could cry too.

Mary bought some chocolate at the milk bar and brought it over to the little girl. The child did not want to take it, and hid behind her mother, who was sitting on the floor. The mother took it for her, and said, "Tell the lady thank you." There were many people all around them, but each family seemed to have a little square of cement that belonged to them. A boy of about twelve, with a white frightened face, crouched near the woman, and would move closer to her and try to take her hand. Sometimes she would pat him and sometimes she would push him away. You could see that she scarcely knew what she was doing.

"Are you going back today?" Mary asked.

"Yes. We have been here since yesterday. We were ordered to leave at four o'clock this afternoon but the train did not go. They say we must wait."

"Two women threw themselves under the wheels," the boy said in a high sharp voice. He looked at Mary with terrified eyes. The mother slapped him and he cowered away from her. She knew what was the matter with the boy, but she did not know how to help him. He had seen it. He had been like a scared dog ever since, whimpering and sick. It was terrible, the screams and the blood, and the hair of one of them.

"Yes," the woman said. "Then they emptied the train and we are here waiting."

"Where is Papa?" the little girl asked. She was happy now, kneeling against her mother, out of sight of the strange lady. She had chocolate all around her mouth.

The woman turned with a quick frightened movement of her head. Her face was long with tight stretched skin and round, aching, protuberant eyes; her hair was scraped back from her forehead. She looked too old to be the mother of the little girl. She reached over and touched their possessions, counting them as she must have done a hundred times, to see that everything was here: a basket, a roll of bedding, a bumpy sack with pots and pans in it, two cloth bundles with clothes, a market bag with the end of the grimy loaf sticking out of it. Then she remembered: it was hard to think or remember, and the children kept straying off, and after she had seen those women.

"He will come," she said.

The man returned, crossing over other families behind them, stepping high to avoid other people's bundles and suitcases. He was unshaved and small and very thin, with gray hair that fell in long flat points under his cap and slanted over his forehead. He was smaller than the woman. He sat down beside her without speaking. The little sticky girl climbed up over him and he took her in his arms. He patted her hair which was yellow but very dirty and matted, and said to her, "Take a nap, child." He made a sort of hammock of his arms, awkwardly, but the little girl wriggled around and would not rest. He sighed and let her go.

"The lady gave her some chocolate," the wife said.

He looked up at Mary dumbly, and nodded. In his own village he would not have allowed his daughter to take presents from a stranger. He worked, he could buy her candy himself.

"They say we will go tonight," he told his wife.

Mary did not move. She had nowhere to go. She could not find Rita.

The woman did not answer; either she had said everything before, or there was nothing to say. No one asked them. They had no choice.

"I showed a man my card but he said he had his

240

orders. It is just as bad for them too." He looked around at the rest of the camp.

He fingered a dark green cardboard booklet; then without speaking, he reached up and handed it to Mary. She saw his picture, looking younger and clean, and his name. It was a Socialist party card.

"I am secretary in my village," he said, with some pride.

"You aren't going back with that?" Mary asked. "You're going to throw it away, aren't you?"

"What is the difference?" he said. "They know me. We all know each other."

"But you can't," Mary began, and stopped. Can't what? There is nothing he can do or I can do.

"Is it true about the concentration camps?" the woman asked. She did not look at Mary. "We have heard the talk. In Eger, in Carlsbad, they say. They say thousands of poor people are in them."

"What is the difference now?" the man asked.

Mary turned and walked away from them. They had stopped noticing her anyhow. They were just waiting for the train, trying to find some position that was at least bearable on the concrete floor.

She passed a young woman, sitting against the wall. The woman was bowed over, with her face in her hands, rocking back and forth, crying. Her hands in front of her eyes gleamed wet in the blue light. She had on a red blouse and her hair had half fallen down, so that one side of the knot pulled away from her head, and the rest of the hair lay on her shoulders. It was pretty hair. She cried and rocked back and forth and no one paid any attention. They had seen plenty of this.

A train whistle blew and a little procession of people straggled and stumbled through the crowd, herded by soldiers. The soldiers were not shoving them—but they were keeping them moving. All the faces looked stupid with exhaustion; the eyes searching around the room, for nothing, were empty even of questions or of fear. They were like old bundles of gray cloth. They had no tickets; the soldiers herded them down a platform and they were lost in the smoke, and the crowd closed behind them.

It was almost ten o'clock. I'll never find her, Mary thought.

12

THERE were looped white curtains at the windows and light came out on to the pavement. There was Czech lettering on the panes and a menu card pasted near the bottom of the left-hand window. Rita walked past and slowly returned. This was the first place she had seen, on all the dark hard streets, where she could rest. It was too early and she would have to wait.

The room was small and steamy, with a sideboard that held glasses and plates, six tables, family photographs and home-made water colors on the walls, and also two of those posters, now outdated, which urged the Czechs to contribute to the National War Fund. There was also, looking everyday and unobtrusive, a gas mask in its long cylindrical container, hanging on the coat rack by the door. Possibly someone had forgotten it, from the time when people carried their gas masks around as simply and practically as they carried pocketbooks or umbrellas. Or possibly it belonged to the proprietress and she had left it in the restaurant, having brought it there to have it handy.

Now only two people were still sitting at a table, a couple, drinking coffee in silence and looking at each other, the tablecloth, the walls, like people who have dined opposite each other for years and for years had nothing to say. Rita went to the nearest table; her legs felt heavy but soft, it was hard to walk without staggering. She slumped into a chair and pressed her hands against the sides of her head. It seemed to her that the pain made her temples bulge out.

The woman who owned the restaurant came through the door that led to the kitchen and looked at Rita crossly. It wouldn't be an order that amounted to anything, she thought, women alone never spent much money and here it was late and she had let the fire in the stove go down and her feet hurt. She crossed the room and asked what Rita wanted.

"It is late," she said warningly. "I can't make anything much. Eggs. Do you want some eggs?"

"No."

The woman tightened her lips. "I can't make anything much now," she said. "You should have come sooner."

"Coffee," Rita said.

"What else?"

"I don't know. Cold meat and bread, anything."

Well, that was reasonable. "I'll make you a nice sandwich," the woman said.

"The coffee at once, please," Rita said. She was afraid she would faint. If she fainted, a policeman might come, or a city ambulance. The coffee made her feel better. Her head ached as much but the cold shaking in her stomach went away, and her legs felt less heavy. She drank another cup, and then tried the sandwich. The bread was soft and fresh but too thick. Her mouth wouldn't open that wide, and it hurt her to chew. The pain went down from her head into her jaw. I must eat, she thought. She forced herself to chew and swallow, wincing as the movement jarred in her head.

She knew how sick she was, and how weak, but this was just a thing that had happened to her, and she must consider it, without excitement, understanding that she could make more mistakes because of it, and that she would be slow when she should be quick. She had no opinion about this disorder in her body, only knowing that she would master it because she had to. It was not necessary to think farther ahead than to-night. She did not have to worry about tomorrow, whether she would be desperately ill or what she must do to get well. There were no problems any more at all; there was one very simple thing left to her. She did not think about the purpose of this or the result of it. Her mind was empty and untroubled. She knew she would have whatever strength she needed to go to Peter.

She beckoned to the woman.

"Another cup of coffee, please. What time is it?"

"Eight-thirty," the woman said.

Too early. "Another sandwich, please."

The couple had paid and left silently, the man holding open the door for the woman. The proprietress stood in the kitchen doorway and wiped her hands on her apron, watching Rita eat, counting the minutes, thinking to herself that people certainly didn't mind how they used up your chairs, paying only a few pennies for a sandwich and coffee. She came eagerly when Rita called her.

Rita asked how to get to the Manes Bridge. If she

hadn't spent money on food, the woman thought, I'd imagine she was looking for a good place to jump from. She has that face, sick and green. Foreigner, the woman thought, German too, none of my business. Good God, why doesn't she go then?

It was easier to walk. If you took a street car you had to stand out in the street and wave and then you had to pull yourself up the steps and stumble down the aisle to a seat, in the light, with a lot of people around, and you had to find change and keep watching to see where you should get off, and there were the steps to climb down at the end. If you leaned forward your legs would carry you on, not fast, but still you kept moving. Just walk, she told herself. It would rain later. The sky was smeary black, and nearing the river she could see the fuzz of mist on the water and the way the mist rose and hung around the houses beneath the Hradcany. A few people passed her, crossing the bridge. Their feet made a sharp clack on the pavement, louder because of the water and the empty roadway. They all seemed in a hurry.

She was alone and she had time and she could not fail. Now she measured the distance between the posts of the bridge, walking slowly, carefully, in the direction she had to go.

There was a policeman standing under a lamppost at the end of the bridge. The rain started, soft as dew, needling the flat black water of the river, making the street shine and shining on the white rain cape of the policeman. The streets sank down here on the other side of the river, shadowy and gleaming in the rain, the small curving cobbled streets that wound around

246

the tall old houses, and circled and climbed above the
river mist and the dim street lamps to the great black
fortress of the Hradcany. She stopped near the policeman and felt the rain blow cool against her face and
remembered what she wanted to ask.

"Please," she said.

The policeman turned to her.

"Can you direct me to Valdstyn Street?"

The policeman took his arms from under his cape,
to point, showing her that she must go to the left and
turn, and then three blocks later turn again.

"Thank you."

The policeman watched her with curiosity. She
walked as if she were very old or lame. Maybe she has
rheumatism, he thought.

The rain slapped on the pavement. The trees that
showed over the garden walls of the old houses slurred
in the wind, and rain tinkled from leaf to leaf. The
wind itself echoed and rattled between the houses and,
in the gutters, the rain gurgled around little drifts of
leaves and sucked as it went down the holes into the
sewers. It is a long way, she thought, listening to her
feet scrape; but she had time and she saw in her mind
the policeman pointing, heard his voice, saw his hand
with three fingers sticking up to show her: three blocks
and then to the right. There was no one on the streets
and no windows were lighted. There seemed to be
more cats than she had ever noticed before, dark and
quick, hiding in doorways and creeping along the wet
high walls. In this time, Prague was a very curious city
at night; it did not sleep but seemed to be full of restless people, waiting and watching behind shuttered

247

windows. It was like a city that listens for the enemy planes, in a cold black tense silence.

This was it. Coming here at last, where she had meant to come, where she had dragged herself with her mind fixed but unplanning, she was suddenly startled to find it true and that the street existed and there were houses on it and one of them would be number four; and she was afraid.

She saw the number four painted alongside a doorway: the doorway was high and arched, closed with heavy carved wood doors. The house rose straight from the street. The lodgekeeper's window beside the door was shuttered. Looking up (but all the time walking past) she saw no light in the windows above. She could not tell whether the windows were closed with wooden shutters or steel blinds, or whether they were curtained from inside. The house looked like all the others on this short street. It was large, four stories high, handsome, with stone fretwork around the windows and a coat of arms above the front door.

Now she had passed it. It would be as hard to enter from the front as a prison or a fortress. At the corner she turned to the right. She was thinking well, now, no longer aware of her fever or the beating behind her eyes. There would have to be some sort of service entrance, she reasoned, for all these houses. She had seen no other door at the front of number four Valdstyn. If there had been a grille gate instead of a door, you might have imagined that behind the grille was a courtyard, and the service entrance would be in there. But this outer door seemed to lead directly from the street into the hall of the house. There will have to be an alley, Rita thought, that runs behind the houses, where garbage can be collected and milk delivered and those things. The alley should start somewhere here, behind this corner house, and run to the right.

Then she saw the entrance, closed with an iron-work gate. She put her face against the bars and looked through. She saw a cobbled alley, about fourteen feet wide and unlighted. On both sides, the alley was flanked with walls, garden walls probably, the nearest one appeared to be ten feet high. Rita could see no opening from the alley into this wall.

She pushed on the gate and it did not give. It was made of close-set rods of iron, each rod tipped with a gilded spear-point at the top. Now she realized that she had not planned at all, and if she could not get past this gate, there was no other possible entry. The iron rods were too close together for her to slip through them. If there is a caretaker for all these houses, she thought, he would lock this alley at night. But usually each house had its own concierge in Prague, there was no need for private night watchmen. She put her hand through the bars and felt for the latch behind the handle. She could not see, so she knelt, close to the gate, to get her eyes on a level with the latch.

Dear God, she said to herself, dear God. It was a very simple bolt; all she had to do was turn the draw bolt and pull it back. The gate opened by itself, slightly, slowly and silently. She got up from her knees and was dizzy, and had to hang on the bars a moment until her head cleared. Then she opened the gate and slid through and shut it behind her but did not bolt it.

She walked down the alley, close to the walls of the

houses that faced on Valdstyn Street. She passed the first gate; it was made of iron bars and iron netting and was locked with a chain and padlock. There was a small garden behind this gate, and there was no house number painted either on the wall or the gate itself. She walked the whole length of the alley and examined each gate or door but they were not numbered and she had forgotten or not noticed the position of number four from the corner.

I'll have to go back, she thought, terrified at this mistake, I'll have to go back and count. The alley seemed very slippery to her now, with a stream of water running in a center trough between the cobbles. She was half running and half walking, and she thought they must hear her in all the houses. She opened the gate again and only when she was out on the street she remembered that she should have looked first. What if she had walked out and run into a policeman on his night beat, or run into any of the servants coming home through this back entrance. She was alarmed by her carelessness and she feared it.

The house numbers ran unevenly: number four was the fifth house from the corner. Now she had to get back in the alley before she was seen, but she did not dare to run. If anyone saw her running it would be worse. She told herself: hurry hurry hurry. How long have I been here, what have I been doing all this time, she thought. There was nothing but doors, gates, doors you couldn't open, high locked gates, a dark street that took forever to walk—though it is only five houses to the corner, only two houses now. She thought ahead to the slippery cobbled alley, and when she breathed

the air cut her throat. Why are there no lights anywhere, she thought. There must not be lights, I cannot
do it if there are lights.

But she did not think of Peter, of herself, or what
she knew about this tall dark house. There was only
the gate to think about, the gate, she told herself in
desperation, forgetting what lay beyond it.

In the alley again, she counted until she came to the
fifth gate. She leaned against the wall in exhausted,
pounding breathlessness and gulped air and then closed
her mouth and forced herself to breathe slowly and
quietly. It seemed to her that her breath screamed out
of her. She saw the padlock but she could climb over
this gate. It was made of wood, and had a crossbar of
wood, four feet from the bottom. The top was smooth,
without pointed palings. Even if there was no crossbar
on the other side, she could hang by her hands and
drop; the gate was no more than eight feet high.

She waited and listened, but heard nothing except
the rain and the nameless creakings like small fire-
crackers that you can always hear in the night and the
little whispering night murmurs that might be anything, rats, water on the cobbles, the leaves of the trees.
In this silence, she would have heard footsteps a block
away.

She ran her hand up the side of the gate until she
touched the hinge. She could grab it to haul herself
up, but she would have to have something to stand on
to keep her balance. Now she was running down the
alley, almost careless of noise. There is no time, she
kept thinking, if I can't do it now I'll never; hurry
hurry.

The second to last house was where she had seen it, not thinking about it before, but seeing it. Possibly the servants in this house put out the garbage at night so that they could sleep later in the morning; it did not matter, it was what she needed. She took off the lid and was sickened by the rotting dirty smell of the food inside. She laid the pail flat on the cobbles, so that food spilled out and the pail was light enough for her to lift. Then she dumped the rest of the food and carrying the pail by the handle, away from her body but stiffly so that it would not sway and clank, she came back to the gate of number four. She turned the pail upside down, close to the wall and the gate hinge, and stood on it.

She stood on the pail and put her left knee on the crossbar and grabbed the hinge with both hands so that she almost lost her balance, pulling herself too sharply to the left. Then she brought up her other knee and was kneeling on the crossbar that was six inches wide, and holding herself in place with both hands on the hinge. The top of the gate was not much more than a foot above her head now, and she reached with her right hand and caught hold, then raised her left hand and pulled herself up from her knees.

Her head and shoulders rose above the gate and she thought in quick panic that everyone in all the houses could see her, outlined against the sky. She swung her right leg over and felt with her foot until she found the same crossbar on the other side, then she had both legs over and was standing inside the gate, and then not knowing what else to do, she jumped backwards with both feet together, landed hard but all right, and turned and ran, bent over low, towards the house.

There had been no time to wonder what she would do once she climbed the gate and she could not stop to plan now. The back of the house was as dark as the front, though, running, she thought she saw a faint irregular line of light down the center of a first floor window, the light that would come through drawn but not overlapping curtains. She was running on a flagged path, lined by a low close hedge. The night and the rain made it impossible to see ahead until she stumbled and almost fell down the basement steps. She stood bent over, with the instinctive reaction of making oneself small where there is danger, huddled and shrinking into herself. The concrete steps led down into an areaway and there was a door here but no light from the small barred window beside the door and no light coming from under the door. She supposed this would be the kitchen entrance and she knew it would be locked and she knew in any case it would be unsafe to try it because people come suddenly into a kitchen at any hour.

She had stepped onto a pavement just before she reached the basement areaway. This pavement banded the house, and now she crawled, so flat against the wall that anyone opening a window and looking out would not have seen her. The cellar windows were placed at regular intervals in the wall; they were four feet square, dark and barred. They were set almost flush with the pavement. She could see no reflection from them and guessed that they had no panes and if they had no panes they must give into the unused storage part of the cellar. But the bars were fastened tight: she did not dare pull and rattle them to make sure be cause above here was the window with the pale streak of light showing between the curtains. Lucky it's raining, she thought, otherwise a window might be open somewhere. Lucky. Lucky. She was thinking of nothing and did not feel the rain slowly soaking through her clothes, nor feel how the rough cement of the pavement tore her stockings and scratched her knees. The sleepwalking serenity of the early part of the evening had gone, and now her mind was sharply fixed on one thing only: a window. She did not consider beyond each gesture: the gate, crossing the garden, creeping along the wall of the house. Each thing she did lasted for hours, each thing was an effort to burst the heart. She had no clear reasonable fear of being caught; it was as if she were alone, but if she broke the rule that forced her to behave in this way she would be stopped from doing what she willed to do. The rule was silence. It was more than she could bear to drag herself along the pavement, close to the wall. The night will never end, she thought, I will never finish. There would always be something else, another window, stairs, gates, always something she had to pass over, cross, push through, in silence.

The only other thing she knew was that she was going to Peter. Not to do anything, not to speak to him or save him. But only to go where she had to go, to do the last free thing she would ever do.

She had almost reached the corner of the house. If none of these windows open, I can try on the other side of the basement steps, she thought.

Now something scratched her hand. She lifted her hand and saw there was black grime on it, gleaming, and she pulled a sliver of coal from her palm where it had cut her. Why? she wondered. Why coal, here? Then she knew and put her hand against the dark hole in the wall where the barred window should be and her hand went through, into the house. She had found the way in.

She tried, practically, to consider this open window to see that she had made no mistake. This was October; at her own house they were getting in the winter coal now, at the office of the Solidarität they had seen the coal being pushed down a chute into the basement four days ago. No matter what the weather, the furnaces were always fired on November first. You paid for that in your rent: heat from November first until March fifteenth. And in the first weeks of October the coal was laid in. Since the pavement was dirty with coal, she guessed that the supply had been stocked today and they had not had time to sweep the pavement and had forgotten to close the barred window above the coal chute.

She sat up and moved close to the open window and looked in. It was too dark inside to see. She felt with her hand and felt the steel of the coal chute; moving her hand she measured it, it was as wide as the window, about four feet across. She pulled herself over the low sill, and laid her feet on the chute, then pushing with her hands, she slipped farther in until she was sitting on the chute with her head inside the house. She had to bend her head because the ceiling was low. Now, moving her body slowly and carefully from side to side, careful not to shake the pillars that held up the chute, careful of noise, she slid down it. Again, she thought, forever, forever long, the noise. Where is the floor? Someone must hear now. Her body dislodged loose lumps of coal and once she stopped, choked with fear, and listened to a piece of coal roll like a pebble down the chute and bump off on the floor at the bottom.

Her feet touched the floor and she stood up. She would not move until her eyes got used to this extra darkness, she must not stumble into anything. She was standing on a crackling layer of coal, but the great gleaming mound had been shoveled to one side of the coal chute. She was afraid of the noise the coal would make, splintering under her feet. To the right she saw a shapeless round many-armed thing, like an octopus, and she knew that would be the furnace. It was a good place to wait, over there, in the shadow of the huge oven, hiding between the curving and twisting pipes. She stepped very carefully, holding her breath to listen, and the coal seemed to make a noise like a landslide. But no door opened, no one called out, no light suddenly shone above her. Then she was close to the cold open furnace, standing on swept concrete, and she heard the voices.

A man's voice said in German, not loud, comfortably, from above her, "You should have come with me and Otto. We had *Gansebraten* like in Munich."

A voice answered, a thin, cold, despising voice, "I do not have time."

"Everything goes good here," the first voice said. "Don't worry."

"You are too fat to worry," the second voice said.

There was a sharp knocking sound, as if the legs of a tilted chair had suddenly been brought down, flat on the floor. "There's nothing against a man eating his dinner," the voice said, but it was not so comfortable, it sounded whining or apologetic.

"We have got nobody useful yet," the cold, pointed voice said.

"We got those two with glasses, and the old one."

"Names," the second voice said with contempt. "It is good to frighten the ones who follow them but it is of no real value. I am going to find out how they work in Germany." There was a hollow short boom, as if a table had been struck hard with a fist or a book. "I am going to pick them up, this way, see, and hold them this way, see, and settle it and finish it and finish it."

"The chief will be pleased."

The second voice did not answer, but there was a little buzz or hum, as if he had breathed with satisfaction, hearing this.

"We have the skinny blond one," the first voice suggested humbly.

"Yes," the cold voice admitted. "He is some good. But he is not the main one and he will not talk."

"We can try again."

"We have tried twice. Once when you were out eating *Gansebraten*."

"He would not talk the second time?" the comfortable voice asked with wonder.

"No. We will bring him in later, when Grüning comes. I am waiting now for Grüning. If we can get nothing from him, we will send him across the frontier tonight. Maybe they can do better at home. But I do not like to fail."

The comfortable voice said nothing and there was a rattling of paper, as if someone had picked up and opened a newspaper.

The cold voice spoke suddenly and harshly, "Do not fall asleep there like a swine that has eaten too much."

"Ach," the first voice grumbled, but did not argue or reply. There was silence.

Rita had not moved. When she first heard the voices, she shrank back against the side of the furnace, hoping that if they were speaking near by in the dark they would not see her. The cold, shaking sickness of fear came over her. She had not actually heard the first words they spoke. Then the fear passed, as she grew accustomed to hearing these voices that seemed to come down towards her and yet sounded to one side, and she listened and recognized the words. Now in the silence she tried to understand how she could hear but not see or be seen. She leaned away from the furnace and took a step, and stopped, sweating, at the loud dry slapping sound of her shoe sole on the cement floor. She bent over and undid her shoes and took them off, and shoved one into each of the wide sidepockets of her overcoat. In stocking feet she moved noiselessly on the floor. She walked around this corner carefully, looking for light, imagining there must be a door she had not seen, and a basement room in which these men were talking. But the wall was flat behind the furnace.

She heard music and a voice announcing something in Czech, suddenly interrupted, and then other music which began in the middle of a phrase. That would be a radio. As she came nearer the furnace, she heard the music more clearly. She walked away from the furnace and the music was fainter. She circled the furnace and listened, it was sharper here but not as sharp as the voices had been. She returned to her first position and heard now clearly the music and a chair scraping over the floor, as if it were being dragged into a different position. She ran her hand over the furnace, then moved two feet to the right and saw, on the level of her chest, the open furnace door. Looking up she saw the pipes like a huge asbestos spiderweb, growing down from the ceiling and twisting into the furnace. But there were two pipes that came almost straight from overhead, into the top of the oven.

She thought, remembering everything, in perfect detail: when the cruel voice said, "You are too fat to worry," there had been a sound like a chair knocking on the floor, as if you were leaning back against the wall and suddenly sat up and brought the two front legs down hard on uncarpeted wood. She had heard that sound, as she heard the voices before, seemingly a little above her and to one side. She would have heard that through the furnace door, like the voices, the sound carried down by the pipes. But she had also heard that chair above her head; you could hear furniture moved, or hear doors slam, through the floor or through walls, when you could not hear words. If I heard that above my head, she thought, they must be in the room with the not closed curtains, the room I saw from the yard. That would be directly above me. And their voices come through the open heat register

259

in the floor of that room, down into the furnace. The comfortable fat voice was the closest of all. He must be sitting in a chair alongside the register, leaning his chair against the wall, she thought. And the other one moves as he talks, because his voice goes and comes.

She had no plan now; she had never had a plan. Even earlier in the evening, waiting first for darkness, then for the streets to empty, walking, finding her way, climbing the gate, crawling through the window and into the cellar, she had not thought she would see Peter or talk to him: she had never thought she would be able to find him and take him away with her. She had done what she intended to do: now she would stay here, quiet as stone, and wait. She expected nothing and hoped nothing. There was no end to this.

She knew where the voices came from and how. She was not afraid, knowing this. She did not imagine what she would do if she were found, she had lost the power of imagining. She sat down on the floor and leaned her back easily against the furnace just below the open oven door. She did not leave because there was no place to go and if she went away, there was nothing to do. Peter was in this house and she was here too; she would be where he was, nothing more.

She heard a door slam, the radio was suddenly switched off, and she straightened up, listening again with violent but uncomprehending attention.

"Heil Hitler," said a smooth voice. That is a Berlin accent, Rita thought. The comfortable voice was from the south, a Bavarian. The other, the one with a voice like a hot cutting wire, spoke all his words clearly and without accent, from Hanover perhaps, she guessed, not Berlin anyhow. But the new one, with the gravy smooth voice, was from Berlin.

"Heil Hitler," said the cold voice.

She could hear feet moving, as if one stood up.

"Good evening, Bauer," the smooth voice said carelessly.

"Heil Hitler, *Herr Hauptmann,*" the comfortable voice mumbled, formal and indistinct.

"So, Hauck," the Berlin voice said, "what is your difficulty?"

The sharp accentless voice answered, "We have got one who could be useful. I thought you would want to see him. He will not talk. We know that he has done underground work for them in Germany, a few years ago. And here he is in charge of some branch of it. He is certainly not the head, but he knows their contact man in Germany and he knows the system of organization. He could give us valuable information."

"Good," the smooth voice said. "Excellent."

Rita hated this voice. It was worse than the other two. She imagined the man smiled as he talked; and she thought of his eyes not smiling. The voice was low, quiet, unhurried, and with a thick syrupy flowing sound. From the way the other two spoke to him, she knew they feared him.

"I will have him brought in," Hauck said. The Bavarian was evidently an underling, he did not speak in the presence of the one he addressed as Captain. "Will you have a cigar, Herr Grüning?"

"Later. Get this man. We will see what we can do with him."

"He has been questioned before," Hauck said.

261

"So? A hero, eh?" Grüning laughed a little, softly, as at an amiable small joke.

The other two laughed politely. The Bavarian coughed, with the effort of forcing his laugh.

Rita heard the door open and heard the Hanover voice calling an order. Then the door shut again and there was silence, with a slurring movement as if someone paced the floor above her. It seemed that the two first voices did not speak to the third, unless questioned. He must be the chief here, Rita thought, the way they treat him.

The door opened and there were many footsteps, an order in the cold voice, "Leave him," and the door shut hard.

The smooth voice spoke again with a teasing irony. He is smiling, Rita thought, not knowing what would happen next.

There was no answer.

"Speak when you are spoken to," the smooth voice said pleasantly, but too slowly. "It is one of the first things we teach. That and respect for the Führer. Say 'Heil Hitler.' "

Rita leaned hard against the furnace. She did not understand this but she felt, in her throat, the way her throat was choking shut, that it was terrible. She half rose to her knees, instinctively trying to crawl away so that she might not hear more. But nothing had been said, there was only the voice, and the way the words were spaced, so slowly, so threateningly.

"Bauer," the man called Grüning said, "what are you waiting for?"

She heard a windy flat sound, smacking, like a blow

on flesh and then a confused stumbling of feet and a chair fell on the floor.

"Bauer is too stupid," the Berliner said, "a fat fool."

The cold hating voice said something low, almost whispering it. Bauer mumbled an apology, beginning, *"Aber,"* and was stopped with a brief harsh command.

"With your permission, Herr Grüning," the cold voice said.

A strange whistling flailing sound came faintly through the furnace door, and a groan, and silence.

Rita stared at the black hole of the open furnace door as if she expected to see in it what made the sound, who groaned.

"Better," Grüning said.

"Now you," Hauck said, "you may as well answer and save yourself. We have caught your dear friend Ludwig and he has told us all he knows."

Not true, not true, Rita said silently, pressing against the furnace. He lies to you, he lies to trick you, do not speak. Then, as if only now her mind waked and she Rita was here, the Rita who had been in prison and remembered places and names, she realized what it meant. Ludwig. Her Ludwig. Then who was this in the room above her, who was standing there not speaking? Who? She refused to know, and she felt the sweat break out all over her body.

"I want to know," the Berlin voice said patiently, purringly, "who is your contact man in Munich? You will now tell me. I want to know where your lying little pamphlets are delivered in Munich. I want to know who receives them, how many men deliver for you, and where they distribute these filthy little documents the Czechs have allowed you to print in their pitiful and disgusting republic. You are going to tell me these things," he paused and said, mockingly, with every syllable pronounced, "Comrade."

Rita counted. Fifteen, she counted, and still no answer. There was a sudden movement above her.

"I will take the cigar you offered me, Hauck," Grüning said, business-like and irritable now. "I do not like these Communist manners."

She imagined she heard a clock ticking on and on, minute after minute. Then she heard steps and Grüning said, "Hold him, Bauer."

There was an instant of nothingness and then a twisted short high scream broke out above her and ended in a sob.

"We will save the other ear," the smooth voice said, "because he must be able to hear us. What is the matter with you, Bauer?"

"The smell," Bauer's voice answered confusedly.

Rita clamped her hand over her mouth. She had slumped down so that she was almost lying on the floor. She blinked the sweat out of her eyes.

"Bauer is no good for this work. Less than no good," the despising voice said. "It is to be remembered."

"It was only for a minute," Bauer said, his mouth seemed to be full of saliva that he could not swallow. "The smell was all. Being so near it."

"This will be excellent training for him," Grüning said.

"As you see, Herr Grüning," the cold voice said, "Comrade Peter Reinick does not talk easily."

Before there had been three men, and a fourth, help-

264

less, not speaking, whose pain she heard and felt, eating into her. And now the fourth man was a face and a body; a face and a body she had known more than any other, and loved. She could not imagine that face now, even the name did not belong to it. She would not think how that face looked, she would not see the grayish thinking eyes, smeared and stupid with pain. She would never know how they had mashed him into something that only moaned or screamed, but would not speak. It was Peter, the body that belonged to her, the fine bones of the head, the gentle hands, the quiet voice, the kindness of him, the mouth. Peter, she whispered, and she began to think it slowly, without words yet: let him die. Let it be ended.

"Wait, wait," Grüning soothed, "we have time. Take off his shoes, Bauer. Be careful he does not try to hit you, the poor little fellow."

"His hands are not of any further use to him," Hauck said with satisfaction. "I was surprised how well he resisted persuasion on his hands."

"Now," the flowing voice said, and Rita could feel the man smiling, "are you comfortable on your chair? What little feet. Your mother was not German, was she? She was a French whore probably. You got your neat little feet from the French whore who was your mother."

"Or a Jewess," Hauck suggested, in a brittle voice for a joke. "One of those topheavy Jewesses with fat legs and little feet."

"Would you like to speak now, Comrade?" Grüning said. "Hold him, Bauer, though he looks too weak to move, a thin weak little man. We could not even use

265

you in our army, Comrade, you are too frail, too womanly. So, would you like to tell me now, because you see what I am going to do, don't you? The name of your contact man in Munich and his address, that will be enough to begin with and then we will rest a bit. Just his name. No? But you see, though this may be no more painful than the hands, it hurts more later. I am not sure you would be able to walk again though I cannot swear to this. I am not a doctor. You do not like it when I touch you? It is just to locate the place right there over the instep. A high instep. Very expensive clean feet you have for a proletarian, Comrade. Now then. I will give you until three to speak. One—two—three."

The sound was a thud and a crack, and before that ended there was a second, and then, rasping and drawn up, deeply, from somewhere inside, horrible to hear, like an animal, the word finishing in a gurgle, "AAAAAH."

Rita's mouth was open and she was breathing in deep pulling breaths, fighting off a darkness that dragged over her, a darkness in which her mind floated, away from her, and the outlines of the furnace shifted before her eyes. Then the sickness came back and the darkness.

She had heard a body slide heavily to the floor.

"Don't kick him, Hauck," Grüning said sharply. "Bring him water, Bauer, and some cognac. We must wake him up. They become too proud, these little rats."

"*Zu Befehl, Herr Hauptmann.*"

"The filth," Hauck said, his cold voice warmer and

louder with anger, "the dirty traitors. Not one of them has talked. Only the fools with names who know nothing. But not one of these. We had three young ones who knew something. And nothing, nothing, nothing. To think that they live outside the Fatherland, plotting and spying and we cannot force them to talk. I would kill them all. I would kill them with my hands."

"And you would learn very little," Grüning said easily. "Do not get excited. Perhaps this one will not talk. We will find another. You must not be so passionate, Hauck. You make a mistake. We are not dealing with people. This man does not exist. He is a thing, like a message in code. He has certain information and we must extract it. But not so excited, my dear Hauck."

"I apologize, Herr Grüning."

The door opened. She heard them, but she heard less well now.

"Good, Bauer. Hold his head and force some of that cognac down. So. A little more. So. Now good. Now are you awake again, Comrade?"

She heard the moan, that was the sound his mouth made as he breathed.

"This room is not well equipped," said the smooth voice, but with an edge of criticism in it. "Attend to that tomorrow, Hauck."

"What shall I do with the cognac? Shall I give him more?" the Bavarian mumbled. His voice had a cottony, clogged sound.

"No, not now. He is all right now. Put him back on the chair."

"Will you use another cigar, Herr Grüning?" the cold voice asked. It sounded nervous.

"No. Now, little comrade, can you hear me? Yes, I see you can. Would you like to say something now? It would be better, you know. We are saving your mouth for you so that you may talk. Would you tell me the name of your contact man in Munich now? We are going to find him anyhow, you may as well spare yourself more discomfort."

Rita knew she would never forget a word, or how the voices changed; she would never forget even their silences. She had seen it all; she knew how the room looked and how the men stood, with their heavy unhurt bodies, so tall around Peter. She could move her fingers, and hear and see out of her eyes (there would be blood in Peter's eyes, the room would be gray for him); but now it was almost over for both of them. It would be over soon now. Be quiet, be quiet, be quiet, she told herself, it is almost finished.

It was as if she had known always that this would happen. All my life, she thought, here was all the torment and the pain you could not escape, all the humiliation and all the helplessness. But Peter had fought against them; Peter had kept the freedom in his mind. Now they had him, as they had always had her, but the last thing remained: silence. He will be stronger than they are, to the end, she thought, he will not speak.

She must be quiet as stone now. They must not find me. They must not take me into that room and use me to destroy his silence. She knew she would cry out if they hurt her; they would use her pain to weaken him, since they could not hurt him enough, ever, not as long as he lived.

We have never won, she thought, but we do not lose. We do not lose because Peter will not talk. Because Peter will never talk and they cannot destroy that.

His body would be beyond healing, but he was stronger than they. He had his triumph. He triumphed for all the brave and unarmed. She said good-by to him, saying good-by to his grayish thinking eyes, and his pride and his faith and to love and to the five months she had had of him that had been her only life. Then she began to say it in her mind, over and over, like a prayer: let him die now, let him die, let him die.

"I suppose that coat rack will do," Grüning said in a conversational tone, "if you hold it to keep it firm. Here, Bauer, tie him to that, so, with the arms spread."

She heard a scuffling, as if they lifted something, feet moving, a chair pushed aside but not knocked over, then a quick tearing sound as if cloth had been ripped. They seemed to be standing directly above her head.

"So," Grüning said, "that is good. Hold the coat rack firm, Hauck, in case he sags. Bauer, take that admirable belt, you know how to hold it. This is the simplest of all, but perhaps it is the best in the end. No, fool, don't hold it by the buckle; the other way around."

"This way, *Herr Hauptmann?*" the Bavarian asked. The words were unclear.

"Of course," Grüning said impatiently. "Now, Comrade, though I cannot see your face I am sure you can hear me. You will get ten lashes and then you will be given another chance to speak. And so on, by tens,

until you answer. I have many things to do this evening, and I am becoming tired of you. You take too
much time. Ready, Bauer? One." It was the same
sound, the quick whistling that ended in a soft cutting
or smacking. Two. The whistling, the soft jerky crack,
then the dull sob; filling her, twisting her body. She
put her hands over her mouth to keep from crying out
and counted, *three,* then waited to hear the lash, then
the sob, louder, higher, longer, *four,* faster now, faster,
she pressed against the furnace, bowing her body in
time to the counts, the sound of leather cutting
through the air, and she beat her hands painfully, uselessly, against the stone as the sobs rose, faster, faster
until at last, on *nine,* the sob was a high, toneless grunt.

"Will you answer me now?" Grüning said.

There was a sound of slow, heavy breathing, as if the
man's mouth were full of blood and he choking on it.

"Again," Grüning ordered.

"One." She could not count now. She saw, so that
she knew it, absolutely, the body that hung in that
room above her head, tied up by the mashed hands,
the maimed torn and dying body. She heard all sounds
as one, the lash, numbers counted in the flat steady but
quickening voice, and she heard the other voice that
cried out in answer to the torment.

She whispered, with her lips close to the concrete
floor, her last hope for all she loved: *Let him die.* Then
she heard the sounds stop suddenly.

"Fainted," Grüning announced.

The Bavarian said something very deep, very low,
three times. It sounded like "God, God, God."

"More than fainted," the cold voice said. It came

from near the floor, as if he were bent over. "Take him down. That was too much. That was badly done."

Then the cold voice sounded differently, farther away, and higher. "He's nearly finished."

She heard a blurred thudding as if a sack had dropped on the floor, very close above her. No one spoke. Quick footsteps came near and stopped.

What spoke now was not a voice, it was a whisper, something like leaves rattling, like the rustle of rain: not a voice, but two words, from a mouth without shape, and from a brain that was almost blackened out. It was so near that she could touch it, just above her head: two words: "Cannot kill . . ." It was Peter's voice.

"Now you see?" the syrupy voice said, but it was cold too, with anger. "Bauer, you fool, were you never taught that you must whip higher? Or lower? You will be taught. You have destroyed the property of the State. You understand?"

Rita closed her eyes into a darkness that did not come but had always been there, a darkness you could not sink into because you were drowned in it, a darkness that was over everything without limit, without end, not soft or peaceful or anything but final.

In the room upstairs they lifted a man's body and carried it out and someone came in with a pail and a rag and there was cold angry talk and apologies and the refusal to accept apologies and a door slammed and then two men alone spoke together, one in a hating harsh voice and the other in a voice near to hysteria, but soggy and thick. In the basement, by the cold furnace, Rita lay on her face and heard nothing.

She woke, very slowly, but it was only her aching arms that woke, her legs that were paralyzed as if they had been long and tightly bound, the pain behind her eyes, the dry throat and mouth. Emptiness had settled on her brain. There was only this unbending, painful, cold and burning thing, her body. And there was the darkness and the strange place where large silent shapes grew from the floor, and everything was silent and stone, and the air so damp and heavy that she could not lift her head against it.

She knew she must go away but she did not know why. She must have air, that was it, she must breathe, she could not lie here and slowly suck in the air until there was none, and then lie here with flattened lungs, gasping for the air that was already gone. From some other time, very far away, she held a memory of water, a smooth, black and beautiful river with a finely starred sky above it. I must go, she thought.

She moved as she had done before, using the memory that was in her legs and arms, not her brain. She crawled along the floor towards the open coal chute. She was stronger as she moved. Every motion, the pulling of one knee over the cement floor, the careful placing of a hand, letting the weight of her body rest on that hand, changing and moving forward, now the other knee, was separate, impossible and could not be measured in time. And then suddenly, her head struck lightly against the edge of the coal chute.

She sat with her back against this support, waiting. I must get out the window, she thought. That was all she had to think now. For one moment, a question hung in her mind: Why? why? No, that was too difficult; you would have to shake yourself alive again and understand and decide. No, she told herself, the window.

She rose and kneeled on the coal chute. Her stockinged feet did not slip; she could push herself up the slight curve, holding onto the sides of the chute with her hands. It was long too, forever high, so that wildly, for an instant, she thought she was still at the bottom, kneeling, pulling, pushing with her toes against the grimy, not steep, not slippery steel surface. Then her head reached the window and she brought her shoulders through into the wet fresh night air and breathed, slowly and deeply, as if she were drinking.

She climbed out the window and sprawled for a moment on the pavement, and she remembered fear from before, when she was running along the flagged path, ducking close against the walls, and the fear hurried her and helped her on. She held to the side of the building to stand, and standing found that this was no harder than crawling.

She did not turn to look but the house was dark behind her. She bent low and moved quickly down the path to the gate. Nearing the gate, there was a sudden pounding in her throat: she had remembered too well. On this side, she had nothing to stand on, she knew she could not pull herself up to the crossbar from the ground. She walked on, because there was no turning back, and coming to the gate, she put her hand hopelessly on the iron latch and it clicked down and the gate swung open.

She could not know that two hours before Bauer had passed this way, deadly frightened. Bauer had only half meant to do it, only wanting it to be over. But Hauck and Grüning knew what he had done. They knew. He had unlocked the gate and shut it, and not stopped to fasten the padlock behind him. They knew he had used the buckle end of the belt too hard to end it. God, to end it as soon as possible. He thought they would begin with the cigar again and he would have to smell how it burned and see, and above all see, and he knew he would be sick on the floor, or scream out; he hadn't been around when they did this sort of thing before, and even now, hurrying down the flagged path, trying not to make a noise with the gate, fearing they would stop him and afraid of what they would do to him later, he only wanted to go somewhere that was lighted and clean and he could drink and lose the smell. The smell was in his hair, he thought, on his hands, he could smell nothing else. He had shut the gate carefully and silently and turned and run towards the street. They did not come after him. He was alone anyhow. But he was alone with his trouble.

Rita stared at the open gate, and suddenly pushed it wide and walked up the alley, not feeling the cobbles bruising her feet, or noticing how she stumbled on the wet stone. She reached the alley entrance and found this gate ajar and walked through it, and turned to the left, always following the memory that was in her body. Then she came to a wide street, lighted with a few blue burning street lamps, and she sat down on the curb, with her feet in the gutter, and rested.

She did not know how long she stayed here. The street was empty, the houses were all dark, the wind had gone down and the night was clear and she did not know what time it was, and time no longer concerned her. Later, she felt into her pockets and brought out her shoes and put them on, seeing without interest her shredded stockings, and her bleeding legs and feet. She stood up and walked steadily, straight ahead, to the river.

She had thought of the river before: she had remembered the few lights splashing in the water, the dark stone curve of the bridges, the furry outlines of the trees on the little islands, and she had remembered the smooth cool unlimited sky. There would be a bench and she would sit on it. She could go no farther.

She found a bench, in shadow, near the wall of the quay. She sat there with her hands in her lap, unmoving, staring ahead and seeing nothing. She was not asleep, but she had gone away from herself, so that she rested there as free as the dead are free.

A policeman walked by and did not see her, silent in the shadow. He passed, later, returning on his regular beat, and noticed the extra darkness where she was. He came close and spoke and pulled out his flashlight and shone it on her face. He called on the Virgin, softly, in Czech, never having seen such a thing as this. By the hair, it was a woman. But where would a woman have come from with a face like that? The face was blackened and streaked, he could see blood on the mouth, and letting his flashlight play over her, he saw the ruins of her clothes. But it was her eyes that he could not understand. They were wide open and they blinked in the light, they were not blind, but they were as flat, lifeless and hard as stone. He stood in front of her, keeping the light on her face, and did not dare to touch her. It was something awful, he thought, not human at all.

But he could not go on all night like this. His colleague would come to relieve him, at dawn, and he did not wish to be seen behaving so stupidly, with such fear, so he cleared his throat nervously and said, "What are you doing here?"

Rita did not answer. She had heard him and she had seen, in the thrown-back light, that he wore the uniform of the police. She had nothing to say to him, or to anyone. She had nothing now ever to say.

"You can't stay here," the policeman said, with more assurance.

He raised his voice and asked the routine question which was always useful in moments of uncertainty.

"Where are your papers?" he said.

She answered him in German, looking for the words as if it were a language she scarcely knew. "I have no papers."

Now he understood better.

"You are German?" he asked.

She bowed her head.

"And you have no papers?"

She answered him with her eyes this time, agreeing.

"You know the law," he said, not unkindly, but just relieved to perform the proper official action. "You should have reported to the police yesterday. The time is up for refugees without papers. There have been notices everywhere," he said, argumentatively, "you must know."

"Yes."

"You must come with me now to the station. You

will have to leave the country. I must report you to the lieutenant."

"Yes," Rita said. And then, with terrible, slow weariness, "Naturally."

The policeman did not understand this. He knew the law and his duty and it was none of his business why she looked this way (let the lieutenant worry) and now he would take her in and make out a short written report and then he could go home.

"Come," he said, reaching over to take her arm.

"Do not touch me," she said.

She helped herself up, holding on to the back of the bench. She swayed a little and put one hand over her eyes.

"Come on now," the policeman said.

"I am coming."

He walked behind her. He wanted to keep his eye on her, to make sure she didn't do anything to get him into trouble.

13

THE breakfast tray was still on the desk, with one un-eaten *croissant*, shiny brown, like cardboard stage bread, and a cool milky half cup of coffee left over. The room had the surprised look of a place that has been robbed. Mary Douglas had taken her three dresses from the closet and the mirrored door stood open; the bureau drawers were partly pulled out; a bathtowel lay twisted and damp on the unmade bed; and powder was spilled across the glass top of the dressing table.

She was packed and ready too soon. She had tele-phoned for her bill and paid it in the room, not to waste time, and now she would have to sit in this ruin and wait for two hours at least, before she could go to the airline office, weigh herself and weigh her light canvas suitcase and her typewriter, present ticket and passport and find a seat in the bus that would take her to the plane.

She picked up the telephone and asked the operator, "No message?"

She had asked three times.

"Will you call the concierge and make sure no one is waiting for me in the hall?" The answer to this was no, too, a few moments later.

I won't think about Rita, she decided. She could think of nothing else.

She sat on the bed and studied herself in the mirror of the closet door. This, being open, presented her with a strange and not too satisfactory view of herself. I can't sit here, ogling my profile, she thought; oh damn, oh hell, why doesn't something happen? Perhaps it would be a good idea to walk down the hall and beat on Tom Lambert's door. But he would either be asleep or packing and besides there was nothing to say: you couldn't hang around wishing people good luck, a fine trip, hope it's fun, let me know when you get back to Paris, you couldn't go on mumbling like that. She had some oldish newspapers from London, but she had looked at them once and it was useless to make herself angry all over again.

Where is Rita, Mary Douglas thought, and her mind became very quiet, and she felt as if she were shrinking within herself. Where is Rita?

There was a knock at the door. She went quickly to open it, calling out, "Rita!"

The woman, standing in the shadowy, carpet-smelling hall, said, "Only me."

"Oh."

"She has not telephoned?"

"No," Mary said. "It must be day before yesterday that I last heard."

"Well," the woman said, "I brought it."

Mary had forgotten their agreement. "Let me see."

The woman opened a black, imitation leather briefcase and pulled out two cardboard folders. She spread these on the bed. The folders were full of tissue thin paper covered with German typing. Here and there a word, or two, or a phrase was blocked out neatly in India ink.

"All that?" Mary asked.

"Yes."

"But it's so bulky."

The woman made a worried gesture. She's changed her mind, the woman thought. She sees what it means today. Why not? Why should she take the risk? But who will do it then, who is there?

Mary Douglas picked up the first sheet. Reading it slowly, because she had difficulty with printed German, she saw that this was a simply worded statement, made by a postman, whose name and town address were inked out, telling of the Nazi invasion as he had seen it. It read flatly, being written with no emotion. He described first the local terror, practiced by the triumphant and unleashed Henleinists in his village, before the actual entry of the German army. He then told, in less detail, of one night and day after the Reichswehr took over, during which Sudeten citizens had been summarily arrested and transported by truck to concentration camps. There were three trucks and they had come half-full from other villages. He did not know whether the trucks were headed for Eger or Carlsbad or over the frontier into Germany. He told also of a little ceremony which had delighted the Henleinists and the invaders. (Mary asked for the translation of two words in a sentence.) The postman stated that his wife had been jostled off the pavement by a uniformed Henleinist. This man stopped to taunt her, announcing, "We are going to make the Czechs so small," and held his hand low, a few feet above the ground. Later the Czech women were rounded up, notably the wives of officials, schoolmasters, policemen and others who, in this humble way, by marriage, were symbolic of the Czech state, and they were forced to crawl forward on their knees carrying pails or bowls of excrement, and forced to throw this ordure on the village statue of Masaryk, and afterwards they were ordered to say, "We thank our Führer."

"Ai," Mary said, shivering with disgust.

"Some of these statements we made actual translations from the Czech; others were in German, from Sudeten German Jews, from Liberals, from Social Democrats, from all types of people."

"What's the rest of it?"

"Like that one."

"All the same sort of thing?"

"There was much more. My husband saved only enough for the book. It is too heavy to take all out of the country."

"It will make fine reading," Mary Douglas said. "Fine, instructive reading."

"We hope."

"But how about the names, and the addresses, are · they all blocked out?"

"Yes. You do not need to worry for that. The poor people, we would not want to make more trouble for them. Though many are lost now, either they are sent back to the Sudetenland or disappeared from Prague and two I know kill themselves."

"So all we have to do is smuggle this out?"

"Yes," the woman said. She knew what she was asking.

"It's worth it, all right," Mary said cheerfully. "But you know, I haven't done this sort of thing much. I get nervous about smuggling a pack of cigarettes. Where should I put it, do you think?"

The woman sat on the bed and watched Mary Douglas. She could not understand this girl. If she hadn't the best guarantees for her, she would have been frightened now. You could always make worse mistakes when you were in a hurry. I know I can trust her, she thought. But she was not used to working with amateurs, and Mary seemed to her dangerously willing, and somehow too gay. Still, she reasoned, they say she is reliable and that is the main thing. Afterwards, it is better that she looks the way she does and talks this way, like a rich brainless American. The customs inspector would be slower to notice her, than anybody else. She will just walk through, tall and thin and elegant, with the expensive clothes, and the handsome, self-confident face, and the voice like somebody who has never even heard of the police. But does she understand what it means, the woman wondered, does she take anything seriously?

Mary was beginning to enjoy herself. We must do what we can, she thought happily, any little thing; how I hope they make really good use of this stuff in Paris.

"From spy stories and all that," Mary said, "I think it ought to be sewed in the lining of something."

"Yes?"

"But it's too heavy. It would weigh down my coat too much."

"Perhaps I cut out more?" the woman suggested.

"Or I could slip the whole business under my girdle," Mary said. "I'd look a little pregnant, but then the customs people might be charming to me."

"You must not make a joke of it." The woman touched the typewritten pages with her hand. "Here is all that will ever be known about many lives, about many good people and brave people. For some, this is all they leave behind, two or three pages." The fine, mourning voice, Mary thought, the little man from Romberg spoke the same way.

"To you, this is only much paper, to be taken from the country with risk." The woman was trying to explain, but she thought: if this American cannot understand, because they are safe where she lives, nothing I say will ever explain to her. "We worked in the night and the ones who were hiding came to us. We met others in cafés and tried to talk smiling and friendly, so no one would notice, and we made notes on the edges of newspapers always afraid someone would watch. Different ones called for letters at the Poste Restante. We tried never to bring more trouble to those who trusted us with their stories. Two men stayed in their villages, though the Gestapo would kill them, to see how it happened there, to tell us, to make this record for all who have no other way to speak. No one has worked without danger, and all have worked with serious hearts. It is very small, you think; we are only two women sitting in a room and seeing how we should smuggle some papers. I do not believe you can understand. We are going on. We are keeping some truth. We are still fighting, each one, and here a few of us together, and we do the only thing we can do. To tell the truth, so that it shall not disappear and be forgotten, is our fighting. In the end, we must win with such papers, in the long end, perhaps, but someday. We believe still," she said, very quietly, "that truth is strong."

The woman did not expect an answer for she kept her head turned away, and from the side, Mary Douglas saw the deep tired lines around her mouth. Mary was thinking of Rita. She was thinking of those very old, unknown pictures that you see all over Europe, pictures of a blood-clear gaunt saint completing his martyrdom against an intricate, flat background. She thought Rita's face would fit very well in such a painting: the great dark eyes, the pallor, the obstinate mouth. In another time, when people seemed to know more about each other, they would have made a legend of Rita, and painted her face, and raised her above the other people whose lives were quiet. You couldn't imagine Rita as a hero because she was too gentle and too small, but she would have been honored as a martyr in the old poems and the old paintings. Mary thought: there are so many martyrs nowadays that nobody notices them.

And here was this middle-aged, drawn, weary and uncared-for woman, whose face you would never notice or remember, and she came quietly and talked a little, and asked a service, and went away. If you had to spend an evening with her, you would probably find her dull, or at any rate sad and heavy. And perhaps she would

be the next hero or martyr, perhaps she was just waiting her moment, until she was caught up without
choice, and forced to be stronger than she could be,
and braver.

Mary saw a little of it already. It was their faith that
set them apart and gave them such stature and such
dignity. They went on with their work, whatever work
came to their hands, and they looked like this, drab
and unmemorable, until the day they paid without
question for their beliefs. On that day you would think
of this woman as tall and proud and unyielding and
you would think of her as being handsomer than other
women.

They have been defeated, Mary Douglas thought,
and they will not accept defeat. This one comes alone
with a sheaf of papers, and through her the others refuse defeat also. They are lost and buried, and they
will not give up; each one has faith enough still to
believe in the power of two or three typewritten pages
that tell the truth.

And maybe they are right, Mary thought, perhaps
not for my life or for hers, but maybe they are right
in the end. Perhaps if you are as faithful as this, you
can see more truly and you can see farther ahead. Perhaps if they will not be defeated, they cannot be defeated. The doubting ones like me do not deserve to
win. We stop fighting. It is not just a bundle of paper
that I am going to have an awful time hiding. It is the
proof that everyone is not beaten yet.

"I beg your pardon," she said to the woman, and put
her hand on the shiny black coat sleeve. "I beg your
pardon truly. And I am honored to do this and I will

do it. Don't worry. I'll get it out all right and take it to your people in Paris. Please don't worry. And you better go now. The less you are seen around this hotel, or calling on the foreign press, the better for you if you want to leave the country without trouble."

The woman had made up her mind. She thought, by the girl's voice, that she had understood; there was nothing to do except trust her and hope she could manage by herself. "I thank you and I pray for you," the woman said. "You are doing a great service."

"No. Not me. You and the others. Good luck. I'll see you in Paris."

Now, alone and with nothing to do, she would have to plan how to hide this wad of typed paper. When you actually thought about it, where to put it, where it would be safe, you began to feel a little shaky. Her suitcase would be thoroughly searched, her typewriter would be opened, she could not sew a rattling mass of paper into the lining of her coat, she could not hold the papers under her blouse, pressed to her side, she certainly could not waddle out to the airport with a stiff crackling package firmly wedged against her stomach and kept in place by the fine silk elastic of her girdle. She thought she might as well read these documents for a while, to know what she was carrying. It would be wise to prepare a good frank lie about the papers, in case they were found on her.

Good Lord, she said to herself, and read faster. How many pages? More than a hundred. Oh, what a story. And then she thought: if I called in Tom and Thane and everybody and let them make copies, they couldn't use it. I can't use it. We wouldn't be believed. We'd be accused of propaganda, the way we always are. She thought: safe people will not believe this and who will dare publish it?

She read of night executions and how the shots sounded to people, locked in their own dark homes, praying there would be no sudden footsteps coming up their paths, no muffled, commanding knock at their doors. She read of the sick being hurried from the hospitals, since even hospitals offer no protection; of concentration camps springing up, and reported in whispers through a countryside where jails had always been small and cozy-looking and uncrowded, and law courts were proud public monuments; of the immediate Jew-baiting, described by a shamed and heart-broken Czech woman who had seen children called Jew in the street, painted with the word, placarded, mocked and hounded, but the children only wept and were afraid and did not understand what this meant; of singular, painless but revolting humiliations, invented to hurt a whole people's pride. As the story broadened out, in minute and ugly detail, her mind closed against it and at last she pushed the typewritten pages across the desk away from her, unwilling to read more.

Is there any place to go, Mary thought, where you don't see or hear or know? She sat in the disordered, blue satin-paneled room and said over the names of the lovely distant places, where people could still live and be troubled only by hunger, sickness or death, the easy, natural disasters. Kenya, Hawaii, Tahiti, Martinique, Mary Douglas said to herself, enjoying the names. Then she thought: what has ever happened to you,

yourself, to make you such an outstanding coward?
What has ever happened to you at all? How many
prisons have you been in, my beauty, how many countries have you been driven from? What would you be
complaining of? Name it. You get an eyeful and it
gives you the horrors and you leave; you just buy a
ticket and take a plane and leave. You're a sufferer,
you are, you have a terrible time. Take a plane and
leave, and leave everybody, and this time Monday
morning, free as air, and bright as a whistle, you'll be
drinking coffee with John on the terrace of Weber's,
and watching him read *L'Auto,* and he'll stop reading and see you watching him and smile, and you'll
hold hands probably for a moment in the sun, and then
he'll go on reading about the boxing at the Salle
Wagram, and you'll look at the women passing to see
if you can pick up any ideas for your fall clothes, and
after breakfast you'll take his arm and walk down the
rue Royale, stopping at all the expensive shop windows, until you get to your bank: and then you'll draw
out francs.

Kenya, Hawaii, Tahiti, Martinique, she mocked herself: if you can't do anything else, you can at least see
and hear and know. Just take your plane but don't
be sorry for yourself, see. And don't feel abused because an unknown woman has asked you to do one
small, moderately risky job for all the other unknown
people. And don't call down punishment on yourself
by whimpering for the South Seas, when you've got
Paris and John. Think what Rita would give to have
Paris and Peter. Good Lord, she thought, I've forgotten
all about Rita for a whole half hour.

She picked up the telephone. It was ten-thirty. The switchboard operator answered her crisply this time; she had other work than to worry whether the gentleman friend of 419 had called or not.

She isn't coming, Mary thought. I'll wait another half hour. I can't wait another half hour. I have to be at the airline office at eleven to catch the bus to the field. If she hasn't come now, she isn't coming. I'm going to take the plane in an hour and a half. What has happened to her? You're afraid to think, she told herself, aren't you? But it's too soon, it's too soon; she'll be all right for another week or two. It doesn't go that fast.

She went to the desk and scratched out a note with the splattering hotel pen.

"Rita my dear,

"As soon as you get this, go straight to the American Embassy and ask for Willard Loning. He's a friend of mine and he expects you. He will tell you what you must do and he will wire me in Paris. I shall send money, by return wire, as soon as he gets in touch with me. It ought not to take more than three or four days to get visitors' visas for you and Peter and I will meet you at the Bourget airport. And we will have a wonderful time in Paris and celebrate.

"With love, Mary."

We will have a wonderful time, Mary wrote for herself, forcing her lips to smile as she wrote, trying to think it was true. Too late, she thought, you're too late. No, she will come tomorrow, maybe she's busy, but she wouldn't leave without telling me. She will

289

come. I will get them out. I will meet them at Bourget. Rita, she said in her mind, come by this hotel just once, just once more.

She looked at the letter. She will come for it, Mary lied to herself. I'll tip everybody heavily so they'll remember to give it to her when she comes. When she comes, Mary thought, and remembered Rita's room with the light still burning.

Now I must go, she thought, and what to do with these papers?

She had papers that she should not have, that was all. Many of them must have been stolen from government files. She had looked quickly at some statements dealing with the unused Czech plans for military resistance, and she had seen a sort of timetable which outlined, by day and hour, the secret and unsavory diplomatic actions of Czechoslovakia's allies during the last crisis weeks.

All in all, in the right hands and used at the right time, she thought, this is deadly information. It certainly makes that Peace-with-Honor, Peace-in-our-Time business look worse than fishy. Stop being funny with yourself, she thought, and stop thinking out of the corner of your mouth. They must be desperate or they wouldn't have trusted me with anything so valuable. They must be very scared too. And so are you, this is no girlish prank. This means bad trouble if you're caught.

There are no copies, Mary Douglas told herself, and this is the small thing you can do for the people who will not be defeated.

Where in God's name shall I hide it? she asked herself.

She stood in the middle of the room and beat her hands together, thinking, but she could devise no miraculous trick or subterfuge which would fool the customs.

They also serve who only take planes and smuggle, she thought, but she did not feel any better.

Then because she could invent nothing, she picked up her bag, a very large smart calfskin square, the size of a small briefcase, and looked inside it. It dated from the year before, and had been an extravagance. Now, with only her passport, ticket, scribbled notes, money and make-up, it was almost empty. In my bag, Mary decided. It's not such a goofy idea as it seems. It's so obvious that no one would suspect it. Or had she read that, in some mystery thriller, about a handsome young British Agent, traveling around on the Simplon Orient Express. Anyhow, she thought, there is no other place, and if they are found, I can insist these are my professional notes, and stick to that story, and I won't feel so guilty and nervous if I'm carrying them in a normal way.

She bent the papers and crammed them into her bag and the bag would not shut. She took her handkerchief and spread it over the smooth rolled top of the papers, and laid her own things on top of the handkerchief. Then she telephoned to the porter to have her luggage carried down, put on her coat and hat, picked up the letter to Rita and walked to the elevator. She was in a hurry to get it over with, now that she had started. I won't feel like myself again, Mary thought, until the plane is several thousand feet up.

"You understand how important it is?" Mary Douglas said to the desk clerk. She still held the letter in her hand. She had hoped, knowing it was silly, that she would see Rita, looking very small and dark and shy, waiting on one of the tapestried chairs in the hall. Then she had hoped the revolving door would swing around and Rita would walk in from the sunny street, making soft apologies for not having come sooner, for not having telephoned. Ought I to wait any longer, she wondered, and saw the clock above the keyboard.

"Yes, Mademoiselle. I shall tell my colleague also."

"It's so important," Mary insisted. "Perhaps she will come tomorrow."

"Do not trouble yourself," the clerk said.

She tipped him heavily, and asked for an envelope, and sealed another bill into it, for the night clerk. She won't come, Mary thought. But she has to come.

The hall was empty except for a bald man drinking chocolate with whipped-cream out of a large cup. Two waiters, wearing aprons, polished the wide front windows.

"Oh, and tell Mr. Lambert good-by and Mr. Thane and Mr. Luther and the others if you see them."

"Certainly, Mademoiselle."

It's not worth telephoning to their rooms, she thought, we'll meet soon enough at the next accident: we, the ambulance chasers.

"You will come back again?" the desk clerk said. She was writing her forwarding address on a printed card.

"Later," Mary said, and then in an uncalled-for burst of frankness, thinking even as she heard her voice that she was being a fool, "when this country is free."

The desk clerk stretched out his hand, smiling so that she saw his eyes for the first time, not as he always smiled, in bored, wooden, polite agreement with the clients. She took his hand and nodded without speaking.

"Business will be bad," he said, as if to himself. "Business will be very bad from now on."

The porter was an old man who bustled and hurried and muttered and seemed permanently stooped under the weight of all the suitcases he had carried. He deposited her luggage on the light tan wooden counter at the airport customs, sighing as if he had just hauled a trunk incredible distances, and left her. The other people, who were taking the plane, fidgeted around their suitcases. There was none of the usual gaiety of departure: no one made a cheerful, loud, pointless joke; no one wore the happy, heated face of someone who is going on a fine trip, though still bothered with what may have been forgotten and where-did-I-put-the-tickets; no one carried flowers; no one had friends to wave good-by and give the final stumbling kisses of farewell. These faces looked strained and hurt, and the people stayed by themselves, in a kind of tight, private anxiety, and watched the customs inspectors and watched the clock with sharp, uneasy eyes, and Mary Douglas thought you could almost hear their hearts

293

beating painfully, jerkily, and you knew they were afraid to go and afraid to stay.

Three customs officials were opening suitcases, up and down the counter, with a new and alarming thoroughness. Behind them, leaning against the wall, were two men in belted raincoats and drawn-down felt hats, who did not move or speak. They had looked at all the passengers, slowly, with no expression on their faces and no change in their steady, impersonal eyes. You could see their eyes examining, carefully, feature by feature, each man and woman who stood by the counter. The two men did not shift their positions or take their hands out of their pockets. They were as controlled and quiet as animals, and their unwinking flat eyes were strange to see. Mary thought they could probably locate the one they were looking for by smell. She turned away. She did not want to see them. Looking at their eyes and mouths, she could feel a prickle run down her back between her shoulder blades.

A woman in black, whose veil did not hide her tear-reddened, nervous eyes, muttered little explanations as the customs inspector pulled out, squeezed and opened a handkerchief case, a shoe bag, and a medicine box. The man beside her, wearing a loose overcoat and a hairy gray felt hat, forced his lips into a stiff smile, trying not to seem concerned as he unlocked his briefcase.

Passports were slowly leafed through and held up to the light, so that even knowing the visas were in order and the passport authentic, the owner waited, speechless and rigid until the passport was stamped and returned. An elderly woman, with little pear-shaped

diamonds in her ears, smiled with an almost sick relief, seeing the round stamp pound down on her passport and leave a purple printed circle which meant she
was free, she was really leaving.

Money was carefully checked. Men and women emptied their pockets and handbags onto the wooden counter and produced the white or pink bank slips which
stated how much money they were taking with them
and how much they left behind.

One of the men, who had stood unmoving behind
the customs counter, nodded and took his hands from
his pockets. The other shoved himself away from the
wall. They turned and walked out the door behind
the counter. Mary let her breath go, very softly. She
knew their eyes were the real danger in this room.

Mary gave the customs inspector her passport first.
It was always wise to establish yourself as an American.
Americans travel all the time, blindly and cheerfully,
and by tradition present no political problem. The
customs inspector was dark, with red-veined cheeks
and he stared at her solemnly through his glasses, and
asked her to open her suitcase and typewriter. He
lifted nothing out, simply patting the clothes and the
silk side pocket, and glancing at the scratched typewriter. He shut the typewriter and helped her push
down the lid of her suitcase and stamped them both.
She was through this formality quicker than any of the
other passengers, who looked at her curiously or with
envy. Then he beckoned and she followed down the
length of the counter to his table, where he took her
passport again, looked through it quickly for the
Czech visa and the French visa, and he stamped this

too, and rose to return it with a bow. Mary smiled at him, holding under her arm always the not shut, large handbag, acting as if she kept her bag open to put back her passport and tickets, as if she always traveled with her bag open this way. She stood as far back from the counter as she dared, so that he couldn't see, outlined beneath her cigarettes, powder, coin purse and notebook, the round lump of the documents. She thought he did look at her bag, and she thought he frowned. She took her passport quickly and smiled with great warmth saying *"Danke schön"* and then moved off, to wait against the opposite wall until the chain would be lowered and they could file through the glass doors to the cement runway and the plane.

There were two more people to attend to, a young man and an older one, both very pale, with fumbling uncertain hands, both Jews. The dark customs inspector asked them rapid questions; it was almost time to leave. Now everyone had been passed, and a little easiness spread among the waiting people. The black-dressed woman made a remark to a man who smiled, someone lit a cigarette, and you could see that they began to feel safe now, they were almost safe, they were almost gone; it was only a question of minutes now, and their shoulders were not held so rigidly, they did not follow the customs inspectors with such fixed and watchful eyes.

A porter had moved over to the chain barrier and was unhooking it. Trying not to seem too eager, the people turned in that direction, ready to push through and hurry into the plane. Inside the plane you would be safer still.

The dark customs inspector called out. Everyone stood still, the faces quiet, stiff, the eyes strained and wary. He pointed to Mary Douglas. She walked back to his desk, and waited in front of him. She could not talk. She felt her face grow cold, but sweat was dampening the edges of her hair. She held her bag as tightly as she could, trying to press it shut against her side. She was shocked at the way her breath seemed to flutter and choke in her throat; she thought surely the man noticed this. She would have to say something, and she must not stammer and she must not let her voice break or tremble.

"You stay in Prague a week only?" the man said, in English, picking out the words and saying each one separately, as if he had memorized them.

"I didn't know you spoke English," Mary said, hoping her voice sounded easy and friendly.

"Yes. Not so many."

"It's very good English," she said, but her throat was dry and she wished he would hurry.

"But you are only a week," the customs inspector persisted. "You do not love Prague?"

"Oh, yes, very much."

"Then you come back," he said happily, "for many weeks. To see our beautiful city."

"Yes, I will. Maybe in the spring."

"In the spring it is very beautiful here. But more than a week."

The chain had been unhooked and the people were filing out towards the plane.

"Good journey," the customs man said.

Mary Douglas, dazed, did not know whether she

should move. Then she turned, without speaking. He was practicing his English, she thought, the laughter so close that she could hardly hold it down. Just showing off before the other customs inspectors; he would say to them that he had a nice talk with the American girl. It's my new lipstick, she thought; he had stood there saying his careful sentences, with a definitely cheerful light in his eyes.

Practicing his English, she thought, and now that she was on the runway, with the brisk light wind blowing her coat open, the sun shining down on the clean concrete, and glittering over the waiting cream-colored plane, she let the laughter come out, and bent over and ran against the wind to the plane.

The peroxided blonde stewardess whom she remembered from the trip in, stood by the portable steps and greeted her warmly, as an old friend. The tail of the plane was painted in stripes with the colors of Czechoslovakia, and on the side it bore the official lettering of the Czech air service: in black paint, two feet high, it was marked O.K. They couldn't have found more accurate code letters, Mary thought. It is O.K. for me, and O.K. for the other passengers. An outgoing plane is about the most O.K. thing they've got around here.

The stewardess was young and happy by nature, and it had been several weeks since she had seen anyone board this plane, laughing. She patted Mary on the back, as she went up the steps, and laughed too.

The propellers spun faster and faster until they were only a grayish, round shadow against the sky. There was a wavering silver line, where the sun caught the revolving metal blades. The stewardess walked up and down the aisle, leaning over the passengers to make sure that their safety belts were properly fastened. The plane turned and taxied along the cement, to the far end of the runway, turned again, and drove forward, bumping a little, but so fast that the windows of the airport building blurred into a long shining band. Then the wheels left the ground and the plane rose, clearing the hangars and the telephone wires and climbed steadily up into a pale wind-streaked sky. Mary swallowed, to break the pressure in her ears, and looking out saw the ground, tipped away from them, and the houses growing smaller and smaller. For a while she watched the land, as it changed into a neat toy, with the perfect clean roads, the little puffs of trees, and the flat, tidy fields.

That's that, she thought. She felt hollow and sick in her heart. Nothing is settled, I am only leaving. If you could leave, and know it would all stop; if you could leave and know the terror and confusion was ended; if you could leave, and the others who did not leave could remain behind in safety. She did not want to think about Paris anymore, there was no pleasure in planning ahead the fine things they would do, in this lovely October weather. If I am going to carry it with me, all the time, she thought, I might as well not leave. John would have managed better. John would have helped somehow. Now she would go back to him and say: John, I left my friends. I don't know what's happened to them. I wasn't any use, John, you can't imagine how awful it is there. Far worse than war, and worse than hunger and worse than prison. And I knew, see, but I didn't do anything. Or would she just say to him: John, John, oh, darling (forgetting everything, shamefully, except how glad she was to be home).

She heard the voices behind her in the plane. She had chosen a seat at the front, where you could look down, over the propellers, and get a clear view of the country. She turned to see that the passengers were gathered together, at the rear of the plane, standing in the aisle, sitting on the arms of each other's chairs, talking and laughing as if they had been friends for years. But Mary was sure they had never seen each other before they met in that tight silence in the customs shed. The two Jews, who had arrived late, smiled as if they could not stop. They were a little frightening to see. She thought that at any moment those rigidly widened mouths would crumple and slump and they would be crying.

The elderly woman shook her pear-shaped diamond earrings at the one who wore a black veil, and chattered in loud incomprehensible Czech, and the one with a veil leaned over and patted her shoulder and laughed and wiped her eyes. The briefcase owner offered everyone cigarettes and was reminded by the stewardess that he could not smoke. In one of the sudden silences, that falls between the roar of the motors, a man who had not spoken said, solemnly, and to no one, "*Gott sei dank. Gott sei dank.*"

Not one of them had looked out the windows behind them at the wand-like church steeples of Prague growing smaller and finer in the distance.

Then the smile twisted and broke on the young Jew's face, and he turned away from the others and groped for a chair, trying to hide his face that had suddenly grown old, and hopeless, and trying to hide his hurt mouth and the tears that stayed in his eyes. The elderly woman, seeing him, put her hand up to her cheek as if she had been struck, and leaned against the window, looking for her city, but it was too late. Prague was gone, and she moved her head slowly, taking in the whole plane, with an expression of wonder and grief on her face. The black-veiled woman stared ahead, and then shut her tired reddened eyes. She did not want to look at Prague. She knew it was behind her now forever. Slowly the others went back to their own seats and stayed alone, and quiet, making their farewells.

Mary Douglas leaned back and let the noise of the motors wash through her mind. The flickering sun-streaked propellers held her eyes. When the plane dropped in an air pocket, she sank with it, relaxed and unresisting.

I'll never see them again, Mary thought. She had already forgotten the names, and remembered only the faces. All the faces blurred in the gleaming band of the propeller, the lined, intent, frightened, bewildered, despairing, angry, lonely; the faces of the lost. I will forget them too. There will be so many others. But I'll remember Rita and I'll remember Peter. And where are they now, *really*.

Rita, she said in her mind, it's not all over yet, it isn't, I swear it isn't. Even if I don't see you again.

The humming rising and falling roar of the motors flowed through the plane. Sun came in the small square glass window and warmed her hands. The shining single line of the propellers began to look like a fountain, spilling up evenly against the flat sky. Mary sank lower into her chair and slept. She was tired, and there were many things to stop remembering.

The movement in the plane woke her. The passengers had all crowded to one side, pushing against each other to peer out the windows. They were not talking. Mary raised herself and looked down. Far beneath them and ahead was the Rhine, dirty green, narrow, and slow. Then they had passed it, so quickly that you could not even look at it once, directly below. They were flying over France. The elderly woman waved her hand, absurdly, knocking against the window pane. The young Jew smiled again. The briefcase man took off his hat, slowly, and threw it up and it hit against the low ceiling just in front of him and fell on a chair. The woman with the black veil said something to herself very softly; it sounded as if she were praying.

Mary Douglas stared down at the neat fields, brown and green, purple brown, yellow. There were the white roads and the white farmhouses and the pompons of the trees. But the land doesn't look any different, she thought. The land doesn't look different at all.

AFTERWORD

I wrote this book in 1939. In 1937 I had become a war
correspondent in Spain because I was there and mailed an
unsolicited article to *Collier's* in New York. *Collier's* published it
and put me on their masthead. I had no qualification except eyes
and ears; I learned as I went. In 1938, I became a foreign
correspondent as well, again because I was on the spot. My
qualification was that I had spent most of my life since 1930 in
Europe, involved in its politics the way a tadpole is involved in a
pond. *Collier's* was a weekly magazine with a colossal circulation,
nine million, thirteen million; I don't remember. This huge
audience gave me the brief illusion that I could affect how people
thought by making them see what I had seen.

When I left Europe in January 1939, I was sure that the
countries I cared about were lost. Before I finished *A Stricken Field*
ten months later, Czechoslovakia vanished into silence, occupied
by the Nazis; Franco and Fascism won in Spain, taking terrible
vengeance on the defeated; Hitler attacked Poland and finally,
tardily, Britain and France declared war on Germany. From
February through October, safe in Cuba, a beautiful bolt-hole, I
wrote out the accumulated rage and grief of the past two years in
this one story, one small aspect of the ignoble history of our time.

To my regret, I never had the sense to build a writer's compost
heap: diaries, journals, notes, photographs, letters. The archive
of my past is a poor thing, limited and fragmentary: those letters
and book reviews that my mother saved. Excerpts from the letters

more or less explain this book, since it is felt that a book so old needs explaining.

A letter dated "June 13 maybe" in 1938, on the stationery of the Hotel Ambassador, Prague, shows that I had been in Czechoslovakia for a week. "This is a very remarkable and exciting country. Without Hitler, it might have been the model democracy of Europe. With Hitler, it is a fortress. And Hitler knows it. I seriously believe that on May 21, when the Czechs mobilized and called Hitler's bluff – the first nation to do so – war was indefinitely postponed. Indefinitely means a year or two but anything may happen in that time: good or bad. I feel hopeful now, though it is inconceivable that this armed peace – with the armaments' burden and the exhausting tension – can endure for long . . . There are four Russian divisions and 1000 planes on the Roumanian frontier and every key road in this country is barricaded and barbed-wired and all bridges mined. The air itself is unbreathable but at least the Czechs are not afraid and confident."

Here my memory turns up an ancient snapshot. I must have heard (and garbled, "1000 planes" indeed) the Russian news from Mikhail Koltsov whom I found on a bench in a long corridor of the Hradcany Palace in Prague, waiting to see President Beneš of Czechoslovakia. When we were in Madrid, Koltsov was officially *Pravda* and, we thought, unofficially the Kremlin's eyes and ears. He was a slight grey-haired man, given to marvellous tough joking, a mocker of dogma and rhetoric. Koltsov had been waiting in that corridor for a week and looked smaller, older, and tired. He said the Czechs would need Russian help to fight the Nazis; if they fought. I was so excited by the mobilization – standing up to Hitler at last – that I had no doubts; of course the Czechs would fight if Hitler attacked.

Koltsov was the only Russian communist I knew but in Spain and Czechoslovakia I knew many European communists: to be a

304

communist then was to declare a personal war on fascism and accept a special danger. The German and Italian communists were stateless; the Yugoslavs and Poles were exiles. When everyone was young I did not notice age, but looking back I realise how young they were, and poor and experienced in hardship, and brave. They were wonderful people, wonderful; they must be long dead.

Since Hitler and Mussolini bellowed against Bolshevism, the Soviet Union became a symbol to anti-fascists. Not to the ruling class of Britain and France who were complaisantly tolerant of fascism but, as always, hostile to Reds. Perhaps to keep the favour of his formal feeble ally France and his informal reactionary ally Britain, President Beneš refused to see Koltsov, a crucial decision.

After Prague, my New York editor wanted articles from France and England: reactions to the Czech situation, European rearmament, etc. A letter dated July 4, 1938, in Paris says that I got back from London the day before and intended to call my report "The Lord will provide – for England."

"I think that England is a kid glove fascism, worse because of its hypocrisy and the fact that all of the people are fooled all of the time . . . As Laski said, 'The first economy an Englishman makes is on thought.' There is no thought, nor is there information, nor is there any set of values a man can respect: there is the Empire and money and the two are perhaps synonymous . . . But day by day, the ten percent who rule that country are practising a cynical opportunism, which is certainly pushing off the chances of peace farther and farther, the while they deny with amusement the mere suggestion of war. I am sure the war will come, though I think there is a possible two year lull during which the English aid their future enemies to become strong, so that the war when it does come will last longer and be worse. Chamberlain is deeply committed to having Franco win . . . He is one of the most hateful figures in modern times, and his whole crowd is disgusting . . .

You only hear what pays, and how all foreigners are muck anyhow and why bother."

Dated August 25, 1938, from Paris: "It is so bad now that one cannot believe it. Edgar (Mowrer) called me up yesterday . . . He had come from the F.O. (Quai d'Orsay) where he had been told that his information from Fodor in Prague was exact. The Foreign Office expects war between the 15th and 18th of September and is acting accordingly. They went on to discuss the evacuation of Paris . . . The uncertainty of all this is enough to break your heart. All Europe suffers with it and the people in the know are going just a little mad . . . The Germans want war: Hitler's entourage that is. The Czechs are so terribly strained by these months of uncertainty and waiting and bullying that they do not much care . . . I believe that if Roosevelt could announce that on the day war was declared America entered with France and England, there would be no war. But he can't do it. And so we'll just get into the war anyhow . . . Everything in Europe now is miserable guessing. Only Hitler knows whether eight million men are going to be dead within the next five years."

For months – it seemed forever – Hitler had been shrieking about the misery of the ethnic Germans in what he called the Sudetenland, the fortified western frontier zone of Czecho-slovakia, a bulge surrounded by Nazi Germany. The cruel Czechs were brutalizing the poor ethnic Germans and it was Hitler's sacred duty to rescue his people. (The Big Lie, always delivered in a prolonged scream, was a winning Hitlerian tactic, usefully adapted by all kinds of governments ever since.) Instead of honoring a military pact and lining up behind the invaluable Czech democracy, Chamberlain and Daladier went, as sup-pliants, to meet Hitler in Munich on September 29, 1938 and gave him the Sudetenland, in return for a piece of paper. "Peace in our time." It lasted less than a year. The moral of that moment in history has lasted for me permanently: never believe

306

governments, not any of them, not a word they say; keep an untrusting eye on what they do.

Cheering crowds greeted Daladier in Paris and Chamberlain in London, when properly both men should have been stoned. President Beneš was a liberal democrat, a decent man in a wrong time. Having rejected aid from the Soviet Union, he lacked the nerve to let the Czechs fight alone. The worst decision and the last he made for his country. From October 1 through October 10, 1938, the German army annexed 11,000 square miles, over a quarter of the sovereign and admirable state of Czechoslovakia. It was clear that the Nazis would annex all Czechoslovakia when convenient.

Letter dated October 7, 1938, from Paris: "I am flying to Prague tomorrow. I got a cable from *Collier's*: they want stuff from Beneš . . . Beneš is in retirement in the country, not talking. The only sensible thing he can do is get out . . . I can do a fine story called 'Obituary of a Democracy.' I am wild with anger and this is my chance . . . Democracy is dying. The disease is called cowardice . . . Everybody's in Prague, waiting for the end."

Again, after those appalling days in Czechoslovakia, I was sent to do postmortem articles on France and England: the general response to Hitler's latest victory. I remember how I behaved in England; I sought out everyone I knew in the pro-Munich ruling class, and promised them that they would get it too, in turn; they would be bombed like Spain; they had sold out the Spanish people and the Czechs and I was never going to set foot on their cursed island again. I was treated with laughing tolerance and told that nobody was in an uproar about Czecho except Maurice Hindus and me. (Maurice Hindus, a respected American political commentator, had already made an indignant visit to London). The words are indelible in my memory though I don't remember which of those pleasant dummies spoke them. When next I set foot on their cursed island in 1943 it was a different country.

This letter is undated; from its contents I guess it was written in November, in Paris. "I have been trying to write my *Collier's* story which I am calling 'Mr Chamberlain's Peace' but it won't come ... The League High Commissioner for Refugees, one Sir Neill Malcolm, showed up for two days in Prague and didn't see a single refugee. But I had seen them, all of them, all over the place and I was sick at heart and very angry. So I went to his hotel and saw him and pounded the table as always and shouted and pleaded and explained and described and then he said what should he do, which kind of surprised me. I suggested he see Sirovy at once and get the blanket expulsion order which was sending these people back to Hitler held up until the Evian Committee could work. He said he'd see Sirovy if I'd get the American Minister at Prague to make the appointment. I telephoned the first secretary of Legation and he agreed to find the Minister and get an appointment and twenty minutes later called back and said, 'After all why should the American Minister do it?' I said damn all of you and I telephoned Sirovy myself, saying I was interpreter for Sir Neill and I got the appointment. Then I went out to see General Faucher, ex-head of the French Military Mission – he resigned in disgust over this betrayal – and he is far the cleanest and best man anywhere and a darling. I told him about the refugees and asked him to build up Malcolm to Sirovy and to go with Malcolm to the meeting; and then I took him back and introduced the two, Major General Sir Neill Malcolm and Son Excellence le Général Faucher. I was there at nine in the morning and stayed with them until a quarter to ten and put them in the car and waited until they came back from the interview, and Sirovy refused to grant a stay for the refugees. It wasn't his fault, the Czechs cannot offend Hitler, they're not free anymore, France and England saw to that ... And now Spain, Spain next. I'll maybe lose my mind with the fury and the helplessness."

General Sirovy was Prime Minister of Czechoslovakia. Who knows what the Evian Committee was; probably window dressing. I wanted a date and found it in the bound files of *The Times* in the London Library basement. A paragraph on an inside page, dated October 12, 1938, stated that Sir Neill Malcolm, the League of Nations High Commissioner for Refugees, had arrived in Prague. I read the smug editorial, praising the wisdom of the Chamberlain government, and anodyne reports of events in Europe and was as outraged by this evil stupidity as if I were reading the news of today. Not that evil stupidity ended in 1938; the supply remains plentiful, with no end in sight.

That winter of 1938, Barcelona was starving. Every day Italian planes flew very high and bombed the city carelessly; more dead, more wounded, more destruction. The endurance of the people was beyond praise. Hunger was killing Spain. Spain was my Cause; Spain was what I loved and believed in and I could not bear to watch the suffering any longer. My work was useless, none of my articles had saved anyone. When I saw the starved withered babies in the Barcelona Children's Hospital and the eyes of the silent wounded children, I decided to get out. Leave Europe, leave history. I could not help anyone; I could remember for them.

In February, in the beautiful bolt-hole of Cuba, I began to write a short story set in Prague. It changed and grew into this novel. Spain was too close. I never wrote about Spain, apart from two short stories much later. I found I could control and use the emotions of Spain in writing about Czechoslovakia. The enemy was the same; the people were equally abandoned, alone, and related by pain.

A letter dated March 18, 1939, Cuba: "Each day I am gladder to have left Europe. It isn't only that one could not work in that havoc but I think, being close to it, by now one would have a broken heart. It is such a miserable collection of lies and chicanery and underneath all such horrible raw dripping cruelty ... The final seizure of Czecho was to be expected but like death, expected or not, it comes as a brutal shock ... Spain is beyond imagining ... I sent money to Maria Osten to pay her passage to Russia where Koltsov, with whom she had lived for nine years, is in jail for 'treason'. It was not my business to judge whether she was committing suicide as I believe she is ... Ailmuth Heilbrunn writes that all Spaniards or people with Spanish passports are to be kicked out of France April ninth and she does not know where to go, where on the map is there welcome or safety ... We live in a world unlike any other at any time. A world so cruel and mad that one cannot believe it will survive ... I think, no doubt selfishly, that right now there is nothing to do about it except help one's friends. And write about it ... as an act of faith, believing still in telling the truth ... and also write to save one's sanity, not to think, to lose oneself in a specific problem of construction, imagination and sentences."

A letter dated Easter, 1939, I suppose early April: "I am sending you herewith the copied part of my novel ... I am past being able to know anything about it except that I love it with passion and adore working on it and am happy inside thinking about it. As to what the present results are, who can say. Not I, surely. It is going to be increasingly difficult to do because it must be kept varied, light and dark, and it is only a dark story."

That loony euphoria is a writer's real reward and rejoices the soul at least once during any work in progress. Apparently only once; I find no other evidence that I was afloat in happiness over this book.

Letter dated September 6, 1939, New York: "I won't write you about the war and please establish in advance that I am not an insensate egoist and don't know what it means to the people who are being bombed and the mothers who sent their children

310

off marked with cardboard tags. But I can't think about that now and get through the days ... *Collier's* wants me to go to Russia first ... The prospect of this final futility of man does not interest me. It horrifies and sickens me and when you get too tired to feel such strong emotions, there is left only a grey boredom. So I shall go to Russia ..." But the visa never arrived and I returned to my novel, while the phoney war went on and on: Poland now vanished into the known silence of Nazi occupation, and the war was at a weird standstill.

Letter dated October 24, 1939: "My book is almost rewritten. I have settled on 'A Stricken Field' as the title. I do not know how well I have done the rewriting and maybe if I had months I would do better but maybe also not. The book is far from me, all gone, I cannot recapture my own emotions in writing it ... So it will have to stand as it is. I hope it is good. I don't know and can't say I care very much."

By November 10, I was on board a small Dutch ship bound for Amsterdam. My editor wanted articles on Scandinavia and suggested a stopover in Finland which I quickly looked up on a map. Years afterwards I remembered that I was eager to go, but my letters prove that I was far from enthusiastic about this dull assignment in the frozen north. I had to earn money; journalism paid for the time to write fiction. All was quiet on all fronts. At sea magnetic mines, that looked like huge basketballs studded with blunt spikes, floated as the waves moved them and sank ships at random. Our ship ploughed safely and slowly past wreckage, bodies and bobbing mines. I arrived in Helsinki on the night of November 29 and the next morning at 9 a.m. the Russo-Finnish war began, so I reported a second war. A letter dated December 10, 1939: "I have again in my life had the unpayable experience of living with a brave nation." Sometime in January 1940, I returned to Cuba.

A Stricken Field was published in New York early in March

311

1940, when the U.S. was still at peace. Funny phrase. There would not have been time for me to correct galley proofs, and from 1940 until now I never looked inside the unattractive beige hardcovers. In 1942, *A Stricken Field* was published in London. I had forgotten this. Paper for books was rationed, why would they be interested in Czechoslovakia in 1942 when so uninterested in 1938? I never saw that edition. Six American reviews and four English reviews have surfaced from the depths of the past. The reviews were filed in my subconscious as bad; I must have been very spoiled. The space given to a novel by a new writer, in 1940, is astounding by present picky standards. All are sympathetic to the subject if not to the form. The *Philadelphia Record* puts the general criticism in one sentence: " 'A Stricken Field' is a compelling piece of reporting and a so-so novel . . ."

I see now why the American reviews offended me; personal references to the author. *Time* magazine reviewed me, not the book. The tone of some reviewers was oddly resentful; I had mentioned this in a letter. Once more from the *Philadelphia Record*: "There is a grim torture scene that will arouse every reader – and then what can you have, war again?" And from the *Boston Transcript*: "I cannot see that this 'novel' can accomplish anything unless it gives some of us a greater sympathy with the refugees whom we encounter – as who does not these days?" I was fairly impervious to reviews but troubled by a secret shame. I had used two of my own small acts in that tragedy as part of the story. It was not my tragedy and I disliked myself for taking a fictionalized share.

I was well along in a new book of short stories when I wrote from Cuba on May 22, 1940: "I know something very wrong happened to me about this last book but as yet I don't know how or why. If you work for a long time on a book you should get something out of it for yourself, some sense of triumph . . . But I had nothing. I had the feeling I had dropped my work, the hard

312

months of my life, into a well, and there they were, muffled and lost. I do not know why this came about but it did and I am surely suffering from it now, both in a sense of personal futility and a lack of confidence in my work ... As I don't know what it is, I cannot write it ... with a little time I will find it and correct it."

But I did not. I buried *A Stricken Field*, never again mentioned it; and got on with the job.

In order to produce this Afterword I had to open the unattractive beige hardcovers and read *A Stricken Field* in print for the first time. And at last, forty-five years late, I have got "something out of it" for myself. Despite its faults, which I see better than anyone else could, I am proud of it. I am glad I wrote it. Novels can't "accomplish" anything. Novels don't decide the course of history or change it but they can show what history is like for people who have no choice except to live through it or die from it. I remembered for them.

Martha Gellhorn, Kilgwrrwg, Wales, 1985

313

VIRAGO MODERN CLASSICS

The first Virago Modern Classic, *Frost in May* by Antonia White, was published in 1978. It launched a list dedicated to the celebration of women writers and to the rediscovery and reprinting of their works. Its aim was, and is, to demonstrate the existence of a female tradition in fiction which is both enriching and enjoyable. The Leavisite notion of the 'Great Tradition', and the narrow, academic definition of a 'classic', has meant the neglect of a large number of interesting secondary works of fiction. In calling the series 'Modern Classics' we do not necessarily mean 'great' — although this is often the case. Published with new critical and biographical introductions, books are chosen for many reasons: sometimes for their importance in literary history; sometimes because they illuminate particular aspects of womens' lives, both personal and public. They may be classics of comedy or storytelling; their interest can be historical, feminist, political or literary.

Initially the Virago Modern Classics concentrated on English novels and short stories published in the early decades of this century. As the series has grown it has broadened to include works of fiction from different centuries, different countries, cultures and literary traditions. In 1984 the Victorian Classics were launched; there are separate lists of Irish, Scottish, European, American, Australian and other English speaking countries; there are books written by Black women, by Catholic and Jewish women, and a few relevant novels by men. There is, too, a companion series of Non-Fiction Classics constituting biography, autobiography, travel, journalism, essays, poetry, letters and diaries.

By the end of 1986 over 250 titles will have been published in these two series, many of which have been suggested by our readers.